Online Wildfire

by Crystal Humphries

BROWN SKIN
B O O K S

BROWN SKIN
B O O K S

First published 2004 by Brown Skin Books
Pentimento Ltd
PO Box 46504
London N1 3YA
info@brownskinbooks.co.uk
www.brownskinbooks.co.uk

ISBN 0-9544866-3-3

Book and cover design: Renée Michaels Design
Cover photograph: Indra Kaur
Printed and bound in Finland by WS Bookwell

Distribution in the UK and Europe by
Airlift Book Company
8 The Arena
Mollison Avenue
Enfield
Middlesex EN3 7NJ
Tel: 020 8804 0400
email: info@airlift.co.uk

'Lord almighty!' Romaine almost choked as her gaze travelled across the velvety chocolate, muscular, well-honed body. He was lying stark, staring, gloriously, buck-naked on a tan leather sofa, his smooth, inviting skin gleaming with baby oil. But this was no baby. His face was turned away from her in profile, his eyes lowered, drawing her gaze towards his prize asset, a mammoth erection that rose magnificently from the soft-focus cloud of black hair that topped his muscular legs. It should have been illegal and, for all she knew, probably was. It seemed to Romaine that his full lips yearned to touch that beautiful penis and she could understand why. She could feel herself almost physically drawn towards it herself as her thighs clenched, shielding the moisture that suddenly flowed. Where had he come from? Like magic. Like obeah! Must be a figment of her sorry-assed, sexually-deprived imagination. Breathe. Breathe. Keep breathing, she reminded herself. She stared in stunned amazement at her computer screen, blinked, looked away and looked back again. He was still there.

Romaine sighed loudly and looked around guiltily, even though she knew that she was alone in the office. Who else would have such a sad, unfulfilling home life that she'd be in the office at 8:35 on a Friday evening? Her fingers furtively glided towards her pussy, but hesitated.

She glanced at the monitor again, but only long enough to find the 'back' button. Not that she was a prude or anything like that, but Romaine had always felt more than a little superior to those pathetic types with no possibility of a real sex life, who sat in their rooms, wearing their dirty macs—and probably little else—fiddling with them-selves, watching whatever it was that people got up to on those sites. What on earth did they get out of it? Some quick, instantly forgettable thrill? Right now she wasn't sure that she'd turn her nose up at some action, however virtual, but she felt a little guilty. She should be getting on with the job in hand. She wasn't even sure that those kind of sites were legal and what if anyone could tell from her computer that she'd been looking at that nude guy, the one she wasn't even going to be thinking about any more, the one she'd nearly forgotten about?

Romaine crossed her legs and forced her thoughts back to the reason why she was sitting in front of the computer in the first place. She'd typed *black men spending power* into the search engine and had just clicked on the first result that appeared. How dumb could she get? It should have been obvious that the combination 'black' and 'men' in any search engine would bring up the more dubious websites. Romaine kissed her teeth and scrolled down the list until she came across a site that analysed data from the last census. That would be more like it. She scanned the data rapidly and made a note of the figures she needed, then e-mailed them to her boss, knowing that the fact that she was still in the office at this time probably wouldn't be appreciated. She rubbed her tired eyes. These days, Romaine could do nothing right as far as her boss was concerned.

Sighing heavily, Romaine shut down the computer, stood and grabbed her coat. She glanced out of the window. It was already pitch black and growing colder outside. Romaine closed the blinds, turned on the answering machine and reached down for her handbag. As she did so, the phone rang, startling her in the stark silence of the office. She could leave it, but instead she straightened up, each vertebra protesting, and reached across her desk. She picked up the receiver just before the machine kicked in and answered with a weary 'Brown, Bartlett and Velasco'. She heard a hint of breathing and maybe a snatch of background music before the line went dead. She held the phone for a moment, listening to the monotonous drone, wondering... Surely he wouldn't? Who knows? This wasn't the first time this had happened. But she was really too exhausted to worry about it right now. She pressed the bar and dialled the familiar number. It was answered a little too quickly for her liking.

'Yo?' Why couldn't he answer the phone like any normal thirty-five-year-old man? Who was he expecting on the other end of the phone? P-bloody-Diddy? A mist of irritation wafted across her brain. She struggled to keep her voice neutral. It was just that she was so tired. A little while ago, she used to think that 'yo' was quite cute.

'It's me. Just leaving the office. Be home soon.'

'Can you pick up a few beers on the way, sugar?'

At least he wasn't asking for a take-away. Maybe he'd bothered to cook. That would be a pleasant surprise. No, not a surprise. That would be like Jesus feeding the five thousand—a miracle.

'Sure. Anything else I can do for you?'

'Well, you could bring some food from Russell's too. Bring plenty. The guys are getting hungry.' She could hear shouts of agreement in the background. He didn't even know when she was being sarcastic! And now she knew what the 'sugar' was all about: the guys had already arrived.

This was all she needed. The takeaway in West Green Road was packed with a disgruntled queue stretching out the door. And she didn't appreciate the couple behind her in the line commiserating about how Russell's was always packed, and how the never-seen Russell must be making a fortune, so why couldn't he employ a few more staff especially on a Friday night when it's so cold anyway and there's not even enough room for everyone to get inside... Their complaints only brought home the uncomfortable reality of every Friday night for the last couple of months. Romaine smiled politely and turned away, glancing at the signed photographs in the steamed-up window. 'Love from Cilla,' 'Thanks from Chris,' 'Best wishes, Lennox.' Did restaurants buy a job lot of these? She couldn't really get her head round the idea of Cilla Black, Chris Tarrant or Lennox Lewis queuing for food from Russell's, good though it was!

As satisfied customers emerged and she drew nearer to the entrance, the spicy aromas made Romaine's stomach grumble. She'd had a sandwich at her desk—gone were the leisurely lunches that she and her boss had regularly shared—and needed something more substantial now. Curried goat and rice and peas, maybe. Or escoveitched fish with food. Perhaps some peas soup too or, mmmm, fish soup. Her mouth began to water and she prayed that everyone in front of her would only be ordering patties or something that could be shoved in a paper bag and handed over, quickly. And may they all have the right change.

Now she was inside the door, at least it was a little warmer, though being able to see the food was almost painful. Like some distant mirage in a desert. Would any of it ever be hers? She concentrated on more photos lining the walls, the signatures smudged by the heavy condensation. 50 Cent. Unlikely. Whitney Houston. Unbelievable. MC Romeo, that chiselled face reminding her of… who? It didn't take long for the memory to resurface and Romaine found herself fidgeting uncomfortably as a flush rose to her neck. That face. That body. The one she wasn't going to think about, the one she had completely and utterly forgotten. The tan leather, dented where his buttocks rested, shadows pooling around it, the contours indistinct, his thighs, speckled with dark curly hairs, rising in a gentle inverted 'V' leading to powerful calves and strangely delicate feet. Every feature was in the background of her memory and in the foreground was that magnificent…

'You going stand there all night? People waiting' y'know. Next, I said!'

And she was being gently nudged by the impatient, grumbling couple.

'Sorry… um, three peas soup, two ackee and saltfish, four pieces of fish, and six of the jerk chicken pieces…'

She could hear the groan from the pair behind. Were they *ever* going to eat tonight? And please, let her have the right money.

❦

Louie would really have preferred to be alone in the house. These Friday nights had become a regular thing and, most of the time, he had fun kidding around with the guys over a few beers and sports on the television, but not tonight. He probably should have cancelled, but against his better judgement, here they all were. And he couldn't concentrate on them. His mind kept straying in the direction he didn't want it to take. It wasn't that he didn't want to spend time with the guys, but tonight he resented the jokes, the easy laughter, their carefree nonchalance while he had to go on as if nothing had happened. *Keep up the front, Louie. You can't let the side down*. Whose side? Louie's side.

Even as he lifted the can to his lips, he was watching them, wondering how they could go on behaving like this, as if life hadn't changed for any of them, as if they were still a bunch of single guys with no responsibilities, no cares, no ties, no heartache.

Look at Sheldon. Friends since college, the same age as him and not a single line on his face. Must be the love of a good woman. Louie almost choked on his beer at the thought. Grace seemed to have his pal under her thumb and just think how many times he'd teased Sheldon about being pussy-whipped. Well, who had the last laugh now? That's why he could never talk to Sheldon about it. Sheldon would either laugh at him or feel sorry for him and Louie couldn't bear the humiliation.

And Colin. Eternal bachelor. Just as they'd all vowed to be. Still no worries for him. He'd been talking about some new chick. French. Blonde hair. Long legs. At least he was consistent. Colin's preferred type hadn't changed since he used to pin those posters to his bedroom wall, way back when they were only just teenagers and knew nothing about women at all. Not that he could claim to know that much more now...

'You quiet tonight, bro. What do you?'

'Nothing, man. I's cool.'

Matthew. His younger brother. Going out with the superbitch from hell. He'd warned him, but the woman must have cast some kind of spell over him. Lord, he could understand why the boy might be tempted to turn his attention elsewhere, but he still felt resentment that Matthew was sitting there, acting like he didn't know the meaning of the blues. Louie could tell from the way Matthew talked about his girlfriend, or didn't talk about her these days, that that particular relationship was terminal as far as his brother was concerned, he just hadn't pronounced the last rites yet. Louie looked at Matthew, the same nose, cheekbones and eyes that he saw in the mirror every morning, but he'd always thought that Matthew was the serious, studious one, his eyes seldom lightening with laughter whereas his own were, more often than not, crinkled with suppressed humour. Now look. How the tables had turned. Whenever he heard his own laugh, it sounded hollow to his ears, even if the others didn't seem to notice.

Romaine. In front of the guys he'd talk to her as if their relationship was just as it had always been. But the pain he kept hidden was like a physical knot, wrenching his guts, clenching even tighter now that he knew she was on her way home. Why didn't he just leave her? He should just walk away. It was now a matter of pride. She had hurt him so bad and he still didn't want to let her know how much he was suffering. He should go. But, hell, he was stupid enough to still love her, in spite of everything. And she would be here within minutes.

❦

Her footsteps slowed to the beat in her head, Aretha singing 'Do Right Woman, Do Right Man' as she neared the Victorian terraced house. It wasn't just tiredness that made her steps falter. She could see the lights blazing in the sitting room. She could never get him to close the shutters. Wanted to show off the widescreen digital television and DVD, the covetable stereo system, the *café au lait* suede sofa, the original artwork that he collected so assiduously. It would damn well serve him right if they got burgled and he lost the lot. She crossed her fingers behind her back, knowing that she should never have allowed those thoughts into her head and hoping to assuage the gods. But it depressed the hell out of her to see those guys settled into her front room, a cloud of blue smoke rising from the ashtrays scattered across the carpet, the shouts as some team scored something in some game or other, the upturned cans raised to thirsty lips. *If you wanna do right woman, you gotta be a do right man.* Shit! She'd forgotten the beers and he'd probably be in a mood all evening as a result. And now the skies were opening and rain was beginning to fall in big, fat, heavy, punishing drops. Well, he could damn well go out himself, or else they could make do with the rum, brandy or whisky that just gathered dust on the sideboard. She'd had a difficult week and now she was getting wet. If she had to come back here each Friday night, why the hell couldn't she return to a quiet house? Just for once.

Romaine turned the key in the lock and stepped into the warm hall, gratefully dropping the carrier bags onto the carpet. She looked up at the coat hooks. Every one taken. She let her soaked coat fall to the ground and took the bags into the kitchen.

As she reached into the cupboard for plates, she felt strong arms envelop her. Warm, soft, welcoming lips skimmed her skin, roaming down her neck, the tongue hot, wet, licking away the tension, the annoyance, all so… very… unimportant… trivial. She turned round in his arms and stood still for a moment, as stunned as she always was by his good looks, the fine features almost like they were painted by the brush of a Japanese artist onto that hazelnut-coloured skin. She looked into her husband's dark, endlessly deep eyes. She stared for a moment, attempting to gauge his mood, praying that something might, miraculously, have changed since this morning. She returned his kiss, her fingers running through his wiry cropped hair.

'Missed you, honey,' she said, pulling away to see the response in his eyes. It was only a half lie. She had missed him, just not the way he had been lately. In just the few daylight hours that they'd spent apart, with the time to think, Romaine had almost forgotten how much she had loved him. So, he'd proved that he could drive her to distraction, make her want to scream with angry frustration, even contemplate walking away, he was still the same man she had married, if a little more careworn—and maybe she was to blame for that. Her fingers rose to smooth away the frown that creased his forehead.

His hand drifted down to her buttocks, pulling her closer to him, lifting her skirt as their kiss deepened, easing into her panties, caressing the warm skin. He bit down hard on her lip, making her wince.

'Um, you taste good, baby.'

She could sense the audience in the doorway and wondered for a guilty moment if that was why he was being so demonstrative. She tried to pull away. Louie held her tight.

'Hey, cut it out you guys. We're here to watch the match, not a porn movie.'

'Hi, Sheldon.' Romaine tugged at her skirt, embarrassed.

Sheldon produced his trademark irresistible grin and kissed Romaine on the cheek, as he reached for a piece of chicken.

Colin stepped into the room and added 'Anytime you want to change the male lead in your movie, you got my number.'

She was disconcerted for a moment, but before anyone could sense her discomfort, she put her hands on her hips and turned to face him. 'Don't be so feisty young man. What you know about them type of film'—she deliberately pronounced it 'flim'—'anyway? You too young, bwoy.' She smiled, even though Colin's gaze always made her feel uncomfortable, as if she should be wearing purdah in his company.

'Lou, didn't you hear what Colin said?' Sheldon shouted, a mischievous look in his eyes, 'You not going to defend your wife's honour? If you're not, then I will.'

As the two guys squared up to each other, both holding chicken legs like swords, fencing with each other, Louie laughed, but there was an underlying tension. Romaine looked away. The laughter brought Matthew to the kitchen doorway and, once again, she was startled by the striking resemblance between Matthew and Louie even though her husband was six years older than his brother and half a foot taller, leaner, smoother, more confident...

When the 'fight' ended in a draw, each man eating the other's chicken piece, they all scrambled for plates, ignoring her and helping themselves to food. Romaine watched, remembering her earlier annoyance. Once again, she was being drawn irresistibly into this circle of friends and she remembered how much fun they all used to have together back in the day. Now, there was the same process each week. She'd start off resenting the commitment she'd made to Louie, the one that forced her to be here, part of this male cabal. And then, little by little, she'd succumb to the charm of these guys and end up drinking, eating, laughing and joking with them, forgetting why she was there. It was her subversive rebellion. She knew she wasn't meant to be enjoying herself. That hadn't been part of Louie's plan and she knew it would irritate the hell out of him. She wasn't petty enough to want to really hurt him or rouse his anger, but these days she took her tiny pleasures wherever she could.

All at once, the guys had all disappeared back to the sitting room and she was left with the remnants of food, which she scraped onto her plate, regretting the peas soup. She shook her head as she joined them and jostled for space on the cushions dragged onto the floor.

Baseball. That's what they were watching on some satellite channel. Each week they teased her that she never understood the rules of whichever sport, cheered at the wrong moment, supported the wrong team, or had even got the wrong game.

'Is not the same as rounders, you know!'

'Looks the same to me. Look at the girlie way that guy's standing with his ass sticking out.'

Sheldon looked at her with shocked horror as if she'd committed sacrilege. '*That guy*! Is that what you said? Don't you know who that is? That's only Sammy Sosa. A hitting god. Girl, you must have too much of a life not to know that! Louie's been letting you out too much.' Sheldon's eyes twinkled behind his unfashionably heavy-rimmed spectacles.

'Did you say *letting* me out? You think I'm in prison or something?' There was an almost imperceptible moment of awkwardness and she could have bitten off her tongue.

Then Colin joked, 'Why else you stay with him? You must be doing some kind of punishment. How many times do I have to offer to rescue you, Rome?' He smiled at Louie, but Romaine sensed a frightening hint of sincerity beneath the words.

'I keep telling you guys,' Louie joined in at last, 'if you would bring your own women round, then we could wife-swap. But you too selfish and want to keep them to yourselves. Or you all scared they might all rush to my feet? Or maybe you don't trust us.' The look he shot in Romaine's direction was full of meaning. 'At least I'm generous with my woman.' He turned his head away although he reached out to caress her leg, his warm hand rising, lifting the fabric, revealing a little too much flesh for her liking.

In unison, Colin and Sheldon downed their plates and fell on top of Louie, pulling him away and then smothering Romaine in stage kisses as she fought her way to the surface. Tears of laughter ran down her cheeks until she noticed the way Colin was looking at her. She knew she was on the verge of hysteria. Louie got up and walked into the kitchen to fetch the last of the beers. Then someone scored and each man's attention automatically returned to the TV screen.

'I know why you don't bring your women. None of them would put up with all this. I think I must be mad.'

'That's why we love you, Romaine,' they muttered in chorus, eyes still fixed and glazed.

❦

'Seriously, guys,' Romaine began ingenuously as she spread the five cards in her hand, 'why *don't* you bring your wives or girlfriends to these Friday-night soirées?'

'*Soirées*? Since when did we get so posh? I thought we were just hanging out at Louie and Romaine's. Next time, I'll wear white tie and tails.' That from Sheldon, Louie's business partner.

'I'll expect no less. I'll change one card. But I'm serious. You never ask Grace?' She wondered how much Sheldon knew. Would Louie have told him, his closest friend?

'Wouldn't want to make you jealous. You notice that, guys? One card. She must be bluffing I'll take three'. His response was automatic, uncalculated. Romaine wouldn't be at all surprised if Louie hadn't talked to anyone. In a way, she wished that he would. He was wound too tight, she knew that the coil needed to be released even if he couldn't see it himself.

'You'll just have to pay to see if I'm bluffing,' she replied. 'Or give up now before you lose everything. So what d'you think Grace is doing while you're here trying to cheat your way out of trouble?'

'Okay, guys. That's me out. I fold.'

'I'm in.'

'Me too.'

'And me.'

'Raise you five.'

'See you and raise five.'

Romaine kept her eyes glued to the cards, not wanting to give anything away. Out of the corner of her eye, she could see Sheldon looking at her as if he had X-ray vision into her brain. She smiled slightly.

'I'll see your five and raise you five. If I know Grace, she'll be at home, in front of the soaps. Friday night is EmmerEnders or something like that, no? Guys, Romaine has to be bluffing, eh?'

'Probably, but I'm not taking any chances. I fold.'

'See your five and raise you ten.'

Romaine looked at the pile in front of her. She wouldn't meet Louie's gaze. She made a rapid calculation. 'See your ten and raise you twenty.' The growing heap in the centre of the table was becoming blurred through the haze of cigarette and marijuana smoke. Romaine felt light-headed, but she was determined to win. It was like a desperate hunger or another subtle act of rebellion. Every week the guys teased her as the sole female and, despite the fact that they'd had to write a list of the winning poker hands for her to consult, she was going to show them that she could more than hold her own.

'How can you be sure? If I were Grace and you left me like this every week, I'd be out celebrating my parole.' She didn't like the way Sheldon was looking at her as if he knew exactly what was in her hand. She wanted to throw him off the scent, if only for a moment. She could sense the way he paused in surprised contemplation of her words, as if this was something that had never occurred to him.

'What was your bid again, Rome?'

'Raised twenty.'

'You know, if Grace was out on the town, it wouldn't surprise me at all. But it wouldn't matter. I trust her.' He paused for a moment as if he'd only just realised that. 'Romaine, you must sure have a good hand. I fold.'

Romaine felt Louie's eyes burning into her. 'So it's just me and you, honey.' Louie was willing her to look up at him, she could sense it, but she resisted. If she met his eyes, she might feel the need to give in to him. She was determined to carry through this small act of rebellion, even if he never understood the message she was sending by doing so.

'Looks like it.'

'You're bluffing.' He reached under the table and his hand was on her knee, sliding up, thumbs describing tiny circles against the soft flesh of her thigh.

'So put your money where your mouth is.' She shifted slightly, moving away from him.

'Okay, see your twenty and raise you twenty.' His toes were between her legs, pressing against her, wriggling against her clitoris. She knew he must be able to feel the heat.

Matthew almost gasped. 'Boy, I hope you know your wife well, or you could lose big time.'

She made the mistake of looking up to see Louie's reaction. For a brief second his eyes were grim, but he smiled at her as she felt his toes burrowing against her vulva as if seeking an entrance. What the hell was he doing? He was now making it so obvious. Was he trying to prove something to the others? Or to himself? Or simply trying to throw her off her stride? Romaine counted to five slowly, forcing herself to hold his gaze and then she smiled too, as calmly as she could though her heart and pussy were both pounding fast.

Out of the corner of her eye, she could see Matthew looking from her to Louie, his gaze intense. 'Careful, Louie. You know, bro,' he fingered the light goatee grown to distinguished him from his brother, 'you sound so confident, but there's always a part of a woman that nobody will ever really know. Isn't that right, Rome?'

Louie's exploring foot dropped to the floor. What was Matthew playing at now? Was he deliberately trying to rile Louie? These two were always in competition, but the younger man obviously couldn't understand how much worse he was making the situation. This wasn't the time to be making comments like that.

'That might be so for you, bro. But Romaine and I don't have any secrets from each other. Isn't that so, Romaine?'

She had to stay out of whatever was going on between the two of them. This seemed like more than sibling rivalry, but there was nothing she could do about it.

Looking down at the table, Romaine wished that she'd never started this contest, but she couldn't give in now. It might only be a tiny, petty victory, but she'd hug it to herself in the coming days. She made a quick calculation. How far could she go without being forced to fold? What if Louie raised by fifty? He had enough. Would they bend the rules and let her borrow from Matthew? No, not likely. They all took this game so seriously. She wanted to get this hand over and done with; the tension was becoming unbearable and she had to concentrate to stop her hand shaking and beads of sweat breaking out on her forehead. She made herself breathe deeply and keep her gaze steady and emotion-free as she looked at her husband.

'I'll see your twenty and raise you twenty.'

Someone groaned. She didn't know who it was. It might have been herself, but she didn't think so.

Romaine glanced to her left. Colin was holding his head in his hands, eyes closed. Matt was shaking his head. To her right, Sheldon was hunched forward, his expression eager. She couldn't surrender now.

'Romaine doesn't hide anything from me,' Louie's voice dripped with sarcasm. 'She can't.'

It was best to ignore him. 'All right. I'll see your twenty and...' She counted them out from her depleted pile, '...and shout.'

'Call!' they screamed at her.

She lay her cards on the table. Two pairs, sixes and queens.

Matthew groaned loudly and she recognised the sound from before. 'Shit! I had a full house, but a low one. You made me believe you had to have a better hand than that. You're good, Romaine.'

'She is, isn't she?' That from her husband.

'So what you got, Lou?'

For a second, Romaine couldn't read the expression on his face. Was he angry? Triumphant? Embarrassed? And then the slow, warm, familiar smile returned to his face and a broad grin lit up his features.

'Girl, I have to give it to you. You had me fooled...' The last four words were staccato, infused with a steely edge that the others could take for disappointment at losing.

He lay down his cards to hoots of laughter from the other guys. A pair of fours.

'...And not for the first time.' A red flush of anger rose to his neck.

Romaine scooped up the pile of matchsticks from the middle of the table, the pleasure taken from her victory, its value diminished.

§

They worked in silence, emptying away butt-filled ashtrays, crumpled beer cans and an empty rum bottles. It was late. 2:30 am before they'd made her lose every last matchstick.

Her body was exhausted, but her mind was whirling. She supposed that she really did quite enjoy being the only female in that group of males. It was like she'd been given access to an exclusive club, as if she had special qualities that the other women didn't possess. Under other circumstances, she would have been able to relax completely and bask in the feeling of being unique, valued. If only she hadn't... but there was little sense in going there. She couldn't change things now.

Romaine fed the last plate into the gaping mouth of the dishwasher and looked across at Louie as he drained the final drop from his glass.

'Tired?' His smile was neutral.

'Yeah, but—'

'Well, I'm beat. I'll go up. Goodnight.'

His kiss was cool. She wondered why he bothered.

He walked out the door. His footsteps echoed up the stairs.

❦

'Part of a woman that nobody will ever really know.' The words echoed around Louie's brain. He smiled bitterly. What exactly did Matthew mean by that? He could have looked up at his brother when he said those words, but he'd chosen not to. If he'd seen any hint of meaning, he might have hit him. Might have lost control. And he had no intention of doing that. He would stay in control, no matter what.

...*That nobody will every really know.* He *had* known her, though. Surely that couldn't have been an illusion? She had allowed him to learn everything about her. It had taken time for him to be sure, but it was because she was the only one he knew inside out and would have trusted with his life, that he'd chosen Romaine above the others.

For a second, his chest swelled with pride as he thought of the others. There had been quite a few of them. Look at Colin now with all those model-girl types. Not a patch on the way he, Louie, had been before Romaine.

She hadn't been the sort he would normally go for. His usual woman had been tall, lanky, fair-skin, long hair and, he was ashamed to admit it now, as few brain cells as possible, preferably just enough to sustain life. He would wine them, dine them and then *grind* them...

Romaine had come to him. Taken matters into her own hands. He'd been momentarily stunned, but flattered to find her there, stirred by the thought that he was so desirable to her, that she had wanted him so bad. And she had crept her way into his heart, damn her. He'd learned to adore her. To admire her strength, her single-mindedness, her intelligence. To be truly flattered that she'd chosen him.

He'd grown to be ashamed of the bimbos, airbrushing them from his sexual history as he'd taught Romaine his preferred moves, receiving tenderness and vulnerability and self-sacrifice and trust from her in return. And then, after all those years together, she'd... He'd thought he knew her body well enough to satisfy her needs. But maybe Matthew was right. Nobody could ever really know… And in spite of what had happened between them, just the sight of her still made his cock hard, he still wanted to touch her, to feel her warm, soft, yielding flesh, cup those soft, silky breasts, bury his throbbing prick right up inside her… He reached for himself.

❦

What the hell was that all about? All evening he'd been pawing her, teasing her, touching her in secret places whenever the guys were distracted—and, more often, when they weren't, like he was getting off on exposing her. Against her better judgement, she'd let herself get aroused. She wanted to make love to her husband. Was that a crime? Surely that wasn't too much to ask on a Friday night! It had been so long. She knew the date off by heart.

Romaine switched on the dishwasher, the dull rumble somehow reassuring. She closed the kitchen door behind her and slowly hauled her body up the stairs, turning off the light behind her and trying to shut down her thoughts. Pale moonlight streamed through the glass panel above the door. How romantic! She stopped for a moment, hesitant. She owed it to him, to them both, to try even though she knew what the result was likely to be. Just one more time. This was her penance, after all. Hot tears rose to her eyes, but she shook them away. Romaine breathed deeply, straightened her shoulders and opened the bedroom door.

Louie was curled up in the bed, his body a three-dimensional question mark. At least it wasn't a full stop, she told herself.

The room was chilly. She undressed quickly and slipped in beside him, grateful for the warmth exuded by his skin. She pressed her breasts against his back and curved her arm around his fortress-like shoulders, her palm flat against his chest. A car backfired somewhere beyond the window. Neither of them flinched, the sound a regular occurrence in this part of town. He didn't move. She didn't move, but thought of moving out.

'Hi, honey,' she whispered, letting her lips and breath linger against his earlobe.

No answer. She knew he wasn't asleep. Romaine let her fingertips drift through the curls of stiff hair on his chest, only stopping to gently unfurl them along the way. Slowly down and then back up, round and round, circling his nipple, pressing the heel of her hand into his flesh, now teasing, now forceful. He couldn't pretend that he was able to sleep through this. She knew what he liked. After all this time together, she understood his body so well. Romaine felt his nipples pucker and moved closer, forcing her pelvis against his buttocks, raising one leg across his hips, making sure that her knee grazed his half-erect penis on the way. And now, as her fingers flickered down his chest, she could feel him stir, his back rigid as if trying to deny the effect she had on him.

She sucked the flesh of his neck into her mouth, tasting the musty, salty after-effects of the evening. He didn't turn. She bit into his skin, nipping him gently. She almost laughed aloud. She was having to turn into a vampire to arouse her husband! Louie lifted his head and moved slightly, as if to shrug her off, but by now, her fingers were on his hips, pulling him round so that she could get access to his penis that was trying its best to ignore her manipulations. Her nails tiptoed across his skin, edging ever nearer and to test his resistance, she raked them across his balls, feeling the tender ripples, hearing him try to stifle a gasp. Romaine smiled to herself. She knew he wouldn't be able to resist. She delved between his legs to stroke the tender, sensitive skin of his inner thigh and as he shifted, restlessly, she could feel her own burning desire as the heat descended and centred itself in her clitoris. She couldn't help wriggling against him, the hungry, desperately sensitive bud aching with want as she rubbed against his buttocks, only intensifying her own frustration.

'Lou?' she whispered.

'Uh-huh?'

Her fingers clasped his familiar cock, thumb tracing the raised vein, wanting so much to feel it pumping into her. Her toes stroked his calves, her inner thighs caressing his tight balls.

'Come on, babe. I'm hot and horny. I want you.'

He couldn't hide the swelling of his prick, couldn't pretend she wasn't affecting him. She knew he loved to hear her talk dirty.

'I'm so wet for you, honey.' She reached for his hand. He resisted, but she held it firmly between her thighs and rubbed herself hard against it. 'That's what you do to me. Remember how it feels? I'm so tight for you.' She grasped his erection and moved her hand fast, up and down, thumb caressing the slippery head. 'I need to feel your big cock inside my pussy. You're buried so deep inside me. Imagine it hot around you. Pretend it's my birthday,' she joked.

He didn't appreciate that. She felt him stiffen, not his penis, his whole body. He abruptly removed her hand and eased his body away from her, attempting to hide his arousal with the guilty nonchalance of an alcoholic who believes you can't smell the whisky on his breath. He curled himself into a tight, silent, defensive ball.

Romaine sighed heavily. Not again, she thought. She was getting more than a little tired of this. For how long was he intending to go on punishing her?

'This is about the matchsticks, isn't it?'

Silence.

'Isn't it, Lou?'

'Don't know what you're talking about,' he muttered. He was moving closer to the edge of the bed. She prayed he'd fall off.

Romaine knew she should back off, but couldn't stop herself. She had been doing that for too long now. 'You're punishing me because I won at poker. Because I showed you up in front of the guys. Because you couldn't control me this time. That's what all this is about, isn't it?'

'Don't be so fucking stupid, woman.' His anger was tangible, a shaft of heat across the cold space between them. He flung the duvet off, got out of the bed, crossed the room in long, angry strides and was out the door in seconds.

Romaine turned on her side, her hands clasped together between her thighs, a knot of icy anger forming inside. She loved Lou, but he could be so bloody childish. Since that night two months ago, every time they came near to physical closeness, each time she thought they could rebuild what there had been between them, he found some excuse to push her away. So why did she go on trying? Her jaw began to ache; her teeth were clenched so tight with rage. Yes, why did she do it? Romaine balled her hand into a fist and punched the pillow beside her. Hard. She stared into the darkness of the room, trying to focus all thoughts on the carved ceiling rose. After a few moments, she felt herself relax, the tension falling away like air from a balloon. Because she loved him, that's why. He was normally so tender, sensitive, understanding and, underneath the glossy exterior, vulnerable, opening himself up to her in ways that nobody else could possibly imagine. And he could charm her into doing anything he wanted, in and out of bed, if he chose. All she needed to see was that tender smile tugging at the corner of his lips, and she'd be like jelly. But it had been a while since he'd smiled at her with any genuine warmth. Now there was this seemingly unbridgeable gap between them and she had to try to find a way through. They'd had five years of fun and laughter, a couple of tragedies thrown in along the way but, on balance, more joy than pain.

It was the last couple of months that had changed all that. And who was to blame? No one but herself! Romaine knew that, and wondered if Louie wanted her to be the one to end it. Maybe that's why he was pushing, pushing at her. She was determined, though, not to lose what they had had just because of one impulsive encounter.

Romaine glanced at the green fluorescent digits on the alarm clock. 4:30 am. Much too late to be able to think rationally about her marriage. She was too exhausted to worry about it all now, to try to tease out the strands of sane reasoning amongst all the mess. She would make another effort. In the morning. Her body was freezing. She got up, slid a long fleecy nightdress over her head and got back into bed. She pulled the duvet up high, holding it tight around her neck as if it was a chastity belt. Why bother? she smiled to herself, her teeth chattering. Romaine squeezed her eyes shut tight, trying to force sleep.

It must have been at least forty minutes later that she heard his footsteps on the stairs and the shaft of light roused her from her stupor. She felt the mattress dip as he threw himself into the bed, wanting her to know that he no longer had any consideration for her. The scent of nicotine and alcohol hit her like smelling salts but she didn't move a muscle, just made herself breathe deeply, in… two, three four, five. Out… two, three, four, five. She closed her eyes tighter as she felt the rhythmic motions next to her. He knew she wasn't asleep. The heat of anger flooded to her face and her fingers clenched. She loved her husband but, Oh Lord, he could make her mad. So mad that she, at times, came close to strangling him.

Romaine listened as the motion intensified and his breathing quickened. She forced her thoughts away from the body squirming beside her, the rapid gasps. She wouldn't give him the satisfaction of letting him know that she knew what he was doing and cared, oh so much. She deliberately turned her mind to the tan leather sofa, the chocolate skin, the long, hard prick rising appreciatively...

CHAPTER 2

Softly-treading, furtive fingers lifted the hem of her nightdress. Disorientated, Romaine felt a shiver of momentary fear skitter along the length of her spine. As he eased the fabric up, above her hips, she listened to his heavy, suppressed breathing, knowing that he had stopped to stare. No matter how much he might think he hated her, the sight of her naked pussy would always have the same effect on him. She kept her eyes closed, wondering what he would do next, whether to let him know that she was awake. Clouds of orange floated across her eyelids and she followed them, needing the distraction, forcing herself to concentrate on the patterns so that she wouldn't move.

She could feel his hot breath as his mouth moved closer to her thigh, nearer to the soft, sensitive spot that had, last night, hungered for just that touch. Against her will, she felt a ripple of desire wash through her body, concentrating itself in the spot that he was so close to… just about to… almost… Oh god… licking with just the slightest flicker of his warm tongue, his hands clutching her hips, fingernails digging into the flesh, hurting her, holding her down, demanding a response as his wet tongue trailed downwards, exploring the groove between thigh and mound. A disobedient 'aaah' escaped from her lips, but still she couldn't, wouldn't open her eyes. She knew this had to be a dream and didn't want to encounter reality. Not now, not when his hand was reaching up, searching for her breast. Another time she might have guided him. But not now. Uncertain of what he might do. Or what he might not do. She didn't want anything to interrupt these feelings he was producing.

Now he'd found her breast and those familiar, gentle fingers circled her already-puckering areola as his thumb flicked across her nipples and then he squeezed hard between thumb and forefinger, eliciting a moan of pain. That seemed to excite him, because he moved himself upwards, still gripping her breast, his cock hard and demanding as she felt it bounce along her calf, her thigh, homing in on her damp pussy.

'Open your eyes.'

No. Please, no. I don't want to wake up. Make the dream last.

'Look at me.'

His hand left her bruised nipple and half-encircled her neck, caressing, squeezing gently.

'Look at me.' Firmer. Commanding. 'Romaine. Look at me!'

Too unsure, yes frightened, to disobey, Romaine opened her eyes and looked into her husband's. She looked away quickly, concentrating on the movement of those full lips. Reading, hardly hearing, what he was saying.

'I'm going to take you, now. You want me now? You wet for me?'

His hand reached for her pussy, the heel bruising her clitoris, eliciting a sharp intake of breath—pain and pleasure mixed in an exquisitely uncertain cocktail. Then his fingers inside her, thrusting hard, demanding, unrelenting. *No*, she wanted to scream, *not like this*, but her mouth formed 'Louie, please!' I'm not going to enjoy this, her mind protested. Not unless you care for me. Not unless you make love to me instead of fucking me. Not if this is just about you and revenge. But she felt the treacherous wetness between her thighs and her unruly hips thrusting against his hand. Damn! He could make her horny even when she was trying so hard to resist.

'I can feel your honey,' he grunted against her cheek. 'Come on, girl, let me feel your hands around my cock. Now!' He took her hand and forced her fingers around his hardness, guiding her movements, sliding her fingers up and down his hot, slick flesh. 'This what you wanted last night? Ooohee! Oh baby! Soooo good. Bet you're glad I waited. I'm even harder now. You know this is what you need. Y'know you love a hard cock. That's it. Faster!' It wasn't a request. A command. His fingers were grasping hers, orchestrating the rhythm. Romaine shifted slightly, creating a physical distance between their bodies. She looked down at the dark red tip of his cock emerging from their combined fingers. That was all this was about: him getting satisfaction. Romaine resented it, but she experienced a renewed surge of desire at the sight of him. She would never get used to the size of him. She wanted to feel him inside her so bad, even though she didn't want him this way. She fought against him to slow the rhythm, not wanting him to come, not right now. Pulling her hand away from his grip, she parted her thighs and reached around him to clutch his buttocks, letting her fingers feather a path up from his tight testicles. Digging her fingers into his muscles, she angled her hips and circled until she could feel the head of his prick against the soft opening of her pussy, a ring of concentrated lust ready to trap him, draw him in.

And then his hands were under her bottom and he was forcing his way into her, before she was ready for his girth, screaming her name 'Ro—mai—ne' as he hit against the neck of her womb. Oh, he hurt her, but he felt so good. So good. He pulled out to the entrance and Romaine knew that she would do anything, anything in the world to have him fill her again. And then he was thrusting hard and fast, pounding harder and faster with delirious passion. Harder and faster even as she cried out that he was hurting her. Cried out for slow and warm and intimate and loving… just like… it… used to be. He was dancing to a rhythm she couldn't hear. But in spite of that, she could feel a distant memory of ecstasy begin to stab at the outskirts of her desire. If only… if only he would slow down, wait for her, take her with him… Oh, fuck, this time… it was possible… she might just… he might let her…

But Louie felt her need, felt each rapid thrust bringing her nearer, closer, no turning back, until… he abruptly, violently pulled out of her. Aaaiiieee!… he was… oooeeee!… coming… shooting… Oh, Lord!

The heavy weight of his relaxed body slumped on top of her and the tears rushed to her eyes. She wanted to scream out 'What about me?' but Louie was almost purring with contentment. Whispering 'Oh, Lord' over and over until he drifted into a perfect, blameless sleep, his chin buried into her shoulder, eyes turned away from her.

❦

By the time he woke, she'd been up for hours, made toast and coffee and cleared away Louie's empty glass and full ashtray from the night before. She had to wonder at the number of tiny stubs and the lingering scent of dope. He must have been feeling real stressed. Well, he was certainly chilled out now, she thought, resenting the soreness between her legs.

She poured his coffee and set a plate, knife, toast, butter, jam and her resentment in front of him. She had to stop herself fingering the knife thoughtfully as she watched his smug grin. He was wearing a short robe and deliberately parted his legs to reveal his heavy, flaccid penis. Romaine couldn't help staring.

'Yo, babe. Haven't lost my touch then.' He fondled her bottom as if he owned it.

There was that 'yo' again. Was he doing it just to annoy her? She tightened the belt of her robe and sat down opposite him, spreading butter on a piece of toast but not raising it to her lips.

'We need to talk, Louie.'

'About what?'

'About us.'

'Haven't we done enough talking about "us"? I just showed you what I feel about us.'

'That's why I think we need to talk.'

'And you don't think you did enough talking already?' His dark eyes narrowed. 'Maybe you shoulda just kept your damned mouth shut.'

'Maybe I should have.'

'Why didn't you?'

'Because you asked.'

'So now is my fault?'

'That's not what I'm saying, Lou. But we can't go on this way.'

Louie stood and walked away from the table. 'I'm going to the office. Meeting up with Sheldon.'

'On a Saturday?'

He looked at her as if she no longer had the right to ask him. He glanced at the clock. 'I'm going to have to run.'

He returned fifteen minutes later, showered and dressed. Unreasonably gorgeous in tight, black T-shirt that caressed his toned chest in appreciation. Black denim jeans moulded to his sexy rear. Caramel skin freshly shaved, hair neatly brushed. The look in his almond-shaped eyes was cold, but still Romaine's body responded. Why was she even thinking of him in that way after what had happened this morning? She picked crumbs from the toast on her plate.

'When will you be back?'
'When I'm back.'

🌶

Romaine had answered the advertisement in the local newsagent's window only because she couldn't wait to move out of home. Two women together. Impossible situation. 'So you think you is big now.' her mother would scream at her. 'You think you full ripe? Well, you only woman enough to fly this nest when I say so. What nastiness you think you goin' get up to outside these walls? Well while you is under my roof...'

This same Victorian terrace in Hillside Road, South Tottenham. Three guys. Wanting a housemate, preferably female. She had been so nervous when she rang the bell, knowing that she wouldn't get this room, not at the first time of trying. She had been demure, eyes downcast, barely glancing at Louie, Matthew or Colin. There had been only one question—an unexpectedly difficult one: 'What can you cook?'

She lied, with her fingers crossed behind her back and in the weeks before she plucked up the courage to tell her mother that she was leaving, she pumped her for recipes, which she wrote down assiduously.

She had brought only one large suitcase to the house along with the pad of A4 lined paper black with scrawled writing, scribbled out errors, curved arrows leading to the corrections and copious footnotes.

They had converted what had once been a sitting room into an extra bedroom, needing the contribution to the rent and, of course, the domestic order they believed she would bring to the house.

The first time she attempted curried mutton and rice and peas—foolishly ambitious, she now admitted—they hadn't even tried to be polite. 'What is this shit?' Louie had asked, dripping the porridge-like, glutinous mess from his fork.

'I'm not used to the cooker yet.' And she'd opened two tins of Campbell's soup, mixing them together, wishing that she was still talking to her mother and could pick up the phone. She returned to her notes and vowed to study well. The ackee and saltfish was no more successful. Nor the jerk chicken. Even when she and her mother were reconciled and she could beg for guidance, they all still agreed that she'd have to take her turn at the takeaway. That's when they started treating her just like one of the boys.

But Louie's room was above hers and while she could ignore the succession of girls that Colin brought home, Gina was becoming a regular fixture. One that disturbed Romaine's nights. Mainly Friday nights.

Gina was voluptuous. No other word for it. Long, dark, wavy hair. Mediterranean colouring. Full breasts, small waist and curvaceous hips. Louie had met her at a pub in town and had brought her all the way to Tottenham, surprising them all. He usually preferred to love them and leave them on their territory. And Romaine had been secret witness to their first night of passion. Paper-thin walls and ceiling. Nothing hidden. First, the pounding rhythm, the simultaneous oohs and aahs. Gina's gasp of surprise that conjured visions of Louie unclothed for the first time. The moans of desire that brought thoughts of nakedness and wetness and hotness and hardness and softness and surrender to Romaine's mind and a flush of want to her inexperienced body. She knew the moment he entered Gina and she clenched her teeth tight, clutching the fabric of her sheet, bunching it between her thighs. She closed her eyes and rocked to their rhythm, her own hand caressing her hip, her waist, her breast, folding around the giving flesh, squeezing harder and harder as their movements accelerated, wanting it to hurt, dreaming of being underneath that pounding.

She'd stopped suddenly. Shocked at what she'd been thinking. Feverish. Unsatisfied, but not wanting, not daring, to take this any further. Oh God, did she really want him? Louie? Her housemate? Lust dissipated, she got up and sat, naked, by the window, guilty, watching the traffic as it passed, needing to concentrate on anything but the sounds emanating from the ceiling above.

It was seven weeks later, on a Thursday evening, that they made love for the first time. She knew that Louie would be back late and prayed that he'd be alone. She waited until the others were in bed, hopefully fast asleep, and tiptoed up the stairs to his empty bed. She undressed, slipped under the duvet and waited, heart pounding, for him to come back. She counted the cars, watching the reflection of the headlights across the curtains, heart leaping each time she thought she heard his key in the lock.

She was, in the end, fast asleep when he returned, woken only by the dip in the mattress as he sat on the side of the bed and caressed her cheek.

'Yo.'

'Oh, hi,' she yawned. 'I was asleep.' As if that wasn't perfectly obvious.

'I know. I've been watching you for a while.'

Oh Lord! Had she been snoring? Or dribbling? She checked the corners of her mouth.

'What you doing here, Romaine?'

'Waiting for you.'

'For what?'

He wasn't going to make it easy. This wasn't what she'd imagined. She guessed she'd hope for Prince Charming kissing her awake and then… and then… and then, what?

'I'm not sure, Louie. I just… I wanted… I want you. I heard you. I mean, both of you. You and Gina…'

'I wondered.'

'Why?'

'The way you looked at her. The way you looked at me.' He stopped. The silence between them became oppressive. 'What do you want from me, Romaine?'

She didn't have the words.

He touched her cheek again, and as one finger trailed downwards, easing back the duvet. 'There's Gina...'

'I know.'

'I know you women always stick together. You wouldn't want me to do anything to hurt Gina, would you?'

But he held her nipple between thumb and finger, rolling it gently, bringing his lips ever nearer. 'Would you?'

'Well…'

He took her nipple between his soft lips and sucked hard, pulling, nibbling gently with sharp teeth as he circled with his hot, pointed tongue. A 'no' hovered in her brain, but a 'yes' invaded, pushing it aside. In any event, Louie didn't wait for an answer. 'You want me real bad, don't you, Romaine? Real bad.'

Her breasts were reaching for him, screaming 'yes, yes!' but he ignored them, uncovering her, lifting the duvet and dropping it to the floor. Leaving her naked, exposed, vulnerable. And he stood, looked into her eyes, then turned away and began to undress slowly, ignoring her, casual, as if she wasn't there. He hung his jacket in the wardrobe. She felt her breathing deepen as he slipped the tie from his collar and draped it over the back of a chair. He pulled his shirt from his trousers and unbuttoned it with a painful casualness. His shoulders were broad, skin gleaming in the pale light from the street-lamps, a blending of golden light and dark shade as the muscles rippled. Romaine watched in awed anticipation, breath held, as the movement of his elbows signalled that he was unfastening his trousers.

He turned his head, looking over his shoulder, his smile unreadable. And then, as if satisfied by some silent, invisible signal. He turned, unzipped himself and in one, swift, confident movement, tugged his trousers and underpants down, over his hips, letting them drop to his feet. Romaine heard her own ragged breathing, but couldn't pull her eyes away. She couldn't look at his face, but heard his 'This what you been hoping for?' as he took himself in both hands and walked towards her.

'God Almighty, what have I done?' she asked herself, wondering if it was too late to run screaming from the room. But she was rooted to the spot. Her eyes never left his erection for a second as he lowered himself on top of her, his weight forcing the breath from her body. He took her hand and led it to his prick.

'You're... so... big,' she stuttered in a staccato whisper.

He smiled. 'I told you I'd been watching you.' His eyes were travelling the length of her bare flesh. 'It turns me on.'

'What?'

'The idea that you were listening. Imagining me and Gina together.'

His fingers were searching between her legs, easing them apart. 'Did it make you wet? You're dripping now.' And she was astonished to find that she was. He didn't sound surprised. Her body was responding to him in a way that she'd never felt before. She was no longer in control. She moved against his fingers, drawing them further into her, wanting to feel them against the ridge of pleasure high up inside, knowing they could never reach that place, needing his cock; nothing else and no one else could satisfy her. Only Louie. Only now. Right now. Her fingers circled him and moved to the tune that was echoing in her head, feeling the heat of his flesh, the moist slickness, the rigid rippling as his breathing shortened and he gasped, pulling himself away from her.

Romaine felt almost bereft without his warmth as he reached into the drawer and retrieved the silver foil wrapper. She watched as, almost engrossed with his own hardness, he slid the sheath over his cock, caressing it down the impressive length. It seemed that it was almost with regret that he turned to her. This was all happening so fast, and before she could react, he was caressing her vulva with his fingers, easing his hard penis between her thighs, grasping them, holding them tight against him as he rubbed himself between the soft valley. And then his fingers splayed her legs as he eased the head between her pussy lips, gently at first and then rapidly, thrusting hard until he bulldozed against the neck of her womb, eliciting a scream of pleasure. Louie waited only for a split second before be pulled out and then thrust hard, repeating the movements over and over, seeming to grow thicker, bigger with each moan of pain.

And then he turned her over. Her face was buried into the pillow, and as one hand grasped her hip, the other reached under and rubbed against her clitoris, producing gasps of ecstasy as he ground his cock deep into her pussy, desperate to fill every space, clawing at her skin, raising himself up, palm pushing against her backside, kneeling, forcing himself into her as her orgasm began to build and he thrust into her, desperate for release, screaming loud as he came, flooding her pussy as his body wracked with spasms.

Two weeks later they changed her room back into a sitting room and Gina was never seen again.

❦

As soon as Louie was out the door, Romaine climbed the stairs and ran a bath. She walked into the bedroom and straightened the bed, wanting to obliterate any sign of this morning. She slipped her robe off her shoulders and looked at her body in the long mirror. A hickey on her neck. Bruises just showing up against the dark skin on her arms and a soreness between her legs that she couldn't ignore when she walked. She dropped the robe onto a chair and returned to the bathroom.

She turned off the taps and relished the steam. Lowering her body into the hot water, she winced slightly but was determined to bear it. She gratefully sank beneath the water and rested there, letting her hair spread like heavy tendrils. She allowed the depth of the water to bear her weight for a second, lulling her into a state of relaxation. She thought of nothing for a few minutes and when she finally did, she allowed a single tear to fall, tracing an unfamiliar path down her cheeks. She reached for the flannel and rubbed briskly at her face.

🌻

He knew he'd been wrong. He had never treated Romaine like that before. But, damn it, the way she'd touched him the night before had made him hard and he'd wanted her so bad, even while trying to pretend to himself that he didn't. So he'd jerked off, wanting to show her that he didn't need her, but that hadn't satisfied him. Hadn't got rid of his need for her. Romaine alone could cure what was wrong with him. He wanted her to love him again, to need him again, but there were visions that he couldn't get out of his head: *the two of them together.* Maybe she did still love him, like she said, but he wanted to be the only one. He just couldn't bear to share her with anyone else. She'd promised it would never happen again and maybe she meant it now, but how could he be sure? Yeah, he could lock her up, make sure she came straight home every evening, force her to join in the Friday night sessions, but how could he stop her thinking of, wanting something different?

The office was empty, the rows of computer screens blank, the banks of servers in rows of brushed steel racks whirring away soundlessly, lights flickering orange behind the glass partition.

He didn't need to be here. Sure, Sheldon would be arriving later, like he did every Saturday, but there was no meeting scheduled, no sense of urgency. He'd wanted to play the big, important businessman. More important matters on his mind than trying to rescue his marriage. What an arsehole he was being. He knew that, but it was like an addiction. He didn't know how to stop.

Louie made instant coffee and rummaged in his desk drawer for a crumbled packet of cigarettes and placed one between his lips. He failed to light it with the first match torn from the small book, nor with the second, but he persevered until he succeeded with the fourth. The taste was dry and stale, and made him slightly nauseous but he needed the crackling, spitting cylinder between his fingers. If only to stop his hand balling into a fist. He took a deep drag and stubbed out the cigarette in a saucer.

He pulled a stack of papers from the tray on his desk and tried to concentrate on each one through unseeing eyes.

❦

As she stepped out of the bath, the phone rang. Not again! This time she might just scream at whoever it was breathing heavily on the other end of the line.

'Hello, this is—'

'Ditch the formality, Romaine. It's me.'

'Grace! I was thinking of calling you.'

'Left in the lurch?'

'Too right!'

'So what we doin' today? Spending their money?'

'Have they got any?'

'Okay, we'll spend our own. Where and when?'

Twenty minutes later, Romaine was in her car driving towards trendy Islington with its over-exuberance of fashionable shops. Grace and Sheldon lived in a three-bedroom flat in Highbury. Big enough to accommodate the occasional visits from Sheldon's twelve-year-old son who had chosen to live with his mother in Stockwell. Sheldon had probably never recovered from the disappointment of having produced a child who valued consistency and affection above the material advantages in life. Well, that was Romaine's slightly flippant judgement. In fact, she knew that Sheldon's concern was for how a young black man could possibly survive in this country without a whole heap of money behind him. After all, money was power and that's why he and Louie seemed to spend every available hour in their office. Romaine suspected that Grace both loved and resented the boy, since he was probably what had stood in the way of children of her own, but she was outwardly too self-assured to admit that to anyone.

Romaine didn't need to knock. Grace must have been standing at the window waiting for her arrival. Each time she saw the older woman, Romaine was surprised anew by her poise and elegance. Gold-coloured skin that seemed to shimmer and thick black hair that had turned prematurely white above one temple. Of the type that still needed to straighten her hair, and couldn't countenance any argument against the practice, Grace had married her 'toy boy', though Romaine found it difficult to think of him as such. It was difficult to guess her age, but Romaine suspected she was somewhere in her early forties, though she often pretended to be ancient. Grace was probably midway between her own age and her mother's, which made their friendship complex, but curiously satisfying.

Grace took her hand, and pulled her along the hallway into the huge kitchen, all brushed stainless steel and old wood flooring, Islington to the core. The routine was the same as always. Grace would kiss her on either cheek, never letting go of her hand, and then take a step back to survey her friend's face, as if mapping the contours for an ordnance survey map. At first, Romaine had been embarrassed, realising how rarely anyone, since her mother's death, had actually really looked at her with the interest and concern that only another woman can show, seeing past the makeup both physical and mental. Today, Grace raised a finger and traced the tight line that extended above Romaine's eyes.

'What's wrong, darling?'

How was it that Grace always knew?

'I'll put the coffee on. I guess we can forget about the shopping today. Do we really need anything new anyway? Let's talk first. We'll see if we need the retail therapy later.'

'You're a witch, Grace. You know that? I didn't think I needed to talk. And then you just ask me what's wrong and I feel as if my whole world is about to collapse.'

'It won't, but tell me what's going on. What's he done now?'

'You mustn't blame Louie. It was all my fault.'

'So you made a mistake—if that's really what it was, I'm still not convinced—and Louie expects you to go on paying the price. For how long? Even a murderer would have got parole by now. And I'm not even convinced that the jury got it right in your case. Or should I say the judge since I ain't' see no jury in this case?'

'I cheated on him.'

'Humph!'

'That's what it was, Grace.'

'Just the once! And because he wasn't giving you what you needed.'

'That's no excuse. He hasn't forgiven me.'

'I think Louie is using it as an excuse to cover his own inadequacies. Have you ever thought that he'll never be able to give you what you want, Romaine?'

'Everything was fine before I…'

'That's what you say. That's what Louie wants you to think. I'm not sure that could have been true.'

'You don't like Louie, do you?'

'Girl, it's not a question of liking him or not liking him. Louie was, and maybe still is, a good friend. I thought that he was a fine man. One who loved you and would care for you.' Romaine wondered if it was possible that her mother's spirit was floating somewhere just above their heads and feeding Grace with her lines. 'But now I just hate what he's doing to you. Look at the way you are now. And all because little Louie got his ego hurt.'

'Grace, you can't possibly know what it's like between us. I love Louie and he loves me too.'

'Okay, okay, Romaine. I'm just the messenger. No need to get annoyed with me. I'm just telling it like I see it, saying the things you not telling yourself.'

'I'm sorry, Grace. I guess I'm really angry with myself. You know, I should have seen it coming. All these years, every single guy I've met has hit on me—'

'Girl, you shouldn't look so hot.'

'You know it's got nothing to do with what I look like or how I am with them.' Romaine sighed. 'Whether they're single, married, straight, bi, strangers or friends, they've just got to try it on. It's a percentage game. They can't help themselves.'

'Does that include Sheldon?'

'Of course. Oh, I'm sorry. I didn't mean to... well... But that was long, long ago. Before he met you, Grace. And Sheldon and I sorted that out.'

CHAPTER 3

'How?' Grace's stare was intense, but there was a half smile on her lips.

'You know Sheldon doesn't play games. He just asked me, straight up: "Do you want to sleep with me?" I said "No." We got that out of the way and we've been friends ever since.'

'Was that before you got together with Louie?'

Romaine hesitated for a moment too long.

Grace laughed. 'So he tried to steal his best friend's girl? Wow! I didn't know he had it in him.'

'You know it wasn't like that. Just something that had to be dealt with before—'

'Honestly, Rome, you don't have to protect him. I kinda like that horny streak in my man! And at least he has good taste.'

'I guess all I was trying to say was that after all those guys, I should have been old enough, wise enough, experienced enough to have seen what was coming, but this was different…'

Grace watched as Romaine twisted the gold band around her finger, her knuckles almost white with the tension. She couldn't understand why Romaine was torturing herself. In her position, she would just have kept quiet and taken the opportunity to have a good time. But she should try to understand what was bugging her friend.

'Well, I suppose the two of you had settled into a strong friendship. There was a bond. Why would you have expected it? Don't beat yourself up. These things happen. The question is: what are you going to do about it now?' Grace touched Romaine's shoulder, a brief gesture of solidarity. 'You can't go on like this, Romaine.' She brushed the hair back from Romaine's cheek.

'I know.'

Grace busied herself with the percolator, using the coffee-making ritual as a firebreak, giving Romaine time and space to calm her thoughts, to retreat from the place where she obviously didn't want to go right now. She poured two cups and placed one before her friend, a neutral smile plastered to her face.

'So how was yesterday evening? Sheldon was home late. What exciting things did you guys get up to?'

'Oh, the usual weekly orgy.' Romaine joked, trying to lighten the mood. 'Sheldon was particularly skilful.'

'I taught him everything he knows!'

'Grace!'

'Well that's the whole point of younger men. You can mould them before they get into bad habits. You know, though, joking apart, I still think it's peculiar the way your husband holds these weekly male bonding sessions and insists you should be there. I know he wants to keep an eye on you, but I still think it's weird.'

'I like the guys. I enjoy their company,' Romaine hedged.

'I wasn't asking about you. What does Louie get out of it?'

❦

Romaine didn't spend as much time as she'd planned with Grace. Too many uncomfortable questions that she didn't want to deal with today. Her head was too fuzzy. When she got back, Colin was waiting in his car, engine switched off, just about to dial a number on his mobile.

'Hey. I was just about to call you. Wondering if I left my wallet in your place last night. I've been looking everywhere.'

This was the last thing she needed. She didn't want to have to entertain Colin. Romaine could deal with him in company, but there was something about him that still made her uncomfortable. Besides, she'd left Grace because she needed to be alone. But what could she say? She couldn't refuse to let him into the house.

'Come in and have a look, Colin. I didn't see it when we were clearing up.'

Colin followed her into the house, unusually quiet now that he was without an audience. This was ridiculous. Normally, a joke would have sprung to his lips by now, but they were unexpectedly dry and he licked them surreptitiously. He'd spent so much time with her over the years, so what was the problem now?

As Romaine walked into the kitchen, he headed straight for the sitting room, to where he knew the wallet would be. He cursorily swept his hand under the sofa cushions in case she was watching and then delved into the sides of the battered armchair, lifting the black leather wallet with a flourish.

'I've been turning my flat upside down. I knew it had to be here somewhere.' He joined her in the kitchen.

'Well, thank God you found it. Do you want a drink, Colin?' Romaine silently prayed that he'd say no.

He massaged his temple. 'Never again!'

'I meant tea or coffee.'

'Sure. Why not? Where's Louie?'

'Working.'

As if he hadn't known. He'd predicted as much; that's why he was there.

Colin perched on a stool, feeling a little like a lapdog, his eyes following her every movement.

'So, how are things, Rome?'

'What? You mean since you last saw me, oh…' she studied her watch melodramatically, 'all of thirteen hours ago?'

He was silent for a while, dredging his mind for something light, frothy, insubstantial to say. 'You seemed… well… on edge. I wondered if everything was okay.' Call that lightening the tone, Colin?

Romaine laughed. 'I was perfectly fine until you guys made me lose all my matchsticks. That was the only thing wrong with me. But you know I'll win it all back next week.' She handed him a mug of coffee.

He hesitated, uncertain whether or not to speak. But he had to keep the conversation going, there was so much that he needed to find out.

'Why do you put up with it, Romaine? The Friday night sessions?'

'Because I enjoy your company so much.' She was obviously determined not to give away anything much.

'I'm serious. Why do you let him force you?'

Romaine looked up at him. His bulk in the room was becoming oppressive even though he wasn't a big man. His dark, slanted eyes were intense and, once again, she felt as if his look was attempting to strip her naked, not just physically, but mentally too.

'I don't believe this. First Grace. Now you. It's like we're holding a witches' coven. Why are our Friday nights so significant?'

'I thinking Louie makes you come.'

'He does not.'

'Or makes it so that you don't have any choice.'

Romaine forced herself to laugh. 'You're joking.'

'No, but—'

'Colin, what are you suggesting? That he uses physical force or something? Or blackmails me? Or shackles me to the table leg? Come on, it's Louie we're talking about here.'

'I've known Louie for a hell of a long time. I know what he's like when things don't go exactly his way. The way he retreats into himself, even when he thinks the rest of us don't know. What did you say to him, Rome? Did you finally tell him that you're not happy with him? Is that it? I can imagine how he'd take that.'

Romaine looked at Colin, a hint of anger flashing in her eyes before she lowered them. She calmly drained the remains of her coffee cup, making time for her anger to dissipate. She made herself look straight into Colin's eyes.

'I don't think you have the right to say things like that to me.' Her eyes flashed. 'Colin, I thought I made myself clear. Everything's fine.'

There was steel in her voice, but he couldn't stop himself. He'd gone too far now to back away. 'I don't believe you, Rome, but you're pushing me away. I know that. But I think you're going to need me some day soon. You know where I am.'

Colin patted his jacket pocket, checking for the wallet. He pulled it out and glanced at it. 'I left it here on purpose.'

'I know.'

'I worry about you, Rome.'

'Don't.'

He watched her for a moment, curious, needing something from her that he didn't find. Her eyes were shuttered. He kissed her on the cheek and left, closing the door softly behind him.

❦

'She likes to pretend that she's so strong,' Colin told himself as he got into the car, 'but, underneath it, she's vulnerable.' He smiled to himself as he thought of the poker game. She had tried so hard not to look at any of them. Didn't dare to raise her head. Not sure that she'd be able to conceal what she was thinking. That was one of the things he found fascinating about her. The fact that you could see the truth of her soul in her eyes. Romaine actually believed that she could hide her thoughts. But if you knew her well enough, and if she let you look into those incredible eyes, there was nothing more that you needed to know. There was nothing that she could hide from him.

She thinks that she enjoys being with all of us. Or that's what she tells us. And probably him too. Every single Friday night for, what, two months now? But she must be doing it for him. No, I don't think that he'd actually use physical force to get her there; that's not Louie's style. But I know him well enough to understand that he'd play mind games that would be hard to resist. I've experienced them myself, many times in all the years I've known Louie. That's why my heart goes out to her now. Soft, achingly vulnerable and believing she's so strong, that's Romaine.

Colin turned the key to start the ignition, but then he was still, not making any attempt to move on.

He could pinpoint the moment when things changed between her and Louie. The moment that brought her into those Friday night sessions. He didn't know what she'd said to him. But the irony was that, whatever Louie had intended, it brought her closer. Every week. Every damned week to torture him. Knowing that he couldn't get near to her when every fibre of his being wanted to be the knight in shining armour rescuing her from the ogre who had imprisoned her heart and soul. If she would let him. God Almighty, since when had he descended into fucking Fairy-La-La land?

It must have been around the time when she cut her hair. He wondered then if it was some kind of penance. And in spite of all that had happened between them, it was like the first time he had really seen her. There they all were, watching some match that was just a pretence for them to be together, getting drunk and they must have missed her key in the lock because, suddenly, she was there, tired lines around her eyes, but smiling broadly. Her hair long enough to just curl around her ears, to frame those huge, wide, trusting eyes, but much shorter than it had been. He had felt a sense of shock. It hurt that she'd decided to sacrifice her hair. But it made her seem so fragile, so vulnerable and he wanted to reach out and take her in his arms. But he couldn't show how he was feeling. Not in front of Louie. She was wearing red, a warm dark red, the colour they call maroon. It was something that came down to her knees, something warm and soft and seductive that clung to her body and outlined the swell of her breasts and the curve of her behind. Something stirred, hardening his cock before he had time to check himself. What the hell was he doing? He knew he had no right to think of her that way.

Colin had just about gained a semblance of control when she turned to him, warmth and wariness both in her exhausted eyes. She walked towards him, the scent of her perfume getting stronger, heady, overpowering, until she kissed him on the cheek with a soft 'Hi!' He moved unexpectedly and the curve of her breast brushed against his arm. Like static electricity.

Colin stayed away from the next Friday session. Took care of business at home.

And then this week, he had watched as Louie took her in his arms, his fingers straying down to the curve of her buttocks and he wanted to challenge him, like a rutting deer, antlers at the ready. He had no right. None at all. But tell that to the marines. And then Sheldon had started the play fight with the chicken legs. Like he'd read what was going on in Colin's head. He wouldn't put that past him either. But Colin wasn't going to deny it. He wanted Romaine. Wanted to have her. To himself. Needed her in a way that spelled d-a-n-g-e-r. He had to stay away. He knew that he couldn't. He turned and looked at the house. She was closing the heavy wooden shutters. Had she been looking at him? The idea excited him. Maybe he should have gone back, tried again with her. As the second shutter closed, he could imagine her bolting it into place. He released the handbrake and pressed on the accelerator, steering away from the kerb.

❦

Romaine closed the door behind Colin with a guilty sense of relief. She didn't know what she might have ended up saying to him if he hadn't left just then. Why did he have to be so demanding? What on earth did he think she could give him? Surely they'd got all that sorted years ago. As she turned away from the door, the phone rang and she raced to answer it. Another hang-up. It must be Louie. She would ignore his games. She turned on the stereo and tuned in to a radio station that was playing blues. Suited her mood. She gently massaged her temples, hoping to stop the pounding. She glanced out of the window. Oh Lord, Colin was still there. What was he doing? Was he watching her? It was too dark for her to tell, but this wasn't funny. She closed both shutters, literally shutting him out. She was shattered and didn't want to think about Colin at all. There was too much else going on right now.

Louie hadn't left any message on the answering machine. She didn't know if he would be at home at all. And what if he did come back? These days, it probably wouldn't make much difference. She'd still feel so alone. If only she hadn't confessed everything! It wasn't as if he would ever have known. She had only told him because he asked where she had been and it hadn't occurred to her to lie. Unashamed, she'd naively told him everything in a rush of innocent wonder. That's how it had felt until she'd seen the expression on his face. Now she wondered if, subconsciously, she hadn't been trying to repair whatever it was that must have been wrong with their marriage for her to have done what she did. Louie, of course, was unaware that anything was wrong at all. And maybe he was right. It might be that, with hindsight, she was now rewriting history. Maybe they had been perfectly, blissfully happy. But if so, why would she have responded to someone else? Maybe just greed.

It worried her now to see the kind of games that Louie was playing. Had he always been like that? Maybe she'd been blind to it. She resented the way her husband could be so charming and attentive when they were in public, but so horribly insular and selfish and angry when they were alone together. She would never have imagined this of him. Or had she driven him to it? It would damn well serve him right if she took her pleasure somewhere else, even if that's how their problems had first started.

Romaine turned off the light in the sitting room and unbolted the shutter. She opened it a crack and peeped around the frame. She sighed with relief. No shiny black Mercedes parked opposite the window. At least Colin had gone. One thing off her mind. And still, it was curious that there was this lingering doubt about Colin. Surely he had proved himself to be a good friend.

It wasn't too difficult to go back to the afternoon of the knock on the door. It was still alive in her mind. Only three hours after the end of her mother's Sunday service. It had taken them that long to track her down. Her mother had neglected to update her address book. Next of kin. Romaine Webster. Absolute next of kin. Nobody else even came close. Her father had disappeared to Canada when she was only three, that country chosen because for what might be a brief period, it seemed to actively welcome immigrants. She had no memory of him. Since then, there had been just Romaine and her mother.

Romaine opened the door to the dark uniform, silver buttons. That's all she could concentrate on. The woman, a female constable, stood in front of the other dark bulk. Looking for a Mrs Ro… Man… Webster. Why? Could they come in? The initial instinct not to let the law in without knowing why. What had Colin done with his stash of dope? Any roaches in the ashtrays? And then looking up to the plastered-on, concerned look tinged with suspicion as the two figures looked over her shoulder and viewed the group of men, palette shading only from light to dark brown.

Sorry to say that… accident… mother hit… car waiting outside… hospital.

Romaine thought instantly of her father, needing someone. How would she track him down? It had been enough years from him to retreat from unwelcome memories, the burden of responsibilities.

The guys all insisted on accompanying her, whether from empathy or instinctive distrust of the police, she didn't know.

At the hospital, it was Colin who took charge, interrogating nurses, tracking down consultants while Louie, Sheldon and Matthew took turns to hold her close. And when she entered the room, it seemed Colin was already there, assuring her that she would be able to bear this latest trauma. Her mother, white with bandages—why hadn't God made them brown? Her mother, eyes opening and flickering as if searching for something, perhaps her only child. Her mother, now a stranger, every breath of familiarity airbrushed away by the clinical atmosphere, the tubes, the beeping machinery, the subdued sirens of death in the air.

She knew that she should rush to the bedside, clasp her mother in her arms, but she was scared. Not petrified, not terrified, just scared. Not thinking of her mother, just worried about how she would deal with the death. Because it was obvious that her mother was dying.

And it was Colin who was the director, orchestrating her movements, giving the cues, prompting her. So that when it was over, Romaine felt as if the curtain had come down and she had played her part, curtsying, accepting the accolade of a well-disposed audience. It was Colin who gave her the strength, taking it for granted that she would do what she needed to do.

But it was Louie who, every night, long after the audience had departed, took her in his arms, rocking and murmuring, 'I'll miss her too, honey. She became part of our lives. She's joined the ancestors and is looking out for you. She's part of you, honey. That can never change. Don't cry, sweetheart. We're still a family. Always will be.'

❦

She walked towards the kitchen, only distracted momentarily by the glow of the screen-saver in Louie's study. It was beckoning her. Tempting her.

She deliberately turned away and proceeded to the kitchen. Romaine poured herself a glass of red wine and returned to the front of the house, not turning on the main light, but instead, a small table lamp by the most comfortable armchair in the room.

She picked up the *Radio Times*, the only magazine in the place, and began to read, seeing it only as a distraction. She turned to today's date. Nothing she wanted to watch on television. It would be so easy to pick up the phone, just to talk. But she had promised herself that she would not do this and it would be like breaking an unspoken vow to Louie. She owed it to him. But Lord, he made it difficult. If he wasn't going to

make any effort himself, what was she supposed to do? Be a martyr for
the rest of her life?

🦌

It was 3:00 before Sheldon arrived in the office. He looked fresh and
carefree. And why wouldn't he? Louie had never been able to work out
what made Grace tick, but he guessed she was good for his friend.
Sheldon had never seemed so contented, so relaxed, so self-confident
before he met her. Grace had been an executive in one of the record
companies that they dealt with. In fact, it had been her decision to give
them the contract. She'd made her interest in Sheldon perfectly clear,
insisting that he should be the one to handle all the negotiations. Louie
had called her the preying mantis, seeing her as a predatory female, with
her long, tall body and thin, bony limbs; one of them ball-breaking
types that would chew Sheldon up and spit him out, but only after she'd
bitten off his head. But he'd had to keep the nickname to himself when
Sheldon stopped laughing at the joke. Sheldon had never been one to
chat too much 'bout the women in his life and, in idle moments, Louie
had wondered if he was, in fact, still a virgin. But that was never the kind
of thing you asked your mate. You could joke about it, tease him, but
never just come out and ask! Anyway, the indication was that he
managed to satisfy the woman's demands because, these days, Sheldon
didn't seem to be frettin' 'bout nuttin'.

'Whassup, Lou? What you doing here? Don't tell me is some emergency.' His eyes behind the thick frames instinctively flickered towards
the bank of servers and Louie almost imagined that he crossed the
fingers of both hands behind his back. But that would have been childish superstition. In spite of endless backup systems, it was a constant fear
that, one day, something would go drastically wrong. They sometimes
still laughed uncontrollably when they looked at how far they'd come.
The idea had first occurred to them when they'd been messing around
in Sheldon's flat, playing with the new software he'd bought, his new toy.
They'd been composing a tune, the one that was going to make their
joint fortune and the program had suddenly frozen. They hadn't saved
up to that point and lost all the material. They no longer knew and
didn't ask who had actually thought of it. It didn't matter. Someone had

raised the question of the number of record companies that had huge archives that weren't backed up. And then what if the same thing that had just happened to them occurred during a recording session? Or equipment failed. Or a fire broke out? They could risk losing tens of thousands of pounds' worth of material. But what if someone, someone like them, could provide constant backup facilities at the end of a line?

The idea was so good that they found the finance with little trouble. They started small with the newly-formed independent companies. They built up good contacts, were recommended to individual artists recording material in their bedrooms, and then in turn came to the attention of executives from the majors, like Grace. On paper the company was worth millions and they employed technicians, sales, finance and admin people as well as a PR company, but they still, totally illogically, feared power cuts or a blown fuse.

'No. No emergency. Just trying to catch up.'

Sheldon gave him one of those looks that said 'You lying bastard,' but he kept his mouth shut. He simply opened a sash window, his protest at the stale nicotine in the air, and switched on the kettle.

He sat at his desk, adjacent to Louie's in the open-plan office and powered up his computer, scanning for e-mails that needed a fast response. Since they'd started expanding overseas, Sheldon made it his business to make sure that the time differences wouldn't present any obstacle to success. They might need to employ even more staff in future, work in shifts, if necessary, but he was currently monitoring the situation.

They worked in almost companionable silence for a couple of hours. And then Sheldon removed his glasses and ran a hand through his cropped hair. He rubbed his eyes, emphasising the dark rings around them. He stood and walked across to the makeshift bar. He lifted a bottle of dark rum in Louie's direction, a question in his gesture. Louie nodded and Sheldon wiped two dusty glasses on the edge of his T-shirt before pouring generous measures, which he topped up with flat ginger ale. They would have to do something about re-stocking the bar.

He passed a glass to Louie and returned to his seat. He rested both feet on his desk and took a sip of his drink, playing for time, not knowing how to start. Louie did the same, almost mirroring his every action. Sheldon and Louie rarely had these types of man-to-man conversations. Left that kind of thing to the women. Sheldon coughed, scratching his head, trying to figure out what to say.

'So…'

'So.'

'So Spurs look like they might be relegated.' What kind of pathetic way was that to open a conversation about, well… personal matters? Especially when they lived on either side of the footballing divide, Louie in Tottenham Hotspurs territory, Sheldon, even today, wearing Arsenal colours.

Louie sat up in his chair.

'You know say is just luck. The way Arsenal don't even have two cents to rub together.'

'Cents or no cents, we have Henry. What you have, bwoy?'

'That's just it, without Henry, what you goin' do?'

'Plenty of other fine players, but the thing is *with* Henry—' Sheldon stopped, realising that he was being too easily diverted. Fun though it might be to enjoy the upper hand, this wasn't taking them where they needed to be. Sheldon thought hard.

'So…' he said. He got up and poured them both another drink. Thank goodness he'd travelled by tube today and wouldn't have to worry about driving home.

This was going to be even harder than he'd imagined and Louie didn't seem to want to help out. He'd been surprised to find Louie in the office today, but last night, in spite of the alcohol, the jokes, the habitual laughter, he'd sensed that there was something wrong between Romaine and him. Her eyes had glittered as if she was on something and Louie had laughed loudly and over-long. There was something simmering under the surface. Sheldon had his suspicions about Colin, had seen the looks he exchanged with Romaine. He didn't say anything to Louie, but had gone home grateful for the uncomplicated relationship he shared with his wife.

He knew well enough that the other guys had laughed at the idea of him and Grace together. When they'd first met, she'd been a big-shot somebody in a record company and he'd been a petitioner at her door.

There had been something in her that Louie had found daunting, but Sheldon had never seen it. She had been a kindred spirit that he recognised immediately. He was the one to ask her out, sending an e-mail message as soon as he got back to the office that first afternoon. He'd gone back to her apartment that very first night. That had been some freaky shit. All his fantasies come true.

She had suggested Granita, joking about the power play that had gone on there between the prime minister and the chancellor. He'd read the stories in the papers and had been curious about the place, wondering if she'd managed to book the same table. In the end, he'd been less impressed than he'd imagined, toying with the food, drinking more wine, watching the movement of her lips, her fingers, the directness of her gaze, and wanting to get out of the place as fast as he could. She must have felt the same way since she skipped dessert and coffee and, without any games or subterfuge, came out with it as soon as he asked for the bill.

'Coffee at my place?'

And the brush of her fingers against his crotch confirmed that she wasn't intending to grind any beans that night.

Her flat was within walking distance, across the road, down Cross Street and right towards the Angel, past Tesco. A left into St Peters Street and she was soon unlocking the shiny black door of a Georgian terrace. As soon it was closed behind them, she walked halfway up the stairs, stopped and, holding his gaze, unbuttoned her coat, lifted her dress and removed her panties, holding them for a moment under her nose. He could only guess at the warmth, the musky odour and yet he squirmed uncomfortably in his trousers, his cock instantly rock-like.

He looked around. There must be at least four flats in the building and she was sitting on the step now, her legs wide apart, the fuzz of black hair unable to conceal the puffy pussy lips, the inviting, glistening dark red flesh calling to him. He shifted uncomfortably, trying to move his erection to a more bearable spot in his trousers.

She licked her lips and wet the middle finger of her right hand. It descended like an arrow into the bushy triangle of hair, stroking her clitoris slowly, gently and then down, further down, it disappeared up to the knuckle into the mysterious hollow between her thighs.

Sheldon could feel the pounding of his heart and wondered if it might not burst right out of his chest. Beads of sweat rose to his forehead, but he didn't dare to wipe them off. He was rooted to the spot, almost literally petrified.

'You scared?' There was a challenge in her voice, but her smile was tempting. She spread her legs wider so he could see her finger moving in and out, slick and wet with her juice. She pulled it out and used it to beckon to him. 'Kneel!'

He was like jelly, like a toddler unsure of how to control his limbs. His brain was trying to tell him that one foot simply went before the other but that thought was being blocked out by the thought of ready, waiting, hungry, freaky pussy.

Grace laughed; a confident, knowing sound that broke the spell. Like a bullet fired at point blank range, he was down on his knees, on the bottom step, his hands around her buttocks, lifting her to him like a luscious, ripe water-melon. And just like a man dying of hunger and thirst he supped and drank and licked and chewed and probed while she turned and writhed and grabbed his head, grinding her clitoris against his lips, bruising him until she pulled away and cried out for him to stop. She raised him up and slid the tongue of his belt from the buckle. She tugged at his zip, reaching inside to grasp him, to free him. He expected her to say something, but she stood, not for one second letting go of him, her thumb fondling him, the tip of her sharpened nail catching against his flesh and she proceeded up the stairs, pulling him as if leading a bull by the horns. He was sure that he heard a door clicking shut somewhere in the darkness up above. He felt his cock twitch at the sound.

He almost knew what to expect of her bedroom. The first time he'd walked into her office and their eyes met, he'd recognised a fellow traveller. Sheldon's sexual encounters had, as Louie suspected, been few. But each had been intense, because he'd selected every one with precise care and discrimination. Emotion hadn't come into it. He'd known what he wanted and had gone after it with the same efficiency that he applied to the business. Discreet ads in specialist magazines. Websites that didn't appear on the majority of search engines. Upmarket London clubs that didn't advertise their services with neon lights or polished door plaques. That's how his babymother had come into his life; a petite redhead who, ultimately, hadn't understood the subtleties and had taken the game a little too far.

Grace turned on a couple of strategically placed lamps that barely illuminated the room, just lifted the darkness enough for him to see the four-poster bed, the dark red satin sheets. The room was almost masculine in its austerity, the only hint of luxury the bed.

She turned away from him and disappeared through a door. Sheldon looked around him. A full-length mirror. Dark panelled doors. No sign of feminine artifice: no creams, potions, lotions. No pictures on the walls. Simple blinds. No frills, bows, ribbons, cushions, furry toys. He silently nodded his approval, but found himself strangely intimidated, by the austerity of the room. He hardly dared to move, his heart was beating fast with anticipation.

Grace reappeared just as suddenly as she'd left. And the transformation made his breath catch in his throat. She was wearing more than before. Something that covered her from ankle to throat, from shoulder to wrist. A gleaming gold leather that caressed every inch of her body making her seem more than naked. Zips in every conceivable erotic position. High heels. Acute points to the toes. She'd done something to her eyes, something that made them more defined, more slanted, cat-like, something that made him shiver. Her lips were red, bright, scarlet red, the colour of blood. A colour that matched the red of her long, sharp nails.

'Scared?' She asked him again. The answer was 'Yes'. And no. He shook his head and took a few rapid steps, closing the distance between them.

He reached out just the one hand and caressed the viscous softness of the leather. He inhaled deeply, taking in the animal odour. He had to raise himself to his full height to kiss her. He wanted to impale her on his tongue, to delve as deep as he could into her body, to possess her, but instead, he brushed his lips against hers and then sucked gently on the fullness of her bottom lip. He took a step away and waited, hands folded against his genitals. He thought he knew the protocol. He'd wait for her command.

But Grace surprised him. She reached out and loosened his tie, pulling it from the collar. Then she unbuttoned his shirt, her nails tickling his chest, flicking against his nipples as they worked their way down towards his groin. She eased the shirt off his shoulders and stood looking at him, like a colonel-in-chief inspecting the ranks. She pushed his trousers down over his hips along with his boxer shorts. Almost stumbling, he rushed to step out of them along with his socks and shoes.

She moved behind him then, fingers smoothing over the muscles of his shoulder, thumbs probing the knots of tension under his shoulder-blades. Her hands were strong, unrelenting as they swooped down his sides and over the roundness of his buttocks, pressing firmly, expertly moulding, as her lips hovered along the trajectory, not touching his skin, but the hot breath letting him know. And then she was pressing her whole body against him, the leather clammy against his back, the zips scratching his flesh.

His hands still guarded his erection and he concentrated hard on trying to contain himself. More than anything, he wanted her strong fingers around his prick, moving slowly, tightly. Or even his own fingers, but he didn't dare. She might stop and what she was doing felt so good. Sooooo good.

And then she did stop.

'Lie down, Sheldon. On the bed.'

He could feel her eyes boring into him as he followed her command.

He lay on the bed feeling faintly ridiculous, his erection pointing skyward as he waited. Grace walked towards him and sat next to him. She opened a drawer by the side of the bed.

'I think I can guess what you want.'

His cock twitched again and Grace patted it gently, almost as if it was a favoured pet.

She extracted a series of velvet-covered boxes with silver clasps, laying each one carefully on the sheets. Without opening them, she discarded several, returning them to the drawer even though, to Sheldon, many of them looked identical. He wondered how she could differentiate, but it was almost as if she could see straight through the velvet into the contents. Finally, she nodded, as if satisfied.

'Open them.'

The first box held a long, dark feather. The second, four black velvet ropes. The third, what looked like a large silver bullet linked by a wire to a switch. The fourth, a short-handled whip. Sheldon gulped with fear, excitement and expectation.

Grace picked up the ropes and stared at his hard-on.

'I think we're going to need these.'

❦

Sheldon realised that his fingers were tracing a line along his T-shirt, over and over. He almost winced as he pressed a little too hard on the welt covered by the cotton fabric. He smiled to himself for a moment remembering this morning… Grace… tall, naked but for the thigh-length leather boots. Grace, dominant. Grace and the severe look in her eyes… He looked up at his friend. Where was he? Oh yes, Louie needing to talk.

'So…' he repeated.

'So.'

It was near enough midnight when Louie finally called Romaine. He probably wouldn't be home. He and Sheldon might have to work through the night.

❦

The phone rang at 2:30 am, waking her. Another hang-up. It was a while before Romaine could drift back to sleep.

The call at 7:30 am wasn't from another anonymous caller. Romaine could only wish it was. Sunday morning. It would be Dolores, Louie's mother. Every Sunday morning the same thing. As if they were likely to forget when they risked her wrath descending upon them. And Dolores' anger was worse than any of the tribulations visited upon King Herod. Romaine picked up the phone. It was, indeed, Dolores reminding her that they were due for Sunday lunch.

'No, I hadn't forgotten, Dolores,' she sighed. 'But Louie's not at home. He's gone into the office today.' Romaine prayed that would be reason enough for her to be excused. How she would love to pull the duvet up over her head and go back to sleep. For years.

'That boy work too hard, especially on the Lord's Sabbath. But no worries, child. I'll get Matthew to pick you up on his way.' And she put the phone down before Romaine could protest.

It was like she was being chaperoned. There was no way that she could get away from Louie's circle. Maybe they all knew. Perhaps he'd told them that she couldn't any longer be trusted to drive from Tottenham all the way to Hackney without stopping off for an illicit encounter. So Matthew would make a huge detour to pick her up. Battersea to Hackney via Tottenham didn't make sense. This was beginning to feel more than a little claustrophobic.

The house felt even more empty and quiet than usual on a Sunday morning. Louie's presence wasn't exactly relaxing these days, but the familiarity of his sheer physical being banished the ghosts that hovered in the corners of a house that was too big for the two of them. Dolores' constant litany was that they needed children to fill this enormous mansion of a home—only three bedrooms, but a mansion to her, nevertheless, a woman who had only recently graduated to a two-bedroom semi-detached in a modern complex, courtesy of her generous first-born son.

Romaine got out of bed and, yawning, walked down the stairs, intent on the day's first fix of caffeine. On the way, though, the door to Louie's study, slightly ajar, caught her attention. She shook her head and made her way to the kitchen. She turned on the radio and shook a generous amount of ground coffee into the cafetière. Her sleep had been restless, filled with the kind of dreams that she didn't want to recall. She rubbed her eyes and as she did so, felt the sudden, sharp prickle of tears that sprang to her eyes for no apparent reason, apart from the dreams that she chose not to remember. She quickly poured a mug of thick, black coffee, sweetened it with a spoonful of honey, intending to take it back to bed.

On the way, though, she made a detour. The study beckoned and Romaine couldn't see why she should deny herself. She hadn't promised him anything about this. And what harm could it possibly do. She didn't turn on the light, but edged her way to the desk, guided by the daylight seeping through the curtains and reflecting off the darkened screen. She sat at the swivel chair and took a few sips of coffee before leaning forward to press the button. She was surprised by the glow of the blue light on the console. In the office, it was orange. Showed how long it was since she'd been in this room. Louie's domain. Damn well serve him right if she invaded his territory. As the welcome screen disappeared, leaving his personalised desktop, Romaine's eyes scanned the monitor, searching for the Internet Explorer icon. There. She wiped her hands against her nightdress and double-clicked.

Now, what the hell was the name of the site? Hell and damnation. She didn't know. It wasn't even that she couldn't remember. She honestly didn't know. She had been so preoccupied with that fantastic body that she hadn't even noticed the URL. Romaine looked away from the monitor, more disappointed than she would have expected. Everything was conspiring against her experiencing any pleasure. She leaned towards the computer, index finger outstretched to turn off the machine. And then it occurred to her: try the search again. What had she been searching for? Something to do with black men. That's all she needed to type in and then she would find the site.

Several clicks later and everything was definitely working against her. Romaine leaned back in the chair and massaged the nape of her aching neck. She rotated her head to ease the muscles and picked up the mug from beside the chair. She took a sip of unpleasantly cold coffee as she tried to take herself back to Friday evening in the office. What had been different? Concentrating on the screen in front of, trying to visualise what she'd done that day, it suddenly occurred to her that she must have been using a different search engine. That was it! Now, which one did they normally use in the office? She just couldn't remember. Romaine glanced at her watch. Too late now, anyway. She needed to get ready for lunch. As she reached to turn off the machine, the name flashed into her head and she typed in the address, lunch with her mother-in-law now the furthest thing from her mind.

Once again, she entered 'black+men' and waited. She clicked on the first result. There he was, her black magic man in all his glory. Romaine breathed out deeply, a sigh that seemed to release much of the tension that had been building for days now. She took her time to glory in the spectacle before her, this time taking in more than the perfection of his physique; the hint of un-airbrushed razor bumps around his chin; the fine lines around his eyes that made her think he was older than he wanted her to believe; the hint of fullness around his waist that suggested a recent re-acquaintance with the gym. But Romaine still wasn't disappointed. She allowed her eyes to linger on his trim calves, the muscular thighs, the gorgeous, stately rod…

It took a while for her to notice the voluptuously naked woman standing behind him, the 'enter' button and the requisite warning. She glanced past the words—a long time since she had been eighteen—and, before she could change her mind, clicked on the button, not knowing, not daring to consider what she might find.

For a moment, she couldn't pretend to be other than disappointed. No more tantalising full-page photos, just a 'quick search' box, demanding to know what she was looking for. 'Couples looking for men.' 'Women looking for groups.' 'Men looking for lesbian couples.' 'Women looking for men.' 'Men looking for women'. No need to go any further down the list. That might be a sensible place to start. So she told the boxes: anywhere, yes she was between the ages of 18 and 99 and lived in England. She pressed on the search button and held her breath for the few seconds that the search took.

Just a list of names with tiny images beside them. Why did she feel let down? What had she wanted to find? Surely she hadn't expected more perfect specimens like the one on the home page? Well, if she was honest, that's just what she'd been hoping for. More bare flesh… like that gorgeous brown gleaming chest, well-defined muscles, the cute smile and okay, naked, erect, enormous, ready cocks. Those were the images that had been floating around at the back of her consciousness: cinnamon, chocolate, hazelnut, golden, ebony, velvety bare flesh, firm, rounded buttocks with that mysterious crease delving between carved, muscular thighs. And then, turning like a statue on a motorised pedestal, revealing penises of all shapes and sizes, but always erect, always turned on by her, the ripples of sensitive flesh, the smooth, dark red bulb at the head, hand reaching for it, lips reaching for it…

Instead, a stark list of names: ActionBoy, Adventurous, Adonis (surely a joke!), AlwaysReady, Balladeer… with those tiny images. Most of them had just posted photographs of their own cocks, strangely unimpressive in their truncated state. Some had used just parts of their bodies, a muscular chest, a firm buttock, sexy eyes. Romaine found herself wondering which magazines they'd been taken from. This was just a downmarket online lonely hearts club. Not what she was looking for at all. She was just about to click on the X in the top right-hand corner of the screen when she noticed Adonis' blurb:

I'll take you to places you've never imagined. I'll suck your tits till you moan, bite your nipples till you scream, nibble your clit and lick your pussy till you faint with pleasure. They don't call me Lizard Tongue for nothing. Satisfaction guaranteed.

Beside it, a tiny photograph of a long, red tongue licking a hardened nipple. Romaine smiled. Much too good to be true. It wouldn't be the first time a guy had made promises he wasn't intending to keep.

She scrolled down the page, glancing at each entry, surprised by some, shocked by a few, amused by many, tantalised by one or two like Ram-Goat:

I'll be your servant. Be my mistress. Use me. I'll sign on the dotted line. I'll do whatever you tell me. I'll bend my will to your desire. Your every wish is my command. My hardened prick awaits your pleasure. It will become erect for only you, or you will be free to punish me. Make me carry out your every desire. I'll fondle your breasts, tease your nipples until you order me to stop. Or lick your pussy for hours and hours until you force me to cease. I expect your punishment if I fail to make you come over and over. Beat me. Hurt me. I await your desire.

Or Kommando:

I can fuck you all night long, non-stop till you drop from exhaustion.

In your dreams! Or Jazz:

Baby, my room is draped in satin and silk. I have a velvet glove. To the sounds of Luther, I'll caress every centimetre of your voluptuous body, a mere glance of softness here, firmer pressure there until you writhe against the satin sheets, offering your breasts to my hungry lips. My gloved hand holds your waiting vulva, one finger melting into flesh, searching your depths. I've created a sable-covered dildo with which I'll tease your clit until I can see the hot juices flowing from your pussy and then I'll plunge it into your clamouring hole, the contrasting hardness and softness driving you to desperation as you cry out for me—

The doorbell rang. Romaine looked at her watch in disbelief. Shit! Matthew. Lunch. Waiting mother-in-law.

The bell again. More insistent this time. Maybe she could pretend that she was out. But Dolores had spoken. Dolores had virtually demanded her presence. She couldn't let herself get into even more trouble. Romaine rushed to open the door, reminded by Matthew's stunned glance that she was still in her dressing gown, which was gaping open. She noticed at the same time as him, that her nipples were erect, her chest flushed. Quickly, she tightened the belt.

'Romaine... I... er... Dolores called... I, um, thought you were expecting us?

'Yes, I was but... I got a little behind. Come in, Matthew. I won't be long.'

He looked a little awkward. 'Elaine's in the car.'

'Bring her in, Matthew. Just a few minutes, I promise.'

Romaine turned away leaving the door wide open. She rushed to turn off the computer in the study and then dashed up the stairs into the bathroom. In less than fifteen minutes, she'd showered, dressed conservatively, lipsticked her mouth and apologised to Elaine for keeping them waiting. Elaine's lips, she noticed, were tight with either irritation or anxiety. They all knew the penalty for being late for Sunday lunch at Dolores' house.

🌶

Matthew's girlfriend was just the type of woman that Romaine would instinctively avoid, given the choice. Unbearably arrogant outside the Hackney house, she was reduced to jelly in the presence of Dolores, her pale face turning almost ghostly with anxiety. Romaine wanted to laugh each time she sat across Dolores' lunch table facing Elaine, watching the wheels turn in her brain as she tried to work out how to avoid offending Dolores, more often than not irritating her by producing no response at all.

Yes, Dolores was a formidable matriarch—why else would Romaine be here at all, attempting to explain her husband's absence? But it wasn't only fear that brought her here. There was genuine admiration for Dolores and a sneaking affection. Tough and uncompromising as she was, there was a deep-seated fairness in the woman and Romaine believed that the only reason that she showed no mercy to Elaine was that she knew how domineering and self-satisfied she became away from her presence. Romaine watched the small, dumpy, freckle-faced woman with warm honeyed skin as she brought the bowls of stewed chicken, jerk pork, yam, banana, rice and peas, green beans, carrots, roast potatoes and fried plantain to the extended table. That was the other reason that Romaine pitched up here every Sunday.

'So, Elaine, you find a job yet?' Dolores knew very well that Elaine worked as a dancer in a night-club, but she refused to consider that a proper job. Week after week, since Elaine's appearance on the scene, she regaled them all with stories of how hard she had worked to bring up she children dem, and the pride she took in not being one of dem lazy good-for-nothing woman dat bleed dey men dry.

'Well... I... I've got...'

'What you saying, chile? Speak up!'

'Dolores... Mrs Roberts...'

'Call me "mummy" nuh.'

Romaine almost choked on her food as Dolores surreptitiously winked at her.

'Yes, Mrs... I mean....Mu—'

'Matthew, I see you spoiling she. Unless you goin' marry she and give she children, make she get up off she backside and find some useful work. I could always find a little something for her to do at the community centre...'

By now Elaine was glaring at Matthew, silently ordering him to come to her rescue. Everyone turned to him expectantly, wondering what he was going to say.

A slow, shy, smile lifted the corners of his lips. 'Mum, you know that Elaine has the most important job in the world: looking after me.' Everyone laughed except Elaine. Her lips tightened into a stiff line. Romaine glanced at Matthew. He looked away from Elaine and as he turned towards her, she noted an evil twinkle in his eyes. She wondered what it might mean, but thought it best to concentrate on the food Dolores was piling onto her plate. Probably just another one of their many arguments. Dolores patted her shoulder.

'Glad to know that you're looking after my boy, at least.' She looked pointedly at Elaine.

They ate their way through the mountain of food in mostly contented silence, broken only by the meaningless commentary from Mr James, an elderly, bald-headed church member whose presence at these Sunday lunches was now taken for granted. No one remembered when he had first been invited or why. No one knew quite what he was to Dolores and why she tolerated his eccentric behaviour, but every Sunday, he continued to provide the light relief.

'They found him in a night-club in Walthamstow, you know. Saw it on the news.'

'Found who?'

'That one from Afghanistan.'

'Iraq?'

'Whoever. The one with the beard.'

'There are plenty of men like that in that part of the world.'

'Yes, but he did kill all the baby boys under two.'

'That was in the Bible.'

'No, this was in Iraq.'

'You talking about Saddam?'

'That's the one. You know they found him in a club in Walthamstow? Saw it on the news.'

It seemed best to ignore him, just as they normally did.

'So, Romaine. What that boy of mine doin' working on a Sunday? Seems like I haven't seen him for weeks now. I hope he have a good excuse for missing lunch.'

'I haven't seen much of him either, Dolores. You know Louie. I guess he's working hard.' Romaine could feel Matthew's eyes on her as she fielded Dolores' interrogation.

'Business going well? I guess it must be if him have so much work to do. But seem to me like him should be taking care of business at home, if you know what I mean. When you two goin' give me a grandchild? You had enough time to practice now. Five years seem like long enough to me, child. You sure nothing wrong, girl? I'll have to feed you some Mannish Water, Cowcod Soup and you must put some cloves in every thing you eat.'

'Dolores, when we decide to try, I don't think we goin' need any help from you.' Romaine smiled to herself, noticing Elaine's astonishment at her boldness. Her mouth opened as if she expected the sword of Damocles to fall.

Dolores laughed loudly and reached across the table to pat Romaine's hand. She was deliberately highlighting the warmth between her and Romaine.

'Child, you know where I am if you want me to talk to that son of mine for you. Seem like him neglecting you.'

'It's all right. I think I can handle Louie.' She crossed her fingers behind her back.

As soon as Matthew and Elaine were banished to the kitchen with the washing up and Mr James was ensconced in the comfortable armchair, fast asleep and snoring intermittently, Dolores took the opportunity to join Romaine on the sofa.

'So! My boy been leaving you alone at home?' She whispered it with such tender concern in her voice that Romaine wanted to bury her head in the woman's soft bosom and weep. Instead, she held back the tears and tried to avoid Dolores' gaze as she muttered, 'No, really. We've both been busy.'

Dolores lifted Romaine's chin and looked into her eyes for a moment before wrapping her arms around her.

'Child…' she stroked her hair, just like Romaine's mother had done when she was little and had nightmares. 'You know where I am if you need me.' And she held her in an affectionate embrace until the others entered the room.

❦

Romaine sat in the back of the car listening to the strained silence between Matthew and Elaine. She couldn't fathom what had brought the two of them together in the first place and, more importantly, kept them together now. Elaine's shoulders were raised high, neck muscles tight as she held her frame away from Matthew, looking anywhere but at him. Occasionally, Matthew lobbed a desultory comment in Romaine's direction, but really not expecting a response, just to cut through the tension. Romaine was in no mood to help them out. She was worn out, physically and emotionally. She wanted to get away from every single member of this family and be alone, truly alone, without any memories, without any regrets.

She stood on the corner, waving just to make sure that they were truly gone. Romaine felt her shoulders return to their more normal level as she sighed. She turned, pulling her keys from her coat pocket, almost running from the gate to her front door. She fumbled with the lock, finally opening the door and slamming it shut behind her as if to create a barrier between this moment and the whole afternoon that had left her so emotionally drained.

The house was empty. Romaine didn't stop to take off her coat. Instead she turned to her right, entered the study and switched on the computer, pacing backwards and forwards while it booted up. This time, there was no difficulty finding the site and she almost ignored the perfect, airbrushed stranger on the home page. She immediately clicked on the 'enter' button, knowing precisely where she was heading. Handy-Man. Her mind had tried to tell her that she hadn't noticed him. But she had. Just before she'd switched off the computer earlier that morning. It was the silk rope that she'd tried to avoid noticing. Piano player's hands holding the silk ropes. She scrolled down the list. Had she just imagined it? No, she'd just momentarily forgotten her way around the alphabet. H came before J, not after, idiot. There he was. HandyMan:

Come to me and I promise you the erotic journey of a lifetime. But you must make a commitment. Everything I ask, you will do. There are rules. You may not touch me. Consider this most seriously. You must not touch me. No other woman has been able to obey this command. Can you be the first? I will give you pleasure, but the silk rope will hold your wrists, bind your ankles, so that you will remain motionless as I worship your flesh with my every touch. Your body will quiver with desire, but you must not touch. You will writhe with delight. But you must not

touch. I will show my appreciation. I will worship. I will adore you. But
you must not touch. I will lead you to ecstasy. But you will not touch.

Romaine shrugged out of her coat and let it drop to the floor. She
sat on the chair and scanned the screen until she noticed the link:
'Contact me'. She chewed her lip and looked around the room as if the
walls might give her permission. It was surprisingly dark outside, the
only light emanating from the screen, shadows cast all around as if the
room was saying 'You're on your own with this one.'

Rather than allow herself the time to think, Romaine clicked on the
link. There, in front of her was a form asking the kind of questions that
were easy. This wasn't going to be as difficult as she'd imagined. 'Register
Free' the banner proclaimed. Just fill in the following details. Password:
She would have to think about this one. How about 'Greta', her mother's
middle name. No one knew that. Safe enough. Age: 28. Easy. No need to
lie. Sex: Wasn't it obvious if she was looking for a man? Maybe not, she
was being naive. She thought of writing 'If only. What do you think I'm
doing here!' and then acknowledged that was too corny. Okay. Female.
And then the question that stopped her: e-mail address. What could she
give? She knew better than to give their address at home and she certainly couldn't reveal the one in the office. What to do? Reluctantly,
Romaine closed down the site.

She thought for a moment. It couldn't be that difficult to create a
new e-mail address, one that she would only access online. Back to the
search engine and with a few enquiries, Romaine had managed to set up
an address for Scarlet, her new online persona. She got back to the site as
quickly as she could, filled in the details again, included her e-mail
address and the box marked 'Screen name': 'Scarlet', just how she felt.
She reached the grey button that seemed to almost fill the whole screen.
'Click here and enjoy yourself'. The point of no return. Romaine hesitated for only a second. She clicked.

Romaine leaned back, her fingers intertwined in her lap, suddenly
paralysed. What on earth was she going to say to 'HandyMan'? What
had brought her here? The answer was simple: Louie had brought her
here. She had made one single mistake and as a result he'd almost shut
her out of his life. It wasn't even as if he was willing to let her go either.

She knew that. No, the truth was that he wanted her there just to humiliate her, to manipulate her, to control her for the sake of his pride. She doubted very much that he felt any emotion towards her right now, apart from a simmering anger. He just didn't want anyone to know that she could possibly have desired someone other than him. She knew he must feel that he had failed her in some way. And no matter how desperately she tried, she couldn't make him understand that what happened had nothing to do with her love for him. Or maybe what *used to be* love. She wasn't certain any longer.

A blank page with just his name, HandyMan, and an empty box anticipating an e-mail message.

What are the rules? she typed. *Let me know what I must do. I'm intrigued. What happens next?*

Pathetic response, but she was new to all this. She pressed the 'send' button before she had time to think about what she was doing. Oh Lord, what the hell had she done? Was there any way that he, whoever he was, could trace her? Had she given any clues? Part of her felt nervous, but another part was excited. She could feel her heart pounding in her chest. Louie deserved this major act of rebellion. She had done everything he asked, had tried every means to make it up to him, but he'd accepted her sacrifices as his due, without walking any of the mile towards her. Well, here she was, alone on a Sunday night, her husband who knows where. She wasn't going to take abandonment lying down. Or rather, she giggled, that's exactly how she intended to take it.

Romaine went to the kitchen and poured herself a glass of white wine. She rarely drank alone, but since it looked as if that's how she was going to remain for a while, what the hell? She took the glass back to the study and sat in front of the desk, sipping. Her fingers tapped on the mouse and she knew that she wouldn't be able to wait for much longer. She was curious. How long did it take to get a response? Impatiently, she dialled up her e-mail. And there it was. Had he been sitting at his computer waiting for a response? Or had he been replying to hundreds of different women?

Hi Scarlet, Good to hear from you. You sound like someone I can do business with. Intrigued? Well, that's just what I hoped to hear. The rules:

You take everything I have to give.
You obey.
You abandon your body to accept all the delights in store.
You are strictly not allowed to touch.
Do you agree?
Do you have Instant Messenger? Talk to me.

He gave his details. Romaine hesitated as her eyes remained fixed to the screen. What had she got herself into? She had asked and he had answered. Isn't that why she was here? The alternative was that she could be lying alone in a cold, unwelcoming bed. What was she going to do now? She minimised the page and looked at the list of programs on the screen. Yes, there it was, Instant Messenger. She launched the program. She needed a password. Now, what would Louie use. She tried his birth date. No luck. Then 'Dolores'. Nothing. She thought for a moment and then, hesitantly, entered 'Romaine'. Bingo. She was strangely touched but didn't want to think about it for now.

There were no contacts in his list. It didn't look like a facility that Louie ever used. That didn't surprise her. It wasn't like him to want to chat. She clicked on the 'information' button, worked out how to enter HandyMan's details and, within ten frustrating minutes, she could see his icon in red. He was online. She was breathing hard, the glass of wine discarded on the floor.

<I agree> she typed. He had been waiting for her.

<Dim the lights, Scarlet. Lock the door. Close the curtains. Concentrate on what I'm doing to you. I'm unbuttoning your shirt, slowly, allowing my little finger to graze the swell of your breasts, which rise towards me as you inhale deeply. I ease my fingertips under the lace of your bra, teasing the dark skin of your areola, almost blueberry black against the delicate cream lace. I reach behind to unhook your bra, allowing your heavy tits to fall from the cups. I stand back, admiring the wondrous sight in front of my eyes. I'm determined not to move towards you, just to watch the rise and fall of those gorgeous breasts as your breathing deepens. You're puzzled, wanting my touch. You move towards me, your hands reaching out. Your finger touches the back of my hand. I take a step back. I must punish you. Remember the

rules. Do you know what you have done wrong, Scarlet? Look at the rules.>

    <I touched you.>

    <You touched me. Do you know what must happen?>

Romaine felt a flutter of excitement. She was enjoying this.

    <You'll punish me.>

    <Right. I take a silk rope and tie your hands behind your back. You must not break the rules. You're new to the game so I'll forgive you this once. But you must not break the rules again. Tying your hands behind your back pushes those gorgeous breasts towards me, like they're challenging me, proud, disobedient. I take up the gauntlet and run my fingers over your breasts, thumbs rubbing against those hard, dark nipples, over and over, round and round until they pucker and harden and I take one between my lips, biting gently. But you've been a bad girl, and I bite harder, making you gasp and pull away. I can see the marks of my teeth against that tender skin. I nibble my way from your breasts down, past your ribs, my fingers preceding until they reach your panties. I smooth them down over your hips, my lips whispering past the mass of crinkly black hair. My fingers skim your feet, your calves, your thighs and embed themselves between your thighs, feeling the heat, the wetness. You are hot for me, aren't you?>

    <Yes!> She didn't have to pretend.

    <I ease two fingers inside your dripping folds, in, out, deeper, deeper forcing my hips between your thighs, holding your legs apart until one foot rises up, as if against your will and your toes graze my calves. I stop. You've broken the rules. Again. I warned you, Scarlet. I lift you and carry you to the table. I tie each ankle to a leg of the table. Tight. The fabric cuts into your flesh. You are spread-eagled. In my power. I'm getting hard thinking about what I'll do to you. My prick is bigger than it's ever been. All because I know you've learned your lesson now and you'll keep to the rules. I kneel between your imprisoned legs, my eyes level with your throbbing clit. I move closer so I can smell the salty, tangy scent of you. You're writhing, struggling to get nearer to my lips, but I catch your gaze. My look is stern, uncompromising. You must stay still. Will you obey?>

<Oh, yes!>

<I push your legs further apart, hold your pussy lips wide open as I bury my mouth in your opening, pushing my tongue into you, tasting the delicious honey that's flowing all for me. And then I'm licking upwards, my tongue broad, hard, unrelenting, up to flick against your clit and then down, pressing hard. Up again, flick, down, up, sucking, getting even harder as I hear your moan of pleasure. I stand up and clutch your breast as I unzip myself. Your eyes widen and you gasp at the size of my erection. You're lifting your hips. 'You trying to touch me with that pussy?' I ask. You shake your head from side to side...>

<No. I learned my lesson. Please don't punish me. Please don't stop.>

By now, Romaine's thighs were clasped around her own hand. She couldn't type any more.

<I'll forgive you this time. Don't let it happen again. I move my hips towards you. I can see the pleading in your eyes. The head of my cock touches your moist entrance. Just a glance, but enough to fill your opening. I watch as the swollen bulb rests there while my thumb rubs your clitoris, driving you into a frenzy and I'm pushing my cock slowly into your pussy and then—>

And then Romaine heard the key in the lock. She heard voices. Louie and Sheldon. Even though disoriented, she had enough sense to quickly shut down the program, turn the computer off and pull her skirt down. As quietly as she could, she closed the door of the study and slipped into the toilet. She splashed cold water onto her face and stood for a second, composing herself.

She stood outside the living room for a moment, trying to still the beating of her heart and subdue her fervid thoughts.

'Hi, honey,' she greeted her husband and accepted his cool embrace. 'Sheldon,' she nodded towards him. 'You guys are late. You want a coffee or a drink?'

'No thanks. I'm not staying. Just delivering your husband to you safely. I'll be off. See you soon, Romaine. See you in the morning, Louie.'

In a way, Romaine wished that Sheldon would stay. There was no telling what would happen now that she was left alone with Louie. She sighed and turned towards the stairs. Bedtime.

She didn't need to think about her and Louie any more tonight. There would be the office in the morning. Another danger area. She didn't want to lie awake thinking about her dilemmas there or at home.

❦

Monday mornings were difficult especially after two days out of the office. Two days away from the tension. Even though there was enough stress at home it was different stress. She had had two days free from having to arrange her working day so as not to stray into potential minefields while having to employ a detector at home.

Romaine wasn't overly concerned that Louie hadn't come up to their bedroom and had left before she awoke in the morning. She was too bleary-eyed. In the end, she had lain awake much of the night thinking, but not about Louie or the office. She had thought of HandyMan. Wondered why she had been drawn to the website. Why her body had been aroused by a complete stranger. Why she had allowed herself to respond. This didn't bode well for her relationship with her husband. It was clear that there was a hell of a lot missing and she would have to talk to Louie. They just couldn't go on like this without the whole situation coming to a head one day. And if she allowed that to happen, it could get very nasty, some of the flak would wound. She might say things that she would regret. He might say things that she would regret. She needed to start the conversation while she was still in control. And yet, now that she had made that decision, in a way there was no more urgency. The knot of tension began to subside in her stomach. The right time would come.

CHAPTER 4

At 8:30, the Monday morning office was empty, curiously aggressive, as if it needed the sharp edges to be rubbed off, a process that would take place throughout the week. Romaine turned on all the lights, booted up the computers and set the coffee percolating. Alison, her boss, would expect nothing less.

Romaine checked the messages on the answering machine. A couple of hang-ups, the usual quota of wrong numbers and the one regular Monday morning call from a client who, unreasonably, must believe that Alison had taken up residence in the office. Romaine typed notes onto the specially-designated file on the networked computer. She knew that Alison would look at it first thing on her arrival in the office. They'd found a way of working together that was easier than long verbal exchanges. More often than not, they communicated via the computer. It wasn't totally satisfactory, and she suspected that her colleagues had begun to notice, but it solved a problem in the short term.

Romaine poured herself a coffee and opened the file titled 'Romaine Webster'. An endless list of minor chores that Alison had devised for her over the weekend. It was just what she'd expected but still Romaine could feel the flush of irritation rising to her cheeks. When she'd first started in the company, Alison would never have dreamed of landing her with such menial tasks: endless photocopying, trivial research, passing on messages, even collecting her clothes from the dry-cleaners, the kind of beast-of-burden tasks that the most junior typists would complain about. But Alison knew that she wasn't likely to complain. It seemed like only a matter of weeks ago that she'd allowed herself a satisfied smile as she'd completed a dossier that formed the backbone to Alison's current research project. She had handed it over with a sense of pride at a job well done. And her boss had been pleased, congratulating her on how thorough her work had been. Now, she'd been relegated to the grunt work and she could sense the sniggers from the other secretaries. She wondered if her back was broad enough to bear all of this, but what alternative did she have? She was in no position to protest, was she? Maybe she should just hand in her notice. But she enjoyed her work, still liked her boss despite this temporary setback, and was convinced that she could get through this. A rough patch, that's all it was.

By 9:15, the surrounding cubicles were nearly all filled and Romaine responded non-committally to every 'Good Morning' and 'Good Weekend?' casually tossed in her direction. She tried to blot out the gossip exchanged across partitions as she felt the tension rise in her stomach. Each time she glanced at her watch, only seconds seemed to have passed. 9:55. Alison would be in the office on the dot of 10:00. Never a minute earlier or later. The knot of apprehension was growing tighter, forming a small, fiery ball. Romaine concentrated hard on working through the list of tasks that needed no concentration at all.

'Morning, Romaine.' Her voice was clipped.

'Good Morning, Alison.'

Romaine looked up, past the tailored, couture suit, the silk scarf casually pinned with an art deco brooch, the rounded face, the gold-touched skin into those stern, dark, severe eyes, no hint of softness, not with her long, brownish hair pulled back into a tight ponytail.

'Good weekend?' she asked, not caring, but glancing around the office.

'Yes. Thank you.'

Alison turned towards her office, pointedly dropping her coat on Romaine's desk. Deliberately making her point. She was the boss and Romaine would have to leave her work, get up, walk round the desk and hang the coat on the hanger that stood just outside Alison's office. People had often argued with her that it was impossible to work for a female boss, and Romaine had remained constant and fierce in her defence of Alison. Now, her lips tightened. She wasn't sure any longer. But it never used to be this way.

She'd got the job by asking the questions she'd thought too basic: how many people in the team? how long to research each commission? who were the biggest clients?

And throughout, Alison had watched her with those penetrating eyes, making her feel uncomfortable even as the words spilled from her mouth. She'd directed her comments to the guy from Human Resources instead, Alison still there in her peripheral vision. When she'd been asked to wait outside the office with two more women, her hopes had been raised, but when she looked at the other candidates, seemingly older and wiser, she thought, maybe the personnel guy was just feeling sorry for her and hadn't wanted to just come out straight with it: you don't stand a chance.

It was late and dark outside the windows by the time the hum of voices in the office died down and the three of them were left there alone, avoiding each other's eyes. He called her into the office and left it to Alison alone to give her the news.

'I argued for you,' she said without polite prelude. 'He would have gone for the blonde.' Her smile suddenly transformed her face, making her seem almost girlish, though she must have been at least five years older than Romaine. There was the hint of a dimple in one cheek, but it quickly disappeared. She could have passed for white if she so chose, but Romaine recognised the texture of the relaxed hair, the fullness in the lips, the inky darkness of the eyes.

'If you want the job, a confirmation letter will be in the post.'

Romaine could only nod dumbly, but Alison seemed to understand.

'Right,' a smile crept into her voice momentarily and then it regained its former brusqueness. 'Look forward to working with you… And Romaine… Don't let me down.'

'I won't,' Romaine smiled as Alison's fingers touched her arm. She returned Alison's glance confidently. There was no way she would waste this opportunity after three years in a dead-end securities firm, being treated more like a clerk than a secretary. Alison Grover had faith in her, had fought for her. She didn't need to explain any further. As she walked out of the building, Romaine raised her chin and lowered her shoulders. It was as if a huge weight had been lifted from her. She would give in her notice tomorrow and look forward to a much more fulfilling future.

It wasn't until she walked into the office again on her first morning that she understood the significance of Alison fighting to employ her. She vaguely recalled the discreet box at the bottom of the job advert:

Brown, Bartlett and Velasco is committed to achieving equality of opportunity. The huge partitioned room was filled with blonde, blue-eyed secretaries and assistants, looking almost as if they were extras from *The Stepford Wives*. Romaine shouldn't have been surprised, but she was when she realised that Alison was the only other black person employed by the company and she was light enough in colouring to have her race ignored even though that was the last thing she wanted. Only the most obtuse visitor to her corner office could miss the African carvings, wall hangings, paintings and photographs that adorned her walls and the framed quotations from Malcolm X, Stephen Biko, Stokeley Carmichael and, most prominent: Florynce Kennedy:

Don't agonize. Organize.

Subtle. Romaine wondered how many of the others would get it. They'd probably assume this was just Alison's reminder to herself to keep her desk tidy! But Romaine got it. Even though 'it' was something they never discussed in the office.

These days, there seemed to be nothing at all that they *did* talk about inside the office or out. Just a series of instructions almost hissed through clenched teeth or typed into the folder on her desktop. She'd have to find a way of talking to Alison too, but how? Her boss had come to seem like the most formidable woman in the world. There sure was a hell of a lot of talking to be done.

Romaine watched as the screen saver appeared before her. She'd been lost in contemplation for some minutes now. She needed to get out of this oppressive office, if only for a few minutes. She got her coat and handbag and knocked on Alison's door. She poked her head round. Her boss seemed to be engrossed in the sheets of computer data in front of her. She looked up and smiled, for a moment having forgotten her annoyance. And then the stony mask returned.

'I'm just off to the dry cleaners, Alison. To pick up your suit.'

She glanced at the clock. 'Fine.' She looked back at the figures, her way of dismissing Romaine.

☙

Romaine's steps slowed as she made her way back to the office, the polythene-enclosed clothes draped over her arm. Suppose she just kept walking, past the high-rise, glass tower. On past the station and turn left. Keep going north until she reached Camden, then Barnet, then Enfield and on to Scotland… Instead, Romaine returned to her desk with a sandwich, determined to serve her time until it was late enough to leave.

Alison marched back and forth from meeting to conference to presentation, her footsteps reminding Romaine of German stormtroopers. And then she left, at precisely 6:00 while Romaine struggled to stay ahead of her most outrageous demands. It was 7:30 before she could relax, after she'd said 'goodbye' to her last remaining colleague. She was surprised to realise that she had subconsciously been waiting for just this moment, when she'd be left alone, unlikely to be interrupted.

She quickly logged on to check her personal e-mail messages. She'd had to log off so abruptly that he must have wondered what had happened. Her instincts were right. Sure enough, there was a message for Scarlet.

❦

You missed the climax, so to speak. Why did you leave? Do you want to know what happened to you? I watched as the swollen bulb of my cock rested at your opening while my thumb rubbed your clitoris, driving you into a frenzy and I pushed my cock slowly into your pussy and then you began to move, trying to lift your hips, to force me into you. 'The rule,' I reminded you and your eyes pleaded with me. I showed no mercy. I picked up a long strip of midnight blue velvet. Your look was wary. I noticed the beginning of a tear. 'Close your eyes, I commanded. I blindfolded you with the soft velvet. 'Do you know what I am about to do?' I asked. Silence. I shouted at you. 'Speak to me! Are you scared, Scarlet? Too frightened to speak?' Your nervousness turned me on.

This was getting a little freaky for her liking.

You were defying me. I decided you deserved further punishment. I raised the whip. Was that pleasure making your nipples hard?

A little too freaky…

You were sweating, my dear. I saw terror. I smelled fear. I was getting harder. I brought the whip down hard across—

Why the hell was she continuing to read this shit? Romaine was shaking, but only for a moment. She had to laugh. Poor bastard was probably a 4ft 11in, mousy wimp in a grey cardigan who collected bus tickets and kept a tortoise as a pet! She navigated her way back to the original website. She really should give up and go home. The heating had automatically switched itself off in the office and it was pitch black outside the window, but she had waited with such high expectation to contact HandyMan again, and she felt let down. Besides, she was here now…

Romaine scanned through the options on offer and zeroed in on FrenchKiss:

I am a student here from Guadeloupe. I'm alone in your country. I need a guide. I want to learn everything about your ways. Teach me.

Romaine wondered whether his imperfect grasp of English had led him onto the wrong kind of site, but she found herself wanting to know more. At least he seemed like a stark contrast to HandyMan.

Welcome to London, FrenchKiss. Tell me about yourself. What do you look like? What are you looking for? Where do you want to go?

Romaine waited for several minutes and checked her messages. No response. She'd try JellyRoll who described himself as mature, well-travelled (she wondered if that was some kind of code), an old-fashioned gentleman and gentle man. This time, she would try the site's chat room.

<Hello. Are you there, JellyRoll? Would love to make your acquaintance, Scarlet.>

Immediately, the tiny icon began to flash. Romaine felt a flicker of excitement.

<Scarlet. What a beautiful name. I suspect you are as lovely as your name. I'm pleased to make your acquaintance. Tell me about yourself.>

<I'm 5ft 5in. Dark-skinned. Large, dark-brown eyes. Almost black. Shoulder-length, straight blonde hair (she lied). Full lips.>

<Long, shapely legs? Tell me about your breasts. I love large breasts.>

Were all these guys so forward? Dumb question, Romaine realised. Why else would they be there? The whole point of coming to this site was that they were both anonymous. They would never meet, so what did it matter? She could be whoever she wanted. However she wanted.

<My breasts aren't large, but they're full and shapely, with large, pink nipples that are puckering now, as I talk to you.>

<My dear Girl,—she could almost feel his shock across the ether. Maybe he really was of a different generation. She needed to slow down, feel her way—you make me blush. Let me pour us both a glass of ice-cold champagne.>

<For God's sake, JellyRoll, just go for it. You've never been that polite in the past.> This came from another visitor to the site, Lulu. Romaine only then remembered that the point of these chat rooms was that other people could join in. She felt a momentary embarrassment until she realised that no one could see her or knew who she was.

<Lulu, just butt out, would you?>

<Your accent's slipped, JellyRoll. I'd watch it if I were you.>

Romaine was amused, but still intrigued by JellyRoll's earlier persona.

<We could just ignore Lulu.>

<Don't say I didn't warn you, Scarlet. You new to this?>

<Don't worry about me. I'm old enough.>

Silence from Lulu.

<How old are you, Scarlet?>

<Twenty-five.> Thank God he couldn't see her. She was never very good at telling fibs. Her guilt showed on her face.

<Married?>

<Perhaps.>

<That means 'yes'. Does he satisfy you?>

Now it was her turn to be surprised.

<Yes.>

<How does he do it? Tell me how he touches you. Remember the last time you came.>

She would have to delve deep into her memory. It had been a while. Or else she could be creative.

<It was this morning...> She paused, her fingers hovering over the keyboard.

<Yes? Yes? What happened this morning?>

<We travelled together on a crowded tube train. More people than

possible squeezed into the compartment. I was wearing a low-cut blouse and a tiny skirt. No tights. No bra. My coat was open. My husband was behind me. We were like sardines. The carriage was hot. The air dense. My body was pressed hard against a stranger who tried to read his newspaper while hanging on the strap with one hand, pretending indifference. As the train swayed along the rails, I became aware of the gentle motion of my breasts against his body. My nipples tightened. They were so hard, I knew he must feel them against his chest. I could smell his lemon-scented aftershave, feel the friction of his cotton shirt. I subtly eased myself nearer to him, wanting him to acknowledge me. The train jolted to a halt and I stumbled against him, putting up my hand against his chest to steady myself. His hand grabbed my shoulder and held me close to him.>

Where on earth was all this coming from? Romaine had never thought that her imagination could be so fertile. She paused for breath and her hand rose to her breast, hurriedly fondling her nipple.

<I knew that he was looking at my body, but I didn't want to see his face. I turned a little as more people crushed into the carriage, so that my breast brushed his chest. He reached for me, hand hidden inside my coat and his thumb traced a lazy circle around my nipple. I almost cried out with pleasure. I slipped my hand over his, forcing him to squeeze tighter and the harder he squeezed, the more I tilted my hips so that my vagina was up against his cock, rotating in tiny circles. I knew that my husband could sense what was happening. I felt his hand against my buttock, guiding the rhythm, the movement slow but accelerating. We had only four more stops before we would need to get out of the compartment. I feared that the rock hard stranger in front of me might leave the train before us. I pulled his hand down along my rib-cage, down to my clenched thighs. He knew exactly what to do.>

<What?>

Romaine rolled her skirt up, over her hips, right up to her waist. She traced an idle line from her pubic bone, across the ridge of her clitoris, a moan escaping her lips as she did so. She needed to get her right hand between her thighs. She desperately wanted to rub against it. She wouldn't be able to type at the same time.

<guess> she managed to pick out with one hand.

<He teased you, running his finger along the leg of your panties.>

<oh, but i wasn't wearing any.>

<Oh my!... You're so brazen. He could feel your hot wetness. Your pussy was slick and tight as he slipped one, then two, then three fingers in and out of you, working his way further and further up, almost lifting you off the floor with his ardour. Your fingers brush against his erection, fumbling to release him, to find the zip. Finally you have his throbbing dick in your hands and you're rolling it between your palms. He pulls away slightly, too excited, and you ease the pressure, feathering brushes against his rampant flesh—>

Rampant flesh? Come on! Romaine smiled to herself. Surely he could do better than that.

<Over your shoulder, your husband is watching every movement. He can see the stranger's dick and feel the movement of your buttocks as you are finger-fucked. He frees his own rod and slides it between your thighs so that it bumps against the stranger's hand. His fingers reach around your waist and descend until he can feel your clit tightening. The stranger pulls his fingers away from you and he's touching your husband's dick. Tentatively at first. And then his other hand is on yours, guiding the motions around his throbbing organ and both his hands are playing the same symphony, and his breathing gets fast and shallow as he's jerking your husband's cock at the same time as his own—>

Hold on. Whose fantasy was this anyway? Still, Romaine's excitement was growing as she pictured the scene. She could almost feel the wet, slippery prick in her hand and Louie's big, heavy cock sliding against her inner thighs. She wet her finger with her tongue and worked harder, faster, concentrating on one single, blissful spot.

<You can feel his balls contracting. Your husband is biting your neck to stifle his moans. As the stranger is about to come, he clasps both hands around his own prick and accelerates the rhythm. Your husband lifts you, thrusts his cock deep into your pussy and spurts hard into your tight, fiery depths. The train comes to a halt. You see the stranger's back pushing its way through the crowd and off the train. He disappears from sight. You never saw his face.>

By now, Romaine was slumped back against the chair, her legs spread wide. She hardly took in the next postings.

<See what I mean, Scarlet. JellyRoll has a way of bringing every-thing round to his own fantasy and it gets fucking boring. The same one all the time. I told you. If you want a really good time, I'd recommend Manchild or QT. Lulu.>

<Or SilverStar. He's really wild. Maggie.>

<Or give me a try sometime, Scarlet. Conductor.>

Wow! She'd done it with quite an audience!

❦

That night, Romaine had no idea when Louie came home and slipped into the bed beside her. She slept well and dreamlessly for the first time in weeks. Must be a clear conscience, she told herself as she awoke and watched her husband snoring gently. It irritated the hell out of her that he could sleep so peacefully, as if he didn't have a care. This situation was getting to her; she couldn't deny it any longer.

Romaine waited until they'd gone through the silent charade of breakfast together. As soon as he left the house, she called Grace.

'You around today? I need to talk.'

'Tell me when and where.'

'I'll take a sickie. I'll call the office and then we can meet. Say, 10:45 at Highbury & Islington station? We can walk. And then do lunch.'

'Wow! Walk *and* do lunch. Must be serious!'

Romaine left a message on Alison's voice-mail. She knew that Alison was unlikely to believe her excuse, but what could she do about it? She wasn't likely to ring to check on her welfare. Besides, the menial tasks that she'd been given to do were so unimportant that they could wait.

❦

Grace was waiting at the station, stamping her leather boots and slapping her gloved hands together. It was the end of November and their wispy breath feathered the air. Grace's skin was almost blue with cold even though little of it was visible between the furry hat and the woollen scarf. Romaine hugged her, reassured by just the presence of her friend.

They walked in silence around Highbury Fields, stopping for a few moments to watch the insane parent pushing his bundled up child on the swings. The two women looked at each other and laughed.

'Only dem mad dog and Englishman…'

'Is 'cos we not used to this cold weather.'

'What you mean, girl? You born here!'

'I know, but sometimes I does like to pretend. It mek me feel frail and vulnerable.'

Grace smiled at her, finally pulling the scarf from across her mouth.

'I think you *are* vulnerable, Romaine. At the moment, anyway. Isn't that why you called?'

'I guess.'

'What's he done now?'

Romaine asked a question of her own.

'Has Sheldon said anything?'

'Sheldon? You think those two guys talk to each other about anything important? And with Sheldon, you'd have to draw diagrams. Subtlety doesn't go down too well with him. Why do you ask?'

'I suppose because I don't know what's going on in Louie's head. I don't know if he even cares any more. I suppose I'm trying to find out, second-hand, what he's thinking.'

Grace took her elbow and steered their steps away from the playground across the grass towards the deserted benches. They were both silent until they sat, hardly noticing the thin layer of frost. Grace waited.

'I think it might be over, Grace.'

'What makes you think that?'

'Well, any cure would be down to me. And I might be ready to give up. I'm not sure I care enough any more. I might, but I'm not sure. I'm so tired of it all.' Romaine was silent for a moment and that was when the tears started to flow. She didn't wipe them away. Like a child, she allowed them to fall, unchecked. Grace waited for a while and then fumbled in her pocket for a tissue to wipe her friend's cheeks.

'Girl, you better be careful them tears don't freeze on your face.'

Romaine sniffled. 'You know what I've done, Grace?'

'You've started up again with—'

'No. I wouldn't know how to, even if I wanted to.'

'And do you want to?'

'I don't know, Grace. I don't think so. It would be too complicated. I'm trying to deal with one thing at a time. No, it's not that. The other evening, I was at work late and I came across this website—'

'Divorce for Beginners?'

'No. It was a… how can I describe it? A…'

'A porno site? Been there, done that, designed the T-shirts.'

'You're kidding!'

'Romaine, why you looking at me like that? Either you think is a crime or you think I'm too old, staid and boring for them kind of thing! Either way, I'm surprised at you. Where you think I met Keith?'

'Keith? Who's Keith?'

'You mean I haven't told you? Over lunch. Is too cold here to be discussing them kind of hot ting. Might just melt and you'd have to scrape me up from the ground.'

'So you know the kind of site I'm talking about?'

'What you think us bored suburban housewives do all day?'

'Don't joke, Grace. I'm serious.'

'About what? You been having a bit of fun on the net? Looking at some fine brothas? What's wrong with that when you ain't getting none at home?'

'I haven't been doing much looking. Just a lot of typing.'

'What's the site?'

Romaine gave her the name and described the workings. With downcast eyes, she told Grace everything. About her shock when she first clicked on the home page, her determination to turn away, the growing tension as she waited to access the site again, her 'conversations' with HandyMan and then JellyRoll.

Grace laughed uproariously, tears trickling down her own cheeks now.

'Girl, you should see your face. You can hardly bring yourself to look at me. What's wrong with you? Look at me, Romaine.' She put her arm around Romaine's shoulder and waited until her younger friend met her gaze. 'Do you think I'm some kind of freak?'

'No.'

'Do you trust me?'

'Of course.'

'Okay, girl. Let's have that lunch—' She looked at her watch. '—Or brunch, or whatever it is, later. I'm going to take you on a shopping expedition.'

❦

Romaine couldn't pretend that she hadn't guessed where they would end up. The moment Grace bought a return ticked to Oxford Circus, she had an inkling. Now that they were inside the shop, it wasn't as daunting as she had expected. Only a selection of sheer black night-gowns trimmed with red feathers, see-though g-strings, furry handcuffs, massage oils and edible body paints. All good clean fun. Ann Summers obviously wasn't as raunchy as she'd imagined. Until Grace grabbed her hand and dragged her down the stairs to the basement.

Romaine felt herself flush as she was propelled to the shelves of dildos, vibrators, ben-wa balls and vibrating eggs. Beside her was a couple obviously hoping to road-test each item before they bought. Over by the videos was a facially-challenged, middle-aged man trying to look as if he was intending to buy for a partner. Not in a million years, Romaine thought. He was looking around furtively. But then she realised that she was too.

'Relax,' Grace commanded, laughing gently at her. 'Nothing's going to bite. Girl, I'm going to sort you out. I'd recommended the Rampant Rabbit Deluxe or the Sensual Vibe. From personal experience. Which do you prefer?'

Romaine glanced where Grace was pointing. 'I don't like the colour of that one.'

'Okay. Decided. My treat.' She picked up the box and headed towards the cash desk, credit card in hand.

Grace paid and handed the discreet package to Romaine. 'For the next time you log on.' She smiled as the blush rose to Romaine's cheeks again.

Over lunch in a crowded British Home Stores, Grace revealed all to a shocked Romaine, having to raise her voice above the bustle. She'd met Keith through a similar internet site, but one that was obviously more adventurous than Romaine's. She couldn't pretend that she'd been attracted to his mind. She hadn't cared, Grace admitted, whether he had

two neurones to rub together. She had intellect at home. She wanted
hard muscles, firm buttocks and a cock that made her think twice. Keith
was the third since she'd married Sheldon. She had chosen with care.

'I'm not exactly unfaithful in the narrowest sense of the word. I don't
let them make love to me. But everything else that we can come up with
between us. Romaine, you can't imagine how hot it gets when we both
know there will be no full sex. We have to find other ways of making
each other climax. New ways each time. Girl, Keith's imagination—and
his tongue—have taken me to places you would never believe.'

'Why do you do it, Grace? I thought everything was cool between
you and Sheldon.'

'It is. This has nothing to do with how I feel about Sheldon. That's
what I keep trying to explain to you, Romaine. I'm not taking anything
away from Sheldon by enjoying a little extra pleasure elsewhere. He's my
husband and I love him. But there's no use pretending that any one man
is ever going to be able to give me everything I need. It's nothing against
Sheldon. I just think that's a very adolescent, fairy-tale way of thinking.
We're grown-ups now.'

'Does Sheldon know?'

'There's no sense in hurting him unnecessarily.'

'You admit that it would hurt him.'

'Romaine, I can't change the way Sheldon is. I don't want to. I love
him, but that don't mean I have to deny part of myself. I do everything I
can to protect him and that's because I care for him. Sheldon knows
who I am and loves me for it, but that don't mean I'm going to rub
things in his face. That's why I'll never understand why you had to tell
Louie. Is not as if he was ever likely to find out.'

'We used to share everything.'

'Don't be so naïve, Romaine. Did Louie share each minute of his
working day with you, his every thought, every interaction with another
human being? Did he tell you every time he looked at another woman's
legs or tits? On the train. On the street. In his office. Did you know every
time his dick got hard?'

'Louie's not like that.'

'*Every man's* like that, Romaine. Wise up!'

'Maybe, but before all this happened, we were happy. Louie was gorgeous, funny, tender, sensitive, caring, sexy, everything I ever wanted.'

'He couldn't have been everything you wanted, otherwise you wouldn't have—'

'A big mistake. It's ruined things between us. I've tried my hardest to make things up to him, but nothing seems to work. We hardly talk any more. The atmosphere at home is so strained, except when there's someone else there. Louie doesn't even want to talk about it. I don't know what else to do, except give him his freedom. I think, secretly, that's what he wants. He's just pushing me to say it.'

'And what do *you* want, Romaine?'

'Whatever's best for Louie. I owe it to him.'

Grace rolled her eyes upwards, losing patience.

'For God's sake, girlfriend, grow up and stop being the martyr. Louie doesn't need another mother. Look out for yourself and consider the silver lining.'

'Which is?'

'You've got a brand new vibrator and a hot website waiting for you.'

❦

Her mobile rang just as she approached the house. Another hang-up. If only Louie could be persuaded to close the shutters. She could see the receiver still in his hand. This was really the last straw. She had guessed a while ago that he'd been checking up on her, but now she could see the evidence with her own eyes. Tonight would have to be the night for the conversation.

Romaine closed the door behind her and strode straight into the sitting room. He thought he was being so clever, pretending to be holding a conversation when she knew there could be nobody on the other end of the line. She waited until he said his phoney goodbye.

'I wasn't at work. Before you ask, I spent the day with Grace. Call her and check if you want.'

He was still holding the phone and he looked up with a surprised look on his face. Trying to play it innocent. As if he didn't know what she was talking about. Staring as if she had lost her mind. His eyes travelled to the package she still held in her hands.

'Is not as if I really care, but what you and Grace been doing together?' He stressed the last word, the sarcasm punctuating each syllable.

Romaine felt her eyelids prickle as the anger she felt turned to cold ice in the pit of her stomach. She circled him warily, like a bullfighter keeping an eye on his prey. She slipped out of her coat, draped it on the arm of the sofa and sat in the armchair facing him. She watched even as he walked to the sideboard, retrieved a glass and poured a generous shot of brandy. He passed it to her.

'No ice?'

'I think we have enough of that.' At least he could still joke.

He didn't make himself a drink. Immediately, Romaine felt at a disadvantage. As if she was the one who was getting hysterical and needed medicinal alcohol.

'We need to talk, Louie.'

'So talk.' He didn't intend to make it easy.

'I've been trying to make it up to you, Lou. To be the person you want me to be. But it's made no difference. I don't know what you expect me to do. It's like you're going to go on punishing me forever. What I did wasn't so bad.'

'No?'

'At least I didn't set out to hurt you. What you're doing to me now is a hundred times worse. It's cold, calculated, deliberate. It's like you've stuck a knife into me and now your twisting it—'

'I didn't draw the knife.'

'You see what I mean? What's the point of just throwing the blame back at me all the time?' Romaine sipped at the brandy. She needed to calm herself before she just exploded at him and said words that she would never be able to take back. She decided to take another tack.

'Lou, you know how much I love you. There's never been any question about that.' She could see that he hadn't been expecting that. His expression softened for a moment. It even seemed, for just an instant, that he intended to move towards her, to bridge the gap. If only they could sit together on the sofa, his arm wrapped around her, her head buried in his shoulder. It would be so much easier to say all that she wanted to tell him. But he held himself back. She could almost see the barrier of pride that stood in the way, but she would go the final mile.

'What happened was nothing to do with you, Lou.'

Romaine put the glass down by her side and stood, determined to close the physical and mental distance between them. She walked towards him, smiling inwardly at the little-boy pout of his lower lip. She placed a hand on either side of his head and brushed a gentle kiss across his lips. No response. She slid her tongue between his lips, along the ridges of his teeth, hoping to find a way in. Her fingertips stroked the nape of his neck, caressing, pulling him closer to her, massaging away the rigidity along his spine. He tried to pull back, but she held him tight and, at last, he opened his mouth and allowed her in. She tasted the bitter residue of alcohol and resentment and explored, determined to wash away the lingering remnants.

He responded, enclosing her in his arms and grasping her hair, tugging, making her cry out as he forced his tongue into her mouth, thrusting as if they were fighting a battle. Then his hands were all over her, lifting her sweater up over her head, forcing their way under her bra, squeezing her breasts, clutching at them, digging his nails into the roundness. Romaine could hardly breathe and tried to move away, to gain a little respite, but he held her firm and now his mouth was on her neck, his tongue licking down to the flesh that he held in his grip. He took her bruised nipple into his mouth and sucked hard, connecting with the direct line to her clitoris that started an electric pulse throbbing.

'Oh, honey,' she breathed. 'That's so good. Harder.'

And he bit into her nipples, taking her at her word and showing no mercy. As his mouth moved to the other nipple, his hands fell to her buttocks, pulling her to him, hard, forcing his knee between her thighs, grating against her hardened clitoris. Back and forth, rubbing harder and harder against her. He tugged at her knickers and, aroused beyond recognition, she reached down and helped him to tear away the fabric. Her throbbing clitoris was almost crying out for his mouth. Lord, she wanted to feel the soft sweetness of his tongue against her. She was crooning a low, rumbling tune, a begging lament and he pulled away from her breast. He knelt before her and spread her legs wide. His eyes glittered as he parted her lips with his thumbs, exposing the tender, rosy tip. He sank one finger into her pussy, churning inside her. Then another finger and another, round and round, his eyes fixed on the movement of his own hand.

Romaine looked down at him, at the beads of sweat forming above his top lip, the rhythmic pulsing of his dark fingers as they disappeared inside her, emerging glistening with the evidence of her own desire. Her hand moved to his, needing to accelerate the motion, wanting to ride those elegant fingers, to feel them deep inside, but he pushed it away, flicking his thumb from side to side across her hardened clitoris.

'God, Lou, faster, please, please…'

He stopped then, for just a second, glanced at her and then returned to watching her body writhe in desperation. His mouth was an inch away from her pussy and he leaned towards her, infinitely slowly, tormenting, torturing her.

'Go on, Lou. Eat my pussy. Now. Please.'

She watched as the tip of his tongue inched from between his lips. He touched her and a scream of pleasure escaped her lips, aaaiiieee, Oh God!

He leaned back on his heels and looked up at her, an unfathomable smile on his lips. 'That what you want?'

'Yes, Oh yes.' Her hips were swivelling towards him.

He stood up then and, still staring at her wet pussy, slowly unzipped his trousers. He reached inside and manoeuvred out his cock, holding it towards her like a weapon, as if he was about to launch an attack. One hand was quickly around her waist, pulling her to him as the other directed his cock to her gaping hole. With a single fierce thrust he was inside her, the length of him buried between her folds. He held her thigh, bringing her knee up above his hips, fitting it into the curve of his waist, hardly pulling out, but grinding deeper. Then the other leg tucked around him and he lifted her, carrying her forward until her buttocks rested against the back of the armchair. With the added leverage, he pounded her, drilling fiercely into her as she clung to him, gasping, fingers biting into his back, scraping at his skin, drawing blood. Her hunger was desperate as the blood pounded in her ears.

Romaine had never felt him this strong, so big. And she told him.

'Lou. Oh, Lou. You're filling me up. You're enormous. So… hard. So, fucking hard. That's it, baby. Fuck me. Harder.'

'Like this?'

'Oh, yesssss!'

'*This* is what you want, isn't it, Romaine?'

'God, yes! I've never felt you like this.'

'This *all* you want?'

'Yes, babe. You feel so, so incredible. So big and my pussy's so tight for you. I can't take much more, honey.'

'Oh yes you can,' he laughed and then he looked into her eyes and stopped all movement for a while. He leaned forward and kissed her then, slowly, gently, tasting the sweetness of her mouth.

And he lifted her, carried her to the sofa and lay her down gently, all the while still inside her. He pulled off his shirt and lay beside her, making small circular motions, only the head of his cock inside her now, teasing the sensitive pad of flesh at her entrance. Softly, so softly.

'Whose pussy is this?' he teased reminding her of the old joke they shared.

'Yours.'

'Whose hot, tight, pussy?'

'Yours. All yours.'

'And whose prick?'

'Mine.'

His thrusts were gradually becoming longer, harder, slower and deeper.

'Whose thick, hard, hot prick?'

It felt as if each stab was reaching her womb, her stomach, her breasts, her mouth, as if she could feel his fullness in her mouth. Her pussy began to clench around him and she could feel the orgasm building in waves, rolling upwards, circling, concentrating like a tornado.

'Tell me. Whose fat… enormous… fucking… gigantic… prick?' He was gasping, each breath forced from his body.

'Oh mine. Mine,' She screamed as the climax hit. She arched her body, rigid against him as her finger found her clitoris and her thumb rubbed against his penis tracing the bulging vein as he shouted her name and exploded inside her.

CHAPTER 5

Romaine looked at her sleeping husband. He looked so young and innocent that she couldn't bear to wake him. He was probably exhausted. He'd stayed late in the office and then he'd done so much extra work when he got home! She smiled to herself feeling the soreness between her legs and enjoying the flutter of pleasure as she recalled their lovemaking. And it had been just that: making love. She wasn't kidding herself that all their problems were over, but something had happened last night to force open a chink in the armour that he'd build around himself.

She would let him sleep. Romaine leaned over and kissed him gently on the cheek. He shifted slightly and reached out for her. She stayed motionless for a while, just staring at Louie's lovely face and then she glanced at the clock.

She eased out of the bed and rushed to the bathroom, showering and dressing as quietly as she could.

❦

There was a renewed energy to her step as she set out towards the tube station, navigating the lines of stalled traffic, inhaling the familiar fragrance of exhaust fumes. Ridiculous how just good sex could change your whole world outlook! She bought a newspaper and gave the newsagent a bright smile. Her smile was infectious and his broad grin made her feel as if it was summer and all was well with the world.

As she walked down the steps to the platform she could hear the whoosh of air and the rumble as a train approached. She jogged gently and arrived just as the doors opened. There were empty seats and she secured one, believing that, this morning, the gods were on her side.

The front page of the newspaper managed to dampen her mood with reports of a plane crash into the Red Sea. One hundred and forty-eight killed. Military atrocities in Iraq. Osama bin Laden reappearing on Arab television. She skimmed the headlines and turned the page. American probe reaches Mars. Increased fear of terrorist attacks. Romaine folded the newspaper, her thoughts considerably more sober.

As she took the lift to the eighth floor of her office building, the nauseous apprehension bubbling in her stomach insisted that she really couldn't go on like this. She'd gone some way to sorting out the situation at home. Now, she'd have to do something about Alison. She couldn't leave things like this. She'd have to start a conversation.

The possible permutations rotated in her head, each one less satisfactory than the last. 'Alison, I think we should talk…', 'Alison, this situation is becoming unbearable..', 'Alison, we can't go on like this...' They all made them seem like a warring couple and the woman was, after all, her boss. 'Alison, can I talk to you.' Keep it simple, that would be best. But then, where would she go from there? A hammer was pounding at her temples now. She scrabbled in her desk drawer searching for paracetamol.

'Glad to see you're feeling bett—' Alison's sarcastic greeting was cut off at the sight of Romaine's face. 'Are you okay?' she continued, her tone softening for a moment, her face, unguarded, relaxing into a gentle smile.

Romaine looked up at her boss, taken aback by the deep concern that showed in her heavy-lidded eyes. She had forgotten how Alison's face could be transformed by that sweet smile. She found herself responding, but the effort to return a smile made her wince.

'I'm fine, Alison. Honestly. Just a headache.'

Alison looked unconvinced, holding her gaze for a moment longer before walking into her office and closing the door behind her.

Romaine remained distracted for most of the morning. Despite her very best efforts, she couldn't stop her thoughts wandering between Alison and Louie. She might have allowed herself the hope that all was on the way to being sorted at home, but she knew that the key to the problem was here in the office. She needed to knock on that solid-looking door and begin the conversation. But did she know what she hoped to get from the dialogue? What did she honestly want the outcome to be? There were, realistically, only two possibilities; break the ice between her and her boss or resign. She knew which Louie would prefer, but she wasn't certain that she was willing to make that great a concession. If he didn't trust her, then it didn't matter where she worked, he would always be suspicious, watching her.

The morning had started so well and now here she was exasperated with him again, but understanding how he was feeling too. After all, she'd been there herself! She remembered how devastated she had been when she first found out. Admittedly, it was naïve of her to assume that, just because Gina wasn't seen in the house again after her first night with Louie, she was off the scene. So Louie was never at home on a Friday night. Well, she couldn't really expect him to give up all his friends for her, could she? Besides, it was healthy for them to spend time apart. Didn't want the relationship to become claustrophobic.

It was Colin who told her.

A Friday. She had arrived home to find Colin back early from work because of a mild cold—Colin described it as a new Asian strain of influenza with no known cure. Romaine had trailed up and down the stairs with chicken soup (tinned), Lemsip, orange juice and increasingly alcoholic hot toddies. She had probably hoped to knock him out altogether. It was on about the hundredth mercy dash to his room that she dumped the pile of dirty clothes onto the floor and collapsed into the chair by his bed, determined to assure herself that he wasn't really at death's door.

'Romaine, could you just get—'

'Colin, just a moment's rest. I beg you,' she laughed. 'One more trip up and down those stairs and I'll end up in bed too and you'll be taking care of me.'

'I'd do that, Rome.' There was a smile on his lips, but his eyes were strangely serious. In a split second, Romaine recognised the look, but refused to acknowledge it. She stood.

'So, what do you want now, Colin?' Her tone was bright but she should have thought before she spoke.

'You.'

She tried to laugh again, but he reached out and grabbed her hand. As he did so, the bedcover fell away and she was aware of dark, ebony, almost bluish skin that glistened with a shimmer of sweat, tight curls of hair speckling his chest. He shifted slightly. She knew it was so that she would see what she didn't want to see: the evidence that he did, indeed, want her. Romaine had never thought of Colin in that way, not as a sexual being. He had always been, well, just an androgynous friend. With his desire staring her in the face, how could she tell him that?

'Colin, we can't do this.'

'Why not?'

'Louie…'

'So where is Louie tonight, Romaine?'

'You know where he is. He's probably drinking with the boys in some backstreet dive. I don't ask for details of what you guys get up to when you're on your nights out together. Not for me to pry...' She knew she was babbling, trying to divert his attention.

Suddenly, Colin let go of her hand and sat up in the bed. He pulled the cover up to his chest.

'Wake up, Romaine. We haven't seen Louie in weeks. The others joke about how you've pussy-whipped him into submission. But I knew he wasn't here. I could almost feel it.'

Colin wrapped the cover around his waist and stood. Romaine couldn't move. Her mind was still processing what she had heard. No neurones available to control movement. He was closer now. Too close. Taking her into his arms, holding her tight. Whispering something, nothing, everything into her ears, hands caressing her shoulder, her neck. 'You needed to know, sweetheart. He's not good enough for you, Rome. I haven't thought about anyone but you. We could be so good together. It's like we're soulmates. I can feel how he's hurting you, even if you can't. I'll take care of you, baby. I want you so bad.' Maybe he did have a cold; his skin was burning up with fever.

For a moment, Romaine rested in his arms. But she was cold. Not only on the outside, but inside too. Icy. Unfeeling. And his erection was pressing against her. She suddenly felt nauseous and, pulling away from him, ran out of the room into her own bedroom, well, Louie's bedroom actually. She quietly closed the door and stood behind it, as if to barricade herself in and keep the rest of the world out. She could hear Colin's gentle rapping on the wood.

'Romaine? You okay? I'm sorry, Romaine. Romaine! I shouldn't have…'

But he had.

She didn't say anything to Louie about it. And she guessed that Colin didn't either. She stayed at home, in that same house, alone on Friday nights. Wondering. Pondering. Seeing him in someone else's arms. Someone else's bed. Until she worked it out. Perhaps it was the perfume he brought home on his skin, or the shade of lipstick that stained his shirts. She asked no verbal questions, but each time they made love, her body came closer to finding the answer. She noticed, for the first time, that they never made love on Friday nights. And it wasn't because he was drunk and incapable. Still, Romaine didn't confront him. Maybe she was too young, too inexperienced, too much in love with him, too calculating, but she found herself being sweeter, kinder, more thoughtful, more understanding until, one night, he confessed.

'I feel bad, Rome. So guilty that I can't go on like this. You're so good to me. We need to talk.'

'Sure, Louie. You know you can tell me anything.'

And so it all came out. How, he hadn't had the courage to tell Gina that it was over. She depended on him. She'd said that she loved him. She was so fragile. How could he hurt her?

Romaine was silent. She looked at Louie, an understanding, concerned smile plastered on her face.

Okay, so maybe he hadn't wanted to end it either. After all, he hadn't known where things would go between him and Romaine. What was the point of finishing with Gina if things weren't going to work out with Romaine? So, yes, maybe he'd been a coward. Maybe he'd been selfish.

Romaine was silent. *No 'maybe' about it!* She nodded sympathetically, head tilted to one side, listening patiently.

But it was doing his head in now. He couldn't cope with the lying, the cheating, the deception, week after week having to make up stories, hiding the truth from both her and Gina. He couldn't cope with it. And besides, he knew now that he loved Romaine, wanted to be with her. Could she forgive him? He truly adored her, wanted no one else but her, needed her.

Romaine rose, kissed him tenderly, stroked his cheek with one finger and smiled. She silently walked out of the room and into the bathroom. She stuffed a towel in her mouth and screamed as quietly as she could while the hot tears coursed down her cheeks.

And she nursed her pain, carefully applying layer upon layer of bandages until the wound healed and the scar barely showed. Maybe she shouldn't have. In the end, they probably didn't have enough practice in talking—well, not about important matters. They should, really, have talked about Gina of the long, dark hair. Perhaps, underneath the plaster, the wound had been festering, resentment growing. Was that why she'd looked elsewhere for whatever it was that she needed? But that would be so unfair. That would mean that she'd used—

'Romaine!'

She could tell that it wasn't the first time that Alison had called her name. She looked up, trying to figure out what she might have been asking.

'Can you come into my office for a moment.' That was all that Romaine needed. She'd been trying to concentrate hard on her work and yet she'd let her mind drift. She hadn't wanted to give Alison any ammunition. And now, just because of her pig-headed husband, she'd failed. Maybe she should take the opportunity to ask for the conversation.

Romaine picked up her notepad and pen and walked through the door that Alison held open. It was like entering the execution chamber. Alison closed the door securely and walked behind her desk. She sat and placed her elbows on the surface, fingers tented, polished nails tapping against each other. Romaine could tell that she was trying to contain her irritation. God knows how long she'd been calling to Romaine. She didn't sit. Just waited for Alison to look up at her.

Finally, she did. The cold ice in her eyes seemed to melt and she sighed and leaned back in her chair.

'I don't think you're really well enough to be back at work, Romaine. Take the rest of the day off.' Her eyes travelled over Romaine's features like a consultant examining a patient for signs of illness.

'Alison, I'm fine, honestly—'

'Come back when you're fully recovered.' Her tone left no room for argument.

As Romaine reached for the handle of the door, she heard Alison almost whisper, 'You know where we are… If you need me.' She didn't reply. Maybe she'd misheard. She gathered up her bag and coat and left the office, not even stopping to turn off her computer.

It felt good to be outside and her head immediately cleared. She had nowhere to go, though. Romaine felt slightly uneasy. Like a fraud. There was nothing physically wrong with her. Nothing that a few days off was going to cure. She headed for the tube station and then changed her mind. The last thing she wanted to do was to go back to the empty house. Louie wouldn't be home for several hours, if at all. She concentrated on her steps, not caring where they would take her. Just counting, easing into a hypnotic rhythm, avoiding other pedestrians by good luck alone. Perhaps she should send Alison an e-mail message. That seemed so cold and formal, or else too casual. But she knew that, at the heart of the matter was the fact that she felt intimidated by the older woman. That hadn't always been the case. Of course, on her first day, she'd been a gibbering wreck, concentrating so hard on getting things right that she hardly heard any of Alison's instructions or the patient explanations. By the time she left at the end of the day, her smart dress was almost drenched in nervous sweat.

Despite the growing realisation that she was resented in the office— the two other women who'd been waiting to hear the result of the interviews were internal candidates—those first weeks had passed in a blur. It was with a certain astonishment that she'd gone home after a month, bubbling with excitement.

'You know,' she'd said to Louie, 'I'm really good at what I'm doing.'

He had smiled fondly. 'I never doubted it.'

'No, but this isn't just secretarial stuff. Alison's begun to give me all kinds of extra responsibility. I felt really nervous about it, and I sensed all the others watching, waiting for me to fail. But I'm coping. I can do it.'

He stroked her hair as he passed and kissed her cheek.

'This Alison woman has good judgement.'

Within months, Alison was taking Romaine with her to the most crucial meetings, relying on her to be a second pair of eyes. They made a formidable team and it was difficult to put anything past them. Together, they ensured that no tiny, but crucial, detail was missed. Alison began to rely on Romaine's ability to accurately assess the different personalities they had to deal with each day. It was one particularly long and tricky meeting that first drove them to the pub after work.

'Wow! Thank God that's over. What can I get you?'

'Vodka and tonic with a dash of lime, please Alison.'

Over drinks, they discussed the clients.

'I think there's a great deal of insecurity going on there. That's why I requested that the most senior executive available should be at the meeting. I knew they wouldn't be able to fault the actual research.'

'But he tried, didn't he.'

'I guess Martin's job was on the line.'

'It was lucky that you'd asked for written confirmation of the terms of the research.'

'Not luck, Romaine. I make it policy not to start a project without having the details in writing. If I'd left it to Martin, who's used to dealing with some of the men in the firm, then a nod would have been as good as a wink. I've learned, Romaine, that we can't be that casual. No old boy's network where we're concerned.'

It was the first time she'd used that 'we'. And Romaine was savvy enough to know that it would not be repeated within the office. The 'we' was like an amber light for what Romaine wanted to get off her chest.

'I guess there are people in the office who think there's an old girl's network operating between us. They seem to think there's an element of favouritism.'

Alison laughed. The first time Romaine had seen her like this, almost helpless with amusement. She searched in her handbag for a tissue and wiped her eyes. Romaine couldn't quite see what was *that* funny.

'Of course there's favouritism,' Alison continued between gasps. 'What the fuck do they expect?.' The expletive was untypical. 'They've been doing it to us for centuries and then they can't take it when, just once, it happens to them.' She looked at Romaine's surprised face and patted her hand. 'Don't worry, Romaine. I'm not stupid enough to risk earmarking you for bigger things if I didn't think you were up to the job. I told you that I fought for you. But that was only because you were head and shoulders above all the other candidates. Remember, you'd have to be to get past the lech from Human Resources.'

'Thanks, Alison. I'm grateful. But what exactly am I being groomed for? I thought I was quite happy being your assistant.'

'The sky's the limit. Or rather, the glass ceiling's the limit. I'm not going to be in this job forever, Romaine. That's not part of my plan. And I intend that when I leave… if you want it, that is.'

'Oh!' was all Romaine could reply.

Louie had thoroughly approved of Alison's tactic.

'We haffe look after we own. Nobody else goin' do it.'

'But you and Sheldon don't do that, do you? You've got loads of white folks working for you.'

'Only because we need to right now. Just wait until more of the youngsters get the experience and the knowledge.'

So that's when Romaine had thought it would be a good idea for her husband and her boss to meet. They seemed to have so much in common. And maybe they really did…

❦

Before she knew it, the sky was darkening. Romaine glanced at her watch. 5:45. She had been walking for two hours, forcing herself not to think. She looked around. Rosebery Avenue. Had she, unconsciously, been heading towards Islington? Perhaps, but her legs wouldn't carry her much further now. As she slowly orientated herself, she realised that she must be close to Matthew's office. She fished in her bag for her mobile and dialled his number.

'I was passing.' Fortunately, he didn't ask how and why. How would she explain it? 'Do you fancy a drink?'

At least he didn't let his surprise show in his voice. 'All right. I'll meet you in The Wilmington Arms. Ten minutes.'

The pub was fuller than she'd expected. Matthew was an advertising sales executive for the newspaper based just across the road. Newspaper office? Journalists? Pub? Two plus two? That explained the crowd. Fortunately, they all milled around the bar, chattering loudly, drinking as if the pub was about to run dry and she found a small table near enough to the entrance. She draped her coat over the chair and fought her way through the scrum to order a vodka and tonic for herself and a lager for Matthew.

She wished she had a newspaper to read. Hated the way she could see the furtive glances from some and the outright stares from others, even though she tried to keep her eyes focussed on the contents of her glass.

Matthew didn't greet her. Just sat and downed half the contents of his glass in one long draught.

'God, it's been a long day. I needed that. Thanks, Rome.' His smile was shy. Romaine often wondered how someone as introverted as Matthew could flourish in the world of advertising. He was silent for a while, looking around as if he'd never been in the place before.

'So, what brings you to these parts?'

'I don't know. I was just walking. Ended up here and thought I'd call you.'

'Glad you did. I needed a reason to leave. Would probably have stayed at my desk for another couple of hours. No incentive to go.'

Romaine thought of his girlfriend, Elaine, understanding why she might not be reason enough to leave, but she said nothing. She sipped at her drink until the silence became awkward. But she didn't know how to break it. Didn't know what to say to Matthew. Didn't actually want to talk to him at all. Just wanted his physical presence. Not to be alone for a while.

'Another drink?'

She hadn't even noticed that she'd finished the first one. She nodded and watched as Matthew made his way to the bar. Had she chosen to be with him because he looked so much like Louie? His walk was identical. The smile. The gestures. The only real difference the beard and the seriousness in Matthew's eyes where her husband's had always sparkled with a gentle, relaxed humour. Until recently. She shifted uncomfortably in the seat and stared blankly into space. She didn't even noticed when Matthew returned. Now, he simply reached across the table and took her hand in his, caressing it gently with his thumb. Anyone looking at the two of them would have thought that they were lovers sharing a secret rendezvous. Or a long-married couple who didn't need the words. Probably the latter since she didn't look into his eyes.

Matthew simply waited until she was willing to talk. The alcohol relaxed her tongue, but she wanted to talk only about Dolores, his work, the new Outkast album, the latest Michael Jackson scandal (this particular jury of two found him innocent, with certain reservations), the likelihood of Arsenal football club winning the cup and the less likely end to global terrorism. It might have been the latter that reminded him of Elaine. Matthew hitched the jacket of his sleeve up and looked at his watch. Too late to be turning up now, he thought. Oh well, in for a penny…

'Another, Romaine?'

'You need to get home.' It wasn't a question.

Matthew walked to the bar.

Strangely enough, that's when Romaine woke up. So what was she doing now? Did she really need any more complications in her life? She didn't know exactly what shape any complications might take, but a tremor between her legs warned her that they weren't likely to be warm and cuddly. She looked up at Matthew as he walked towards her, a glass in either hand, and wondered if the only reason she was feeling like this was the alcohol and the fact that, even with the goatee, he looked so much like Louie and she had always found the sight of her husband so incredibly arousing.

Matthew swallowed his drink fast. Too fast for her to think.

'I'm not going to get home at this rate.'

'What about Elaine?'

'I'll call her.'

He was tactful enough to turn away as he made the call. She could decipher the low muttering. At least it wasn't an outright lie. '…spending the night with Lou and Rome. Speak to you tomorrow.' She noticed the order in which their names were linked. So innocent-sounding. So, he'd drunk too much with the guys from the office and the sensible thing would be to stay at his brother's place… That's what she imagined Elaine would think.

❦

The silence in the taxi hinted at awkwardness, but not quite.

'He won't be at home, you know.'

'Wouldn't surprise me. He's a workaholic, my brother.'

Both their mobiles rang at the same moment. He answered his. 'Yes. Sure. Goodnight, honey. Talk to you in the morning.'

At least he had answered.

The silent key turned in the lock and Matthew closed the door behind them. The ghost of her mother insisted that she offer the customary hospitality. She didn't. No tea, coffee, brandy or even Ovaltine. Romaine had drunk enough to want to rebel a little.

She merely led him to the guest bedroom. Stark, but lovingly decorated with too much of her in it. She watched as he moved away, deliberately presenting her with his broad shoulders and firm buttocks, and pulled back the covers. He turned back to her then. Romaine closed the door. Silence between them.

She lay in bed for a while. The inability to sleep had little to do with Matthew. Or so she told herself. Louie was not by her side. She couldn't deny that she felt hurt. After last night, she had hoped that he would come home. Would want to continue where they'd left off. He must be determined to deny his feelings for her and that thought depressed her terribly. But just for a moment. Well, if he didn't need her, then she didn't need him either. Hell she didn't. If that was so, why the fuck was she lying awake at 1:30 in the morning, hearing every breath from Matthew in the next room, wondering at last if, maybe, she wanted him just a little? But only because he reminded her of Louie, who wasn't there. Surely that's all it was. Well, that's what she hoped.

Romaine waited for a while, too long, staring at the ceiling, archiving in her mind the changing patterns of car headlights reflecting across the central rose.

Eventually, procrastination was futile. She got up, shrugged into her robe and stealthily eased open the door, the package in her hands. Prepared. Why was she acting so furtively? This was her own house. Her husband had left her alone. She was free to do whatever she wanted. Still, she glanced at the door to the spare room. No light. No sound. Romaine hesitated before taking a stealthy step and then another, and another towards… where? She descended the stairs and veered in the direction of the study.

It didn't seem right to turn on the light, so she navigated by moonlight towards the console and pressed the button, summoning the blue glow. She waited. It was chill in these unfamiliar, early morning hours. She waited. Not desperate. No longing. Just hoping for satisfaction that was unlikely to come any other way.

Romaine typed in her password to get her messages. And there it was. FrenchKiss.

I have twenty-two years. Long hair, like sable. Skin the colour of, how do you say it, marrons glacés. Eyes that are hazel. The build of a warrior and the speed of an antelope with the strength of a lion and the cunning of Anancy. You, I know, are the queen who demands a worthy champion such as I. Your skin is golden, shimmering in the moonlight. I pledge my devotion to you. I need to learn how to satisfy you. I know there are many others. What should I do? Tell me urgently. I cannot wait. Even now, I take myself in hand. My penis stirs, knowing you are thinking of me, watching, stirred by my passion.

I imagine you, a proud African princess, examining your troop of devoted warriors. You reach out a hand to test our muscles, your eyes showing no emotion as your fingers trail biceps, assaying the strength of each man, knowledgeable eyes judging our worth, our strength, our staying power. You stride along the ranks, never satisfied, searching for something more. Until you reach me. You stand in front of me and stare, your eyes travelling from toe to head and then, slowly, infinitely slowly, back down to the centre of my body. You stare for a moment, a delicate flush rising to your cheeks. And you turn to the commandant and nod in my direction. I am made to take a step forward. All eyes are on me. A thousand eyes on my manhood. This will be my initiation.

Romaine wondered at how quickly his accent had changed and his grasp of English had improved. She forced herself to stop there. She smiled and, almost as if in a trance, obeyed her own steps as they took her into the living room, to pour a generous shot of brandy. And before she knew it, she was back in the study, intrigued, wanting to know where his imagination would lead her. She eased the door shut behind her.

I'm prodded from behind, urged towards your quarters. The room is empty aside from a couch and a quartet of pipers playing a joyful, but uncertain, melody. I am made to lie on a silken couch while your hand-maidens cleanse me and anoint my body with fragrant oils. I have been taught that I must not, on pain of death, show any sign of arousal. It would be like treason to suggest that I find a mere handmaiden in any way comparable to your royal highness. I struggle with my feelings, desperate to hide the swelling of my organ as a trio of hands fondle me, caressing every private, sensitive, grateful morsel of flesh. My teeth are clenched, my fingers curled into tight fists. I know that I have to pass this test. On pain of death.

You enter the room and walk forward slowly, until you are standing before me. Your look is contemptuous. Your handmaiden stands by your side, her breasts bared, her hips covered by gossamer threads. As you stare at me, she reaches for you and slowly, infinitely slowly, unbuttons your robe, letting the silken material fall. Her hands are pale, gleaming, as they follow the ripples of material, stark against the dark, melting, enticing, seductive velvet of your skin. I gasp as the white fingers, the scarlet nails, press into the voluptuous softness of your breasts and the fabric reveals the inky black peaks of your nipples against the honey sweetness of your breasts. They shrink and pucker, hardening under her touch.

Your eyes meet mine and you turn to her slowly, lips demanding. She moves towards you and I watch the fullness of her breasts crush against yours as her tongue seeks an opening and finds it between your full, ripe lips. Your hard, glittering nails seek out her breasts and squeeze, drawing a moan of pain as they sink into her soft, giving, tender flesh. You laugh, eyes glittering and turn back to me, your gaze

seeking out my cock. I move to cross my legs, hide my shame, but the
guards clutch my thighs, pulling them apart, revealing my guiltiness, the
hard rock that is my lust for you.

In the silence of the early hours, Romaine could hear her own
breathing as it deepened and quickened. Almost without thinking, she
reached down into the package, past the flurry of tissue paper until she
felt the giving hardness of the latex. She didn't look down, but her
thumb eased slowly over the rounded head. She grasped its firmness as
she read on.

The young maiden's eyes are also on the enormous fullness of my
prick. I squirm away, but there is nowhere to hide. She smiles, blushing,
as her hands reach round and lift your large breasts, presenting them to
me, squeezing the nipples, proud, confident, boastful in her ability to
touch what I long to feel between my lips.

By now, Romaine's legs were spread wide, her nightdress up above
her waist, revealing cream silk knickers pulled taut against the swelling
of her mound. She rested the vibrator against her pussy, reluctant to
move, not wanting to precipitate any premature release. She stared at
the letters on the screen, black against white, seeing instead a young
man's golden skin, body splayed, perhaps wrists and ankles imprisoned, sex hidden by a suede leather loincloth. She almost felt, rather
than saw, a glimmer of light, maybe a polished sword hanging above
his head, waiting for the merest transgression, waiting for her
command. She glanced at the vibrator, hard, constantly erect and she
let it rest on the fullness of her pussy lips, nestling between them,
barely kissing her clitoris as it throbbed, longing for some kind of
release.

She awaits a silent command. A slow, cruel, triumphant smile
crosses her lips as her fingers, infinitely slowly, trace the curve of each rib,
travelling the length of your body, sensing every pore until they encounter
the border between tantalising flesh and promising curls. She delves into
the forest that guards the sweet torture. Her ruby tongue flickers across
her lips as her mouth opens to form an 'O' of surprise and delight as she
reaches between the expectant curve of your thighs. I watch as your hips
gyrate and your body writhes against her gentle probing. Her hands press

*against your mound and you are climbing her body, as if seeking to ride
an illusory cock. I'm moaning in delight and despair and my prick feels
as if it will burst, the blood rushing to it, swelling it beyond bearing.*

Romaine touched the switch, hesitating for just second, prolonging
the moment for as long as she dared before flicking it and sending a
wave of electric pulse sweeping into her clitoris, up through the muscles
of her pussy, making them clench involuntarily as her body arched,
thrusting forward to clutch at his imaginary phallus. She tried to stifle a
moan, and it turned into a strangled gasp.

*She buries her fingers into your cunt and your writhe against them,
twisting and turning to get your fill. She is fierce in her fucking, her eyes
cruel as if with vengeance.*

She turned to one side, tugging at her panties, lifting one leg as she
touched the vibrating organ to the opening of her pussy. She held the
lips wide with the fingers of one hand as she eased the quivering object
into her, twisting slowly, the delicious friction almost unbearable.

*And then, Oh God, she's kneeling before you. Your eyes burn into
mine as your fingers circle your large nipples. Her lips reach for you,
waiting, and you bend your knees, tilting your dripping, wet pussy
towards her hot, pointed, lizard tongue. Your legs buckle and she
grasps your ass, clutching as she licks and sucks your lustful pussy,
burying her snake-like tongue inside you, pushing as far as she can,
lapping at your juices and my cock is bouncing, my balls heavy as
they tighten…*

Romaine pushed harder, the minuscule vibrations sending acute
waves of pleasure radiating out from her sensitive clitoris into her vulva,
through her womb, up through her breasts into her feverish brain. Her
breathing was heavy, ragged, uneven.

From the corner of her eyes, she sensed movement. Heard a sharp
intake of breath. She didn't look. Couldn't stop. Couldn't turn her head
as she watched the ridged latex twisting in and out, disappearing into
the depths of her clutching flesh and re-emerging almost unwillingly,
glistening, slick. She pushed deeper, her pussy lips clenching, sucking it
deeper, the pulsing faster, more desperate, irresistible, faster and faster
until her body succumbed, erupting with months of pent-up frustra-

tion and every single muscle tensed in grateful release as she sagged, totally spent, against the rough fabric of the chair, unable to read any more of the words on the screen.

A few blissful minutes later, she turned towards the door. In the empty darkness, it was open. She thought she hadn't left it that way.

CHAPTER 6

Louie returned home before she was quite asleep. It was late enough and early enough to be silent on the streets. Tonight he was considerate. Kind. He eased his body into the bed, almost furtively, spooning himself against her back, gently cupping her breast as he slipped his penis inside her, moaning at the wetness that he found. He made love to her and when he was done, Romaine slept. Not dreamlessly, but at least she slept.

The next morning, she simply explained to Louie that she hadn't been feeling too good and would give the office a miss for the day. A rare enough occurrence for him to scrutinise her face, a fleeting glimpse of distrust on his face.

'So what happened?'

'Nothing. I came home with a headache yesterday and I'm feeling a bit off now. Might be a cold coming.'

'It's so unlike you not to go in to work, Romaine. You must really be feeling bad.' He sat by her and put a palm to her forehead. She knew that she wasn't running any kind of temperature. 'You want me to stay and look after you?'

For one nasty, treacherous moment, Romaine wondered if the offer had anything to do with her indisposition, or more to do with him not trusting her any more. Wanting to keep an eye on her.

At that instant, the door to the spare room creaked open and Louie jumped, startled, body rigid in fight mode.

'It's okay. Just Matthew. He stayed here last night.'

'Had a skinful with them guys from the office, eh?' Louie didn't ask anything more and Romaine didn't volunteer any further information. Anyway, the momentary distraction seemed to have made him forget his offer of nursing care.

Thirty minutes later, both he and Matthew had left the house. Romaine curled into a tight ball beneath the duvet and forced herself back into sleep.

🍒

They walked to the station with Louie taking one step to Matthew's two. He was in a hurry and wasn't about to make any concessions to anyone else. By the time he took the stairs down to the platform three at a time, Matthew was out of breath and gasping for air.

'Bro, you need to do something to take care of yourself. Elaine not giving you enough of a workout?' He punched Matthew gently in the arm, causing him to wince. 'Boy, you're really out of shape, you know.'

'So what's wrong with Romaine? Why she not going to work?' Matthew had his own theory, but wasn't about to expand. He suspected a combination of alcohol overdose and a very late night. He hadn't got too much sleep himself, not after he'd heard her tiptoeing past his door and down the stairs. Who could blame him for biding his time and then following her to see what was happening?

Louie stared straight ahead, his voice low, lips hardly moving.

'I guess she's been stressed out lately.'

Matthew was shocked. This was more than his brother would normally volunteer unless his body was tied to a rack. He hid his surprise and asked calmly, 'With what?'

'Work, I suppose. That bitch of a boss—'

'I thought you guys were all friends?'

Louie wiped a bead of sweat from his forehead even though it was cold in the carriage.

'You had a falling out?' Matthew pried gently.

'You could say that.'

'About what? You all seemed so tight.'

'Well, that's what I thought.'

'So, she's been making life hard for Rome?' Matthew was still puzzled. 'But Romaine's normally so strong. Surely she could handle the toughest high priestess of hell.'

Louie was silent. As if he hadn't heard. Matthew didn't push and didn't ask any questions when Louie followed him off the train and up the escalator to The Angel. He strode ahead to St Johns Street, but stopped awkwardly outside Bliss.

'Fancy a quick coffee?'

They sat at a small table at the rear of the tiny café. Matthew wolfed his croissant and watched as his brother picked morsels from his scone, rolled them into balls and dropped them back on his plate. The coffee was untouched too. Matthew surreptitiously glanced at his watch. Louie had better start talking soon otherwise he would have to think up a good excuse for his lateness this time—the mother of all hangovers was wearing pretty thin now.

'How did she seem last night, when you got there?' Louie's voice was a monotone, as if he was dragging himself from the depths of some profound meditation.

So, she hadn't told Louie about them meeting up. He wondered if that was significant, but he wasn't about to rock the boat. How was Matthew going to phrase this? 'Well, Lou, she seemed a little... edgy. Happy enough, but thoughtful. Why are you asking me, Bro? What's up. Something going down between you two?' He expected a quick denial, but instead, Matthew just nodded slowly.

'It's been hard. I didn't know if I could take it. I wanted to smash something. To break something. Or someone. To lash out blindly at anything that came my way—'

'Whoa! Steady on, Lou.' Matthew held his brother's shoulder, the closest physical contact they'd had in years. 'What happened?'

Louie's eyes held a mixture of wonder and fear, like he was experiencing his first high and it wasn't going well. 'She's been screwing around.'

Matthew almost laughed. 'Romaine? I don't believe it.'

Louie hung his head. 'Well, maybe I'm exaggerating. According to her, it was just the once.'

Well, well, well. Matthew didn't look at his watch again. This was going to be worth waiting for.

❧

Romaine groped for the alarm clock until she roused herself enough to understand that it was the telephone ringing. 'If it's another bloody hang-up...' she thought. But it wasn't. Alison's voice held a gentle concern that she hadn't heard in a while.

'You still don't sound good, Romaine.'

'Believe me, Alison, I'm fine. It's just that I've been sleeping and you—'

'I was worried about you. You didn't look too good yesterday.'

'Probably looked a lot worse than I felt.'

'That's just not possible.' At least Alison was joking with her again. 'You got anyone there to look after you? To bring you chicken soup?' Romaine had forgotten that she'd told Alison all about the incident with Colin and the chicken soup. In fact, over the months, there had been very little that she hadn't told Alison. And vice versa.

'Louie would have stayed.' Why did she feel the need to defend him? 'I made him go. I just intended to sleep.'

'So you don't need anything?'

It was difficult to say 'no', to reject the olive branch, but she had to.

'No, honestly, Alison, I'll be fine. But thanks for asking.'

'Well, call me if you do need anything. You know where we are. I can always send Byron round with a food parcel if that would be easier.'

There was a click on the other end of the phone and Romaine smiled, a warm, cosy, relaxed smile, for the first time in months. She replaced the receiver and turned onto her stomach, arms tucked under the pillow. Life had just got a whole heap easier. She closed her eyes and immediately fell into a peaceful, dreamless sleep.

❦

The first meeting went better than she could possibly have hoped. A summer barbecue at Alison's home, an Edwardian terrace with a huge, lovingly-tended garden in Kentish Town. Romaine the only one from the office invited, and Louie too. Even though they got on so well, Romaine had been surprised; Alison seemed to fight hard to keep her home life private. It was like a badge of initiation that she'd been invited to the party.

Alison was resplendent in a vivid scarlet and orange African dress with matching headtie. Her husband was at the other extreme of the clothing spectrum wearing torn, faded blue jeans and plain white shirt of soft, worn cotton.

'You'll have to excuse Byron. I haven't quite got him house-trained yet. Even after twelve years.' Her teasing smile was relaxed and affectionate and she touched his arm as she introduced them both to her husband.

She was the consummate hostess, immediately leading them to a group of friends waiting patiently by the barbecue. Neighbours, colleagues of Byron's, Alison's brother and sister and their spouses and children. The afternoon was turning into early evening before Alison finally relinquished her duties and came to sit with Romaine and Louie, a glass of white wine in her hand.

'It's good to finally meet you, Alison.' Louie was at his most charming, a gleaming smile offered to Alison. 'You've become a household name. Well, certainly in our household.'

'I hope your wife's only been saying good things about me. I enjoy working with her. We make a good team.'

'May I say you show great insight yourself. You couldn't have picked a better secretary.'

'Personal Assistant, you mean.'

'Hey, cut it out, you guys. I'm here you know. You're making me blush.' Romaine's protests were dismissed straight away.

'If you don't want to listen to us talking about you, then you can go talk gardening or decorating with Byron. I can see he's all by himself and looking lonely. Why don't you rescue him while I find out all your hidden secrets from your husband.' Alison waved her away.

'Ha!' Romaine laughed. 'What makes you think he knows my secrets?'

And she had left them together and gone to the other side of the garden in search of Byron, a giant of a man who looked strangely vulnerable standing alone against the backdrop of overblown dahlias, a frown creasing his forehead.

'Alison's kidnapped my husband.'

He smiled fondly as he looked towards his wife.

'She has a way of doing that.'

There was a moment's silence during which Romaine realised that the reason that Byron had been standing alone, strangely apart, was not that he was unfriendly or aloof. Because she was so used to Alison's easy self-confidence, it had never occurred to her that her husband might be shy. But he was. She could see it in the way he twisted the stem of the glass between his fingers and the blush that rose beneath the dark colouring of his skin.

'You have a beautiful garden,' Romaine said sincerely, touching his arm. She smiled as she noticed that the tips of his ears turned bright red.

'Thank you. It's taken a long time.'

He took her on a guided tour. By the end of it, Romaine felt privileged. It was as if Byron's garden was a special, secret gift, the Crown Jewels, that he'd allowed her to witness. As he talked of how he'd transformed the land from a barren waste, he'd warmed to his subject and had spoken fluently, large, surprisingly elegant hands describing patterns in the air, creating a vivid picture that she could clearly visualise. He talked of visiting his grandparents in Grenada as a child. The little patch of land that had been given to him and his sisters. His grand-daddy teaching them how to cultivate the soil. Returning each year for the competition to see whose patch was doing best. Being left the clear winner when his sisters lost interest in the dasheen, tannia and cassava, the dry peas and tomatoes, the sweet potatoes and corn and took to boys instead. She could almost smell the dry earth.

What a lovely man! Romaine kept thinking as he spoke. His warm eyes sparkled with the recollections. She no longer wondered what someone as outgoing and confident as Alison saw in Byron. In fact, she felt a little jealous, knowing that this rock solid bear of a man was the secret treasure that Alison went home to each night.

'You have a real talent, Byron.'

He blushed. 'You've let me ramble on. I must have bored you solid.' He looked slightly dazed, as if he'd just woken from a dream. 'Alison tells me I have a tendency to do that.'

They were interrupted by guests saying their goodbyes and Romaine scanned the garden until she found Louie. She caught his glance and passed the subtle signal that said it was time to leave.

They chattered enthusiastically in the car on the way home, both surprised by how much they'd enjoyed the day. Romaine was happy that Alison seemed to have found a real fan in her husband. That was only one of many perfect days that the two couples shared that summer.

❤

Sitting at her desk, the door closed, Alison, too, was thinking back to that glorious summer. *I guess it really was too perfect,* she thought, finally giving up with the report she'd been trying to complete. She pushed the keyboard to one side and flexed her fingers. She stood and glanced through the glass towards Romaine's desk. She noticed how neat it was, nothing out of place. Typical Romaine. She'd even bothered to clear her desk when she hadn't been feeling well.

That must have been what had prompted her to make the call: the sight of that perfectly ordered desk and the knowledge that she needed a viable working relationship with Romaine, if nothing else. What had happened was not Romaine's fault. Nobody's *fault.* That word shouldn't even really come into the equation. It had been up to her to do something and she'd known that for a long while, had been meaning to talk to Romaine. But somehow, and this was so untypical of Alison, it had never happened.

And then she'd walked into the office yesterday and had been genuinely shocked by the unhappiness—no, 'misery' was a more accurate word—that she'd seen in Romaine's face. She had felt a stab of pain or guilt.

She had thought long and hard before inviting Romaine and her husband to her home for that barbecue. As was her way, she'd done her research carefully: the lunches outside the office, drinks after work, gentle probing, all designed to find out about Romaine's lifestyle, her friends, family, husband. She needed to be able to trust her, to make sure that her assistant wouldn't take advantage of their growing friendship, wouldn't make waves in the office. As in every other aspect of her life, Alison was prudent. She collected her friends carefully, harvesting them only after meticulous groundwork.

Her instincts were accurate about Romaine and though it amused her to see how her own introverted husband blossomed with her, she was equally pleased at how well she herself got on with Louie. Alison didn't seem to make many friends in the business world and their interests didn't clash. Their work ethics were similar and their determination to succeed, or rather, the refusal to contemplate failure, was identical.

They had recognised kindred spirits immediately and it became not unusual for Alison to call Louie for advice or contacts if she was working on anything to do with the music industry or computers. She was always amazed by his generosity of spirit.

'Hey, no skin off my nose. Girl, we have to stick together without letting them know 'bout it. Look back in our history. We're masters of the secret code. We should get practising on the djembe drums. We have to keep we "ting" to weselves lest they wan' come mash it up!' She would laugh. No one talked to her the way Louie did. He had a sardonic humour that she immediately appreciated.

And nearly a year ago, she and Byron had been invited to share their anniversary dinner at Cotton's, the Caribbean restaurant in Camden. They had almost overwhelmed the place with their laughter, Byron joining in readily with one or two jokes of his own after a few rum punches. Alison had been the one driving, so she'd been able to sit back and dispassionately assess the group. She had seen something of her own husband in Sheldon; the bumbling exterior, his thick glasses concealing a sharp intelligence, just like Byron's, which both guarded carefully, as if to reveal it to the uninitiated would risk having it snatched away. She liked his straightforward, no-nonsense attitude and could understand why he and Louie would work extremely well together.

She wasn't so sure about Sheldon's wife. Oh, there was a warmth and liveliness about Grace, but Alison sensed a feline wariness, nothing sinister, just a hint that there was something lurking beneath the surface that she would let no one else perceive, something she hugged to herself, something that made her smile whenever she thought about it. On balance, Alison liked Grace but knew this was someone she could never get close to. They were too similar in many ways, and yet so far apart.

Louie had teased his brother mercilessly with a humour that verged on being malicious. Her own brothers behaved in much the same way towards her, so she supposed that Matthew had got used to it. The two of them were so physically similar and yet there was something shadowy, unformed, in the younger man's contours that made him just miss out on Louie's fine good looks. At least that's how it seemed to Alison.

And Colin. Alison had to laugh out loud whenever she thought of Colin. She immediately picked up on the way he looked at her, nothing conscious, just a glance that lingered a little too long now and again, one he'd practised on a million other women. He didn't even notice her amusement, but she played a little game. Knowing exactly what to expect from his type, she made a little bet with herself as to how long it would take.

She was only out by a couple of minutes. As soon as Byron left the table in search of the loo, Colin moved into his seat, slipped an arm around Alison's waist and whispered into her ear, his alcohol-laden breath serving as excuse enough. 'What you doing later, after the old man gone to bed?'

'Getting my lover out of the closet!' She said it loud enough for everyone else to hear.

'Colin!' they chorused. 'Get off that woman. Put her down!' And they proceeded to shower him with morsels of fruit from their cocktails. He laughed too. You couldn't really blame Colin. He really couldn't help himself. Nevertheless, Alison found herself avoiding his touch for the rest of the evening. There was something unsettling about him. Something that she couldn't quite put her finger on.

But they both had a good time and she noticed again how easy Romaine and Byron were in each other's company. It was like Romaine had kissed him on the nose and transformed the frog into a dashing prince. She smiled to herself as she watched them. No, she would never refer to her dear Byron as a frog. He had always been her prince.

So, Romaine not being at her desk as usual reminded Alison of how much she missed the relaxed friendship they'd shared. A friendship that Romaine had never abused. She had always remained so professional in the office. And that's why Alison had to be the one to pick up the phone and offer not the whole olive branch, but at least a single leaf.

❦

A harsh wintry light filtered through the curtains by the time Romaine woke. She got out of bed immediately feeling incredibly refreshed, amazed at how much difference a day and one single phone call could make.

She bounded into the kitchen intent on coffee. As she waited for the grounds to percolate, she glanced out of the window into the garden. The lawn was covered with shiny wet leaves that, she knew, shouldn't be there. Byron had taught her that much. Before she could have time to think better of it, she put on a thick coat over her nightdress, slipped her feet into Wellington boots and got the rake out of the shed. She spent a good forty minutes clearing the lawn, swooping the pile of leaves into black plastic bags before the rain began to fall again. She dashed into the kitchen and surveyed her garden again. A job well done. Byron would be proud of her.

The thought of Byron made her inexplicably sad. She wondered where he fit into all this mess. Maybe she could fix things with Alison, but would she ever be able to regain the easy friendship she'd shared with them both? She longed to pick up the phone and talk to him, try to explain, but it wasn't her place. She had just begun to mend fences with Alison; to call her husband would be pushing it.

Romaine pulled off her boots, dropped her coat, picked up the cup of luke-warm coffee and headed for the sitting room. She deliberately ignored the study with its beckoning screen. Now that her life was back on track, she didn't need any of that stuff.

She turned on the television and flicked through the channels. She always nagged when Louie did the same thing, but she was alone at home and could do whatever she wanted and, besides, there was nothing that kept her attention for more than twenty seconds. She left the television on while she glanced through the CDs stacked in the rack. She picked up the new Alicia Keys and scanned the tracks. Putting the disc into the player, she switched off the TV and picked up the *Radio Times*, dropping it again when she remembered going through it before. Nothing new to watch. There were plenty of things she *could* do to keep busy, like the washing or ironing, or dusting or, if she was feeling really devout, cleaning the kitchen floor. But then, what was the point of having a day off work if you spent it doing drudgery like that?

'You don't know my name and I mmm mmm mmm...' she hummed along to Alicia, wondering what to do with her hands.

Romaine got up and wandered to the kitchen. She opened the fridge and surveyed the contents. She could, possibly, prepare some gourmet delicacy for supper. She closed the fridge. No use pretending that her culinary skills had improved over the years. She made more coffee and discovered a tin of shortbread biscuits at the back of a cupboard. She dunked listlessly.

The phone rang and she rushed to get there before it rang off. Someone conducting a survey on behalf of the major high street banks. She debated keeping him on the phone for as long as possible while he totted up the phone bill from a call centre in Delhi, but decided that she didn't feel motivated enough.

Alicia Keys was silent now and there wasn't anything else that Romaine felt like listening to. Nothing that quite matched her mood.

Maybe a shower and getting dressed would energise her. She moved towards the stairs, but the blue light of the computer tower winked at her. Well, what would be wrong with just seeing if there were any messages for her? She had no intention of replying to any of them, but it might be quite amusing to check on her cyber dates. Romaine pushed a stirring of guilt back into the bulging box in her head.

She paced the room as she waited for the machine to power up. Romaine sat as the screen lightened, went through the routine of checking her e-mail.

Several messages from HandyMan:

Where are you, Scarlet? You are disobeying me. Remember our contract. I know you are deliberately making me angry. You want more punishment. You are forcing me to cause you pain. You want it. Don't pretend.

And then:

Answer me now, Scarlet. My rage is growing. Don't underestimate me. You know what I can do. Respond. Or else…

And:

I have prepared the hairbrush to spank your pert backside. You will beg for mercy, but I have the whip by my side. You are in my control and there will be no respite. You will feel pain such as you have never known as the leather flicks across those sensitive nipples. You will wince, trying

not to scream, but with each lash, you writhe more and more, attempt-
ing to escape. I ease up momentarily to remind you of what the absence
of pain feels like. It's ecstasy to you. But soon, I start again, the whip
cracking as it connects with the soft area between your thighs. Your body
is on fire, the heat rising with each touch of the tendrils. I'm getting
hard as I watch the red welts rising on your breasts, your stomach, your
thighs. The pain is so intense that you're crying out for me to stop. But I
won't. That's what's in store for you. Are you ready? Let me know.

The final message from HandyMan made her nearly choke with laughter:

Please Scarlet. I can't get off without you. Please, please tell me
what you want me to do.

Romaine was almost tempted to respond. She felt so sorry for him, but she wasn't a social worker, she reminded herself. She checked for messages from FrenchKiss, but his last entry had ended rather prematurely and there was nothing new. Nothing from JellyRoll, either. Romaine felt curiously disappointed; the site hadn't failed her before. She returned to it and searched again through the list of candidates. There was no one who tempted her. Maybe it was her change of mood, but she couldn't get into Sucker who was looking for a nanny or Well-Heeled who had a thing about boots (she thought of her muddy Wellies) or even Stiffy, who was into groups. So what exactly was she looking for? It suddenly struck her that that might be what she needed to decide.

Romaine clicked her way back to the home page and scanned the various buttons. She hesitated for a moment and then pressed the button marked 'create profile'.

Another blank form presented itself to her. Where to start?

The first couple of boxes were easy. She'd already decided on a name and age. Description was a bit of a poser. Who did she want to be? Romaine sat back in the chair as she riffled through all the possibilities in her mental filing cabinet. She had the shade card spread out in the forefront of her mind when she suddenly realised that she could be whoever she chose. She could be blonde or a red-head, green eyes, or grey. Tall, leggy, shapely. Big breasts and butt. And, of course, long hair. But she had to be careful in case she created some kind of freak, or forgot the details. No, it would be best to stick as close to the truth as possible, without giving too much away.

Medium height, firm, full breasts, shapely legs, rounded buttocks, skin the colour of Virginia tobacco, long, dark, waist-length hair,—no sense in wasting an opportunity to fantasise!—*elegant fingers. Eyes almost black, thick brows, nose a little too broad, lips a little too full.*

She could always come back to the description, refining it as necessary. The most difficult part was going to be the section marked 'Seeking'. Yep, that was the biggie. Just what was she seeking? There was no point in continuing until she knew that. Strangely regretful, Romaine clicked on the X button, closing down the site. She felt oddly restless.

❧

Louie was home earlier than she'd expected. Just because she hadn't been feeling too good. Things were looking up. He was no Mary Seacole, but at least he brought a takeaway with him. They curled up on the sofa afterwards, his strong arms wrapped around her.

'Feeling better, honey?'

'Uh-huh. Feeling good.' His fingers massaged the muscles of her back, pressing hard as she sagged against him, the pleasure instantly obliterating the pain, only for it to return as he circled lower, knuckles prodding, probing, down, down to the base of her spine where she hadn't realised that the pain existed. She moaned against him. Massage had always been his million-dollar speciality, his genius, his ask-the-audience, fifty-fifty and phone-a-friend rolled into one. At this particular moment, Romaine would have paid him a million dollars to continue making her feel so good. She was melting into a puddle of ecstasy when the phone jangled. For several moments they both wished it away and then, when it became too intrusive, Louie reached over and lifted it to his ear, cradling it between chin and shoulder before he answered, still massaging her neck.

'Yo.'

The freeze transmitted itself to Romaine through his fingers. She knew exactly what was coming.

He handed the receiver to her, stood and walked out of the room, physically and mentally distancing himself.

'Hello?'

'Hi, just checking on how you are.'

'Alison!'

'He couldn't bear to talk to me, could he?'

'I'm sorry. It's just that he—'

'It's okay, Romaine. You don't have to explain.'

'I'd like to try.'

'Maybe not now. How about a drink when you're better?'

'Tomorrow? After work?' She couldn't miss this opportunity. She had been trying for so long to engineer a conversation.

'As long as you don't think you have to come to work.'

'I'm fine, Alison.'

'No arguments. See you at six-thirty. Usual place?'

'Okay. See you then.'

He'd obviously been waiting someplace outside the door. He didn't say anything, just slouched on the sofa and grabbed the remote control.

'She just wanted to know how I was.'

No response.

'Louie. I said Alison just called because—'

'I heard you.' His eyes remained fixed to the television screen.

She stood and deliberately placed her body in front of the television.

'We can't go on not talking about this, Lou.'

Without a word, he stood up and strode into the hall. She heard his footsteps rapidly climbing the stairs, thuds across the ceiling, silence for several minutes and then echoes down the stairs and past the sitting-room door. Romaine walked to the hallway and watched as he reached for his coat, a plastic carrier bag in his hand.

'Where you going, Lou?'

'I need some space.'

'Don't be like this. You know we have to talk sometime.'

No response. Romaine's eyes narrowed with impatience. She felt as if she had just been plunged into ice-cold water.

'Wait a few minutes. You can't go like this.'

Watching the grim set of his face, Romaine debated for a second whether there was anything to be gained by pursuing the lines she'd rehearsed so often for the last two months. I'm sorry. I'm guilty. It's all my fault. You're the innocent party in all of this. So beat me, punish me, whip me (she thought of HandyMan and had to suppress the hysterical laughter—she could never make him understand).

Romaine turned away from him and ran up the stairs, hurt and angry at his rejection. She packed as many of his clothes as she could into an overnight bag and returned to where he stood, rooted to the spot. She touched his arm gently, and when he shrugged away her touch, she handed the bag to him without a word.

❦

He didn't call. Romaine wanted not to care where he'd taken his pathetic scrap of a masculine ass. But she found herself dialling Grace's number. No, he wasn't there. She called Matthew, probing discreetly, not wanting to admit what had happened. It was clear from Matthew's light-hearted teasing that Louie hadn't turned to him. Colin? She couldn't possibly call him, although she knew he would know immediately what had happened. It was like he had some kind of sixth sense where her relationship with Louie was concerned and he'd probably come running. And besides, her husband would need to be desperate to admit the situation to Colin. Dolores? How would she explain to her that she was looking for her husband?

Romaine slept remarkably soundly given the circumstances. She guessed she'd got used to the empty bed over the months. But on waking, a tiny alarm bell went off in her head. What if something had really happened to him? How guilty would she feel then! But, hell, Louie was a grown man, big enough to look after himself. Even so, what if…

She got into the car and drove carefully, but fast, into the early-morning gloom.

She reluctantly pressed the bell. The light flickered on in the hall and she could hear Dolores putting the security chain in place.

'It's me, Romaine,' she tried to reassure her mother-in-law.

Dolores fumbled to open the door.

'What is it. Is it Lou?' Her face was pale as she clutched the neck of her pink cardigan around her throat.

Romaine felt guilty at how inconsiderate she had been. Of course Dolores would think of her son first. She should have called instead.

'No, Louie's fine. I just, um, thought he said he was on his way here. I need to get a message to him.' Dolores was obviously not convinced. Her eyes were saying exactly what Romaine immediately thought: so what's wrong with his mobile?

Dolores opened the door wide. The droop of her shoulders signalled that the last thing she wanted to do at this time of the morning was listen to another person's troubles, but years of church-going had made it impossible to deny someone in need.

Dolores led the way to the kitchen, the heart of this home and Romaine thought she could hear voices in the kitchen as the scent of frying bacon and sausages wafted through the flat. She was surprised to find, ensconced at the head of the table, Mr James, looking as if he was in his rightful place. Less surprising was the fact that Dolores waited on him like an Egyptian handmaiden; it was her chosen role in life. Romaine was mildly amused.

'You want some breakfast, child?'

'No thanks, Dolores. Just coffee for me.'

'You need to build youself up, girl. Look 'pon you. You been losing weight?'

'No, honestly. I'm fine, Dolores.'

The radio was blaring. A news channel. It seemed that Mr James needed to keep abreast of what was happening in the world.

'You hear say that George Carey send up a man on Mars?'

'George Bush.'

'Whatever. Him put man on Mars, send him all the way there. Them find that little planet all them thousands of miles away and yet him and that Tony Bennett—'

'Blair.'

'Well, with all the try them try and they still can't find that Osama Ben-Gurion.'

'Bin Laden.'

'Whatever.'

Dolores raised an eyebrow as if she was used to ignoring him. She shook her head at Romaine, warning her not to prolong the conversation. Romaine sipped her coffee while the others finished their breakfast. She wished that she hadn't come, that she could leave, that she wouldn't have to give some kind of explanation to Dolores.

As they stood together at the kitchen sink, one washing, the other drying, Dolores did her best to explain about Mr James.

'Him don't have nobody else. And I just couldn't bear the idea of him sitting alone in that small room every day. So him come here for his meals. Is no more work for me. And anyway… is a little bit of company.'

Romaine understood. And she knew that each meal cooked would be added to Dolores' mental tally of good deeds she'd be able to confess on Redemption Day.

'Does he actually have a first name?' She didn't know why she asked.

Dolores looked up and was still for a moment, as if the idea had never occurred to her. 'You know, I think I did know it once, but that must have been a very long time ago. I can't remember, child. To me, he will always be Mr James. Anything else would seem rude.' She chuckled gently.

The two women worked in companionable silence, Mr James' muttering a not unpleasant background to their activity.

'So, what's happened with that boy of mine.' Dolores finally asked, her drying motions in sync with the rhythm of her voice. Romaine noted the neutrality of her voice, no hint of blame in her tone. 'Don't tell me "nothing". Why else you would be here at this time of the morning?'

Romaine didn't answer for a while, debating how to explain. Dolores was patient, stacking the plates in the cupboard, pouring more tea for Mr James. Eventually, she turned and placed a hand on Romaine's arm, her touch gentle, her eyes affectionate and sympathetic.

'You young things believe I'm too old to remember what those men can be like. Don't worry, child, you don't have to tell me anything you don't want. Much as I love my sons, I still know that they're men. And…' she smiled, 'I learned long ago not to expect too much from them.' Her gaze seemed to turn inwards and Romaine wondered, once again, what the story was with Louie's father. She didn't know if he was dead or alive. No one ever spoke about him.

'You want me to have words with Louie?'

Romaine almost laughed at the idea, but she felt too guilty. She was going to have to find a way of making it clear that none of this was Louie's fault, that it had all been her, but she didn't feel that Dolores would understand the tale.

'No, Dolores, thank you. It's great to have you on my side but, honestly, Louie hasn't done anything. It's more to do with me. I just needed to have some space to think. That's why Louie's going away. Just for a few days.'

'Well, if you do talk to that boy of mine, tell him say I'm still expecting him to be here for lunch on Sunday, so maybe the two of you can patch things up by then. I hope so.'

Mr James' own mumbled news bulletin was getting louder, more agitated and provided a welcome distraction.

'Don't worry,' Dolores, glanced at the fragile old man whose hands trembled as he lifted the cup to his lips, 'I'll take him out for a walk in a minute. Get him away from all this doom and gloom before him have a stroke.'

As she helped Dolores usher her ward out of the door, Romaine wondered what the future had in store for her. Would she and Louie be living in companionable, if arthritic, harmony? She smiled at the thought, but wanted to weep too. Why did her husband have to be so unbending and unforgiving? And then she felt a certain degree of guilt that she had driven a kind, caring, sensitive man to this.

Just when she'd thought her life was getting better, everything had suddenly gone so horribly wrong. And faster than she could possibly have imagined. What exactly had happened? What had she said to upset Louie so much?

Romaine trawled through her memory, analysing each moment, trying to see it all from his point of view. But whichever way she looked at it, all roads were going to lead to the one point: Alison.

❦

Them young girls must think we never lived, Dolores thought as she took Mr James' elbow and chaperoned him across the road, turning to wave to her daughter-in-law as the car drove off. They headed to what was called a park but was more a handkerchief of muddy land with a couple of wrought iron benches, a slide and three swings. This morning, the play area was empty, the lonely swings swaying with the wind.

Mr James sat and Dolores eased her creaking bones into the space beside him. *Lord, I don't know why she trying to protect that boy. I did my best with the two of them, but what can you do? You can't win against the genes. Whatever I tried to do, they would have to grow up to be men. No way to prevent that. And is no use she try to keep the truth from me. What she think goin' happen? He's still my child and I will still love him whatever he might have done, but my shoulders broad enough to accept that he is no angel.*

She thought back to the times she'd seen Louie recently. He'd sat at the lunch table hardly able to look his wife in the eye. Or his mother either, for that matter. Seemed as if he was being tortured and wanted to be anywhere else but there, with them. A sure sign of guilt. And she'd seen the dark circles around Romaine's eyes. Knew that she must have been awake all night long. Dolores recognised the signs. How many times had she done the same thing herself? She couldn't really blame Louie: he must have got it straight from his father. It was always inevitable.

The boys had got their colouring from her, but their handsome features from him. In fact, every time she looked at Louie, the spectre of her husband still rose before her. For twelve years she'd put up with his womanising, allowing his charm to win her round each time because she told herself that she still loved the rogue. How could anyone resist him? And each time he'd promised that it would never happen again. She'd take him back because she knew he couldn't help himself. Of course, he loved her and his sons, Dolores was confident of that, but the old goat really had no control over his urges. It was like a drug and she didn't have the cure. In the end, she'd only thrown him out when he strayed a little too close to home—their upstairs neighbour—and she didn't want him setting that kind of example to the boys…

Mr James coughed beside her and she automatically turned to make sure that he was all right. She wrapped his scarf more securely around his neck and tucked the ends inside his coat.

Funny how, even though she knew her errant husband had loved her, once he had left, they had never heard from him again. For all she knew, he could have been run over by a bus!

So what could she say to Romaine? Tell her to forgive Louie? That they could work through it? What did *she* know? And what if Louie didn't want to give up whatever little bit he had on the side? Maybe that's where he had been on Sunday when he was supposed to be in the office. She'd heard all those excuses in the past, knew them well. But if that was the case, he would certainly get a piece of her mind. Not only was he lying to his wife, but to his mother, too. Strange the way she had thought she knew her two sons so well. If she'd been asked to bet on it, she would have given odds that Matthew would have been the one to take after his father. Quiet and a little bit secretive. She knew Louie was no saint, but he had always seemed so devoted to Romaine. She had been the only one that lasted after a string of women. What more could he want than Romaine, a darling, treasure of a girl? She had been convinced that Louie had grown up at last. Just goes to show what she had forgotten: boys never do grow up.

So now she was torn between her devotion to her child and her deep affection towards Romaine. And the poor girl didn't have nobody else in the world. She would never be able to turn her away…

Dolores stood and offered her arm to Mr James. This was only the beginning of their morning constitutional. They had to walk round the path at least three times before they deserved to stop off at the local café for tea and a bun.

❦

Romaine arrived at the wine bar first. She was given a cheery welcome by the staff. They knew her and Alison well. She made her way to their usual table, up a few steps, with a view out of the window.

She ordered a mineral water even though she longed for alcohol to calm her nerves.

She looked around. The place hadn't begun to fill up yet, but small, chattering groups had gathered by the bar. Obviously colleagues, bitching about their day or bad-mouthing their bosses. Romaine knew she'd missed out on this after-hours winding-down ritual. She'd been politely shunned by the others in her office, probably because of her closeness to Alison. And then she couldn't complain about the boss when she was sharing drinks with her! It struck her then that for quite a while now, probably since her mother had died, she had been profoundly lonely. She had never really noticed before in the midst of the bustle of her life. And what a place to come to the realisation: in a crowded, smoky bar on a rainy, wintry evening! A lump rose to her throat.

Romaine looked up from her glass and it was at that moment that Alison walked through the door. Impossibly elegant at the end of a working day, she made her way unerringly towards Romaine, totally oblivious of the admiring glances in her direction. She wore a long, dark coat with a bright, flaming orange scarf covering her dark hair. She smiled gently at Alison, the dimple appearing and retreating almost like a mirage. She dropped her briefcase by the side of the table and shrugged off the coat to reveal a beautifully tailored grey suit and black polo neck that did nothing to conceal her generous curves. Without speaking, she headed towards the bar, the crowds parting before her like the Red Sea.

She was back in minutes. If that had been me, Romaine thought, I'd have been waiting for hours to be served! She handed a glass to Romaine who could smell the gin immediately.

'Thought you needed something a little stronger. Cheers!' She clinked her glass against Romaine's. 'How are you feeling now?'

'There really is nothing wrong with me, Alison. I'm fine.'

'Oh?'

Romaine refused to look up at the other woman. She twirled the glass around the tabletop, creating wet figures-of-eight.

'I tried to call you today. There was no answer. Your mobile was switched off. I was worried, Romaine.'

'He's left.'

It was Alison's turn to be silent. Romaine finally raised her eyes and met the other woman's gaze. She knew that she would have to truthfully answer the question that Alison was bound to ask.

'Because of me?'

❦

They had grown closer. Alison was so contained, so secure in her world, so wise that Romaine had trusted her completely. She'd felt able to talk to Alison about her most secret dreams and desires and although the older woman was never as forthcoming, Romaine knew that she was privileged to have been allowed into the inner sanctum of warm friendship. She knew that Alison's cool, guarded exterior concealed a warm, caring, generous core that bound her friends to her with a fierce loyalty. In a strange way, Alison made her feel safe.

And together, they were a formidable team with Alison coming to rely more and more on her assistant, knowing that she could leave the details to her more often than not. Within the office, though, they maintained an arm's-length, professional relationship, keeping their friendship a closely-guarded secret.

And two months ago, everything had changed, maybe irrevocably.

The project they were working on was turning into a nightmare. The client changed his mind each day that passed, making more and more impossible demands, each of which they met as he continued to up the ante. It had been Romaine who had suggested the strategy that she hoped would save them a great deal of anxiety and fruitless effort.

'Alison, I think, maybe, we should try to figure out where he's heading, what exactly he wants the research to show. If we know that, then maybe we can do a little extra digging and head off his next demands.'

'Good idea. We've spent enough time in those offices to be able to work out where he's hoping to end up. You've talked to the staff, what do you think?'

Romaine hesitated. Alison had always told her that she concentrated too much on personalities, but she thought she knew what the key was in this particular case.

'Well, I've spent more time than you in the canteen and you might want to take this with a pinch of salt, but…'

'So what gossip have you been listening to now?' Alison chuckled.

'It's a family business, right?'

'Right.'

'From what I hear, there are three sons, all set to inherit.'

'Yep. That's hardly a secret.'

'No, but we're dealing with the youngest one. The hothead. Apparently, he's been trying to modernise the company for years and has met quite a bit of resentment.'

'Not surprising, really. Most of the staff seemed to be nearing retirement age.'

'Yes, but they're still incredibly successful at what they do. They have a loyal customer base and get most of their new business through referrals and word of mouth.'

'Which won't be enough forever.'

'Exactly. So I think we're being used to come up with the research that would justify selling up, taking the profits now and running...'

'…When the others want to plough any profits back into the company. I see.'

'So I think we need to plug every gap in the research.'

'Okay, let's get to it.'

Even as the light faded outside the windows and the office gradually emptied, they'd continued to work, Romaine tapping words on the keyboard while Alison sat by her side taking notes and making suggestions. It was near enough midnight by the time they'd got the report into a shape ready for their meeting the next day.

Romaine had been exhausted, but exhilarated, bubbling over as she explained to Louie how she had come up with the idea.

'Wow, clever!' he'd ruffled her hair. 'Maybe I should poach you from Alison!'

'You'd have to make it worth my while.'

'I think I could just about manage that,' he'd whispered into her ear as he fondled her ass. She leaned into him.

'Okay, big boy. What you offering?'

'A huge rise!'

The meeting had gone just had Romaine had anticipated. Any bluster, posturing and new demands cut short by the figures they were able to produce. All already covered in the report. As soon as they walked around the corner from the office building, they turned to each other and high-fived. Alison impulsively hugged Romaine.

'Congratulations, Romaine. You did really well.'

'You were so firm and decisive with him.'

'Wouldn't have been able to do it without that extra bit of research and that was all down to you. Well done! Let's go celebrate.'

They ended up in the same wine bar and Alison ordered a bottle of champagne, which they drank over an animated post-mortem. By the time the bottle was empty, they were both totally relaxed, the adrenaline of the last few days draining away. Alison's face was flushed and her eyes glittered. It was like she was a gladiator who had just slaughtered the lion.

'I'm hungry now. How about you?'

'Starving. Must be the alcohol.'

'There's food in the fridge. I could make us something. Byron's away for a few days.'

Romaine couldn't hide her surprise.

'Don't look like you didn't know I can cook. Byron's a better, more adventurous cook than me, but I do manage not to starve when he's away!'

'That would be great. Louie won't be home till late and I didn't really fancy a takeaway on my own.'

'I think I can offer something better than that. I promise I won't poison you.'

The house felt different without Byron's huge presence. Romaine had never been in Alison's house when it was quiet. There was a chill to the air, too, as if the house had been sulking all day. Alison turned on the central heating and lit the gas fire in the sitting room.

Romaine followed her to the kitchen as she opened the huge fridge and emerged with a bottle of white wine. She found a corkscrew and handed it to Romaine.

'Glasses in that cupboard just to the right.'

As Romaine poured, Alison retrieved lettuce, cucumber, watercress and spinach leaves, which she handed to her.

'You'll have to work for your supper.'

'But I don't *do* cooking. Louie must have told you.'

'A salad is hardly *cordon bleu*. Just wash it, cut it up and put it in this bowl. I think you can manage that, Romaine. I'll do the dressing.'

They sipped wine as they got to work, Alison preparing a spicy, creamy tomato sauce for a pasta dish that turned out to be surprisingly good.

They stacked the dishwasher and took their glasses, and the bottle, into the dimly-lit sitting room. Alison put a CD in the player, the new album from Aretha Franklin, and sat cross-legged on the carpet, in front of the fire. Romaine joined her and they drank in silence for a while, all talked out.

Then Alison laughed, shattering the silence. 'Did you notice his face? Outmanoeuvred by a couple of black broads.' Her giggling was infectious and Romaine soon joined in.

'We'll be in his nightmares for months.'

Alison sobered up and clinked her glass against Romaine's.

'Well done and thank you. It's been a good day.'

Romaine could almost feel her head swelling with pride. 'It's been a great day,' she said and turned to Alison.

Something happened then.

They didn't know who leaned forward first.

Their lips hovered millimetres from each other, breath mingling. She could have pulled away, might have turned her head. If she'd wanted to. Soft lips touched. And then the tips of tongues. Each waited for something more to happen and when it didn't, Romaine closed her eyes and pushed her tongue between Alison's teeth, stealthily, cautiously exploring. All the time in total wonderment at the softness, the uncertainty. Where she would have expected to feel hard, strong arms around her, a muscular body forceful against hers, their bodies didn't meet. Just the gentle pressure of full, searching lips, warm tongue questioning in wonderment. And then a surge of something molten, hot, unbearably sweet, filled her and Romaine pulled away to catch her breath. She noticed the rapid rise and fall of Alison's breasts and looked into her eyes. She smiled but Alison didn't, her lips open, breathing rapidly, eyes focussed but unreadable. There was a seriousness that might have been daunting and Romaine rose to her knees and touched Alison's cheeks, her fingers tracing the line of her jaw, running the pad of her forefinger down the length of her neck, absorbing the glistening moisture that beaded in the crevice between her collar bones.

She stopped and placed a gentle kiss right there, the spot that Louie always left out. But she didn't want to think of her husband right now. This was nothing to do with him. Her tongue slipped out from between her lips and she licked the space as Alison lifted her chin, lengthening her neck, presenting it to Romaine almost as an offering.

Romaine reached between them and, with trembling fingers, fumbled with the buttons of Alison's shirt. Alison's hands covered hers, stilling any movement for a while before continuing down as she opened the shirt, letting it drop from her shoulders, baring her flesh. She reached behind to unbutton her bra, and Romaine watched in amazement as her breasts were thrust forward. She kneeled back and stared. Alison, as if suddenly reticent, cupped the bra against herself, fingers lifting her breasts, covering them, but drawing attention to them at the same time.

'You too,' she whispered, almost shy and Romaine quickly undid her own buttons and tugged her arms from the sleeves of her shirt. She dropped it to the floor. She wasn't wearing a bra and she followed Alison's gaze to where the firelight flickered against the dark glaze of her small but rounded breasts, the nipples tiny, but hard now. She reached for Alison, taking her hands, pulling them away and letting the undergarment drop. She inhaled sharply. Alison's breasts were large and full, bigger than she would have expected, the skin amber in the reflected light, areolas as large as saucers, freckled, the nipples rounded, puckering.

They sat, staring at each other, as if uncomprehending, not knowing what to do next. Romaine bridged the gap, summoning all her courage and edging forward awkwardly on her knees. It was as if her hands were drawn to those breasts and she lifted them gently, one in each palm,

feeling the unexpected weight, her thumbs caressing the surface, edging
nearer and nearer to the dark circle surrounding the nipples. Her middle
finger moved then, drawn to the brown bud of her nipple, circling it
with an infinitesimally gentle touch. She knew that she wasn't breathing.
Her head was feeling light, as if this was some kind of dream, but the
softness of Alison's unblemished skin was a reality, like velvet, or satin or
silk but smoother, like, well… like her own skin that she'd only ever
touched this way in secret, unwatched. It was as if she was hypnotised by
how Alison's body responded, her nipples shrinking as her breasts
pushed forward, eager for her touch.

She looked up then and caught a glimpse of emerging desire in the
other woman's eyes. It sparked something somewhere deep inside her
and her arms circled Alison's waist, her mouth seeking hers, tongue
hard as it thrust into her mouth. She heard a long moan and she forced
her body against those pillowy breasts, shocked again by the corresponding softness, just the hard points grazing her skin. And then suddenly,
Alison's tongue was against hers, fighting for space, pushing into her
own mouth, exploring, tasting, pulsing in an out and her palms were
between them, hot against her breasts, rubbing, teasing Romaine's sensitive nipples. She breathed a soft 'aaah!' as Alison pulled her tongue
away and her fingers grasped her breast and her lips touched her,
enclosing the tight, aroused nipple. Her teeth bit down, sharp but
gentle, scraping against the tip and then sucking hard, tongue swirling
around the peak. Romaine held her head, keeping the pleasure just
where she wanted, but there was no need, because Alison wasn't going
to stop. She pulled away just to tease the other nipple, to get it just as
wet and hard. Romaine was panting now as she watched those full lips
around her nipple and saw the sway of Alison's full breasts. She couldn't
help reaching for them, squeezing, fondling, caressing, scratching gently
with her nails.

Alison reached behind her then and unzipped her skirt, smoothing
it down over her hips, still swirling her tongue around Romaine's erect
nipple. She pulled away then, stopping to gaze at Romaine's body. She
ran her finger around the waist of Romaine's panties and then stopped,
fingers resting against her hips.

'You sure about this?'

Romaine thought for a moment, looking into her eyes and nodded slowly.

'Because if we go any further…'

'Yes?'

'I don't think I'll be able to stop.'

Romaine lifted Alison's skirt and slipped her hands into her panties, enjoying the roundness, clutching at her and pulling her hard against her own body.

'What if I don't want you to stop?'

They kissed briefly and Alison let her lips trail downwards, descending the length of Romaine's body, detouring only to plant a gentle caress on the underside of each breast, continuing to the cavity of her navel, swirling her tongue round until she writhed as if to escape.

She slipped her fingers into Romaine's panties, the texture of crinkly hairs sending a shock along the length of her arm and down into her own vagina. She let her tongue lick the expanse of flesh above her waist as she explored with her fingers, teasing, gently tugging at the pubic hair until she could feel Romaine tilting her pelvis towards her, directing her fingers in the direction of her hungry clitoris. She waited for as long as she could and then, as she bit into Romaine's flesh, her middle finger darted like an arrow to the hard pebble between soft, wet lips.

'Oh! Oh! Ooooo!' Romaine squealed.

Alison rested her finger there, unmoving, allowing her thumb to play in the tangle of curls, knowing that Romaine wouldn't be able to keep still for long. She waited for the slight tilt and then she followed the motion with the gentlest of touches, letting the rocking guide her, slow, building, faster and faster, thumb delving into the wetness of her pussy, pressing gently, then further and further inwards until she got the response that she expected, a gush of a hot wetness. Alison sat up then, hands still between Romaine's thighs. She gently forced her backwards until she was lying flat on the carpet, the red, glowing firelight caressing her skin. Alison spread her legs, watching as her thumb continued its path in and out. Her eyes were bright, fixed, fascinated as if expecting something, something miraculous. She stopped suddenly and touched her own breasts, fondling as she returned her attention to Romaine, slowly inserting one finger into her pussy, twisting, pushing as high as she could, then two fingers, then three, carefully, gently and then harder and faster as she squeezed her own nipples hard, hard enough to cause pain.

'Wow!' Alison breathed, her voice sounding distant.

'What is it?'

'You wouldn't believe how wet I'm getting. My pussy's feeling so tight.'

And with that, she bent forward and, as if scared of what might happen, quickly touched her tongue to Romaine's clit. Incredibly, she immediately felt her vagina muscles clench around her fingers. She pushed her fingers deeper. She licked again, once more feeling the rapid response. Again and again, she flicked the tip of her tongue against Romaine's hard clit, feeling a corresponding reaction deep inside her. She pulled out her fingers and, lying flat between Romaine's thighs, pushed them wide. With her thumbs, she gentle spread her pussy lips, exposing the glistening, oh so sensitive tip. She kissed it. Aroused by the sudden bucking of hips, she sucked, her own pussy tightening at the sound of Romaine's wailing. She licked, broadening her tongue, pressing hard, moving down until the tip rested against the opening of her vagina. She dipped just the tip in, tasting the salty tang, surprisingly bitter. She slipped her tongue further in and then out to the edge again, round and round, shaking her head, letting her hair tease, and then up to her desperate, waiting, throbbing clit. Then slowly down again, as slowly as they both could bear, then up until Romaine could stand it no longer and she grabbed Alison's head, pressing down, bruising her lips, forcing a rapid rhythm, soft, wet tongue slipping, flickering against her clitoris, distilling the sensation in pure, unadulterated desire until Alison could sense the tightening and she sucked Romaine's clit into her mouth, holding down her hips as she screamed a high-pitched wail and a stream of ecstasy flooded through her and her body froze as she orgasmed with a strength that shook them both like an earthquake.

Alison slid alongside, her body moulded to the younger woman's back. She kissed her chin and buried her face into the curve of her neck, inhaling the lingering fragrance of her perfume. They were speechless, Romaine caressing the curve of Alison's hip with one finger as she stared into the flickering coals.

Romaine couldn't speak because the most incredible thing had just happened to her and she didn't know how to express it. Something profound had stirred in her soul. Something akin to understanding what true passion meant, true ecstasy for the first time ever, something near to mature, adult, uncomplicated... affection or, maybe... love. At the thought, she was hit by another sudden, unexpected wave of desire, unprecedented so soon after. She turned towards Alison, holding her tight in her arms, legs entwined, the soft giving of her flesh, wondrous.

Alison raised herself up on one elbow and brushed a tendril of hair from Romaine's forehead. She smiled into her eyes.

'So what was that about?'

'I don't know.' She nuzzled Alison's neck. 'Maybe we need to do some research, but it felt good.' She licked the cleavage between the full mounds of her breasts and then lifted her head, letting the other woman's nipples graze against hers, marvelling at the contrast in skin tones, the darkness of her own body making Alison's gold almost shimmer. She ran her fingers along the length of Alison's side, slowing as she reached the curve of her waist, detouring around the tight buttocks and then round and down past her thighs, pulling her leg across her own as she reached down to the gentle slope of her calf. She could feel Alison's shivering as their pubic bones met and the movement sent an instant surge of desire through her, flooding her vagina again.

'This doesn't usually happen, you know. It's so soon.'

'That makes me feel good.'

'I want you again.'

Alison reached for her hand and placed it between her thighs, slick and hot with longing. Romaine rubbed hard and fast, sensing from the bucking of Alison's hips that she was past subtlety. She plunged two fingers into her churning pussy, rubbing her own clitoris against her thigh, clenching her muscles to delay the sensation. Alison's eyes were still staring into hers, her mouth breathing a series of staccato 'oh's. Romaine pulled her fingers out for a moment and touched one to

Alison's bottom lip. She looked confused for an instant and then licked, the red tip of her tongue flicking from between her lips, eyes fixed to Romaine's as she sucked the finger deep into her mouth. When Romaine pulled it out, she slowly licked her lips, as if savouring every last drop. Romaine plunged deep again and this time, slipped her finger into her own mouth tasting the flavour that was so similar to how she imagined her own. She reached again for Alison, spreading the other woman's legs until their clitorises touched and a burning fire shot through her. She rubbed gently against her, feeling lascivious as she watched Alison's eyelids droop slowly until they suddenly closed and she arched her neck, a dark flush rising to her cheeks.

As if waiting for a signal, Romaine slithered down Alison's body and buried her head between her thighs rubbing her lips, her nose, her forehead into her vagina, loving the scent, the taste, the feel of her, tasting the softness of her pussy lips, the tiny, hard pulsing of her clitoris, the tenderness of her opening, the rigidity of her pubic bone pressing against her lips. And as if searching for nectar, her tongue dived into the flowering circle and thrust in and out, Alison's gasps conducting the rhythm, until the pitch rose an octave higher and Romaine, delving as hard and as deep as she could, frantically whipping her head from side to side, created an unbearable friction until she felt Alison's release, the shudders reverberating, eliciting echoes throughout every fibre of her being.

❦

'He called me a fucking predatory pervert.'

'I know. I heard him. I was there.'

'Why did you tell him?'

'Because I thought he was my best friend. Didn't you tell Byron?'

'Byron *is* my best friend.'

Romaine looked away, the emotion expanding her heart to breaking point.

'Look,' Alison said, her fingers moving to touch Romaine's hand, and then resisting at the last moment, 'there's no point in us being here, meeting again, if we're not going to be honest. So I'll go first. It was special, Romaine.'

'What do you mean by "it"?'

'What was most important was that we didn't play games. So let's not start now. You know what I mean by "it". ' This time, her fingers did touch the back of Romaine's hand. 'Making love, passion… friendship, finding each other… whatever you'd like to call it.'

'I guess I told him because I couldn't believe what had happened. It was important to me. Magical. I needed to share it with him... What did Byron say?'

'Byron loves me.' Alison waited for a moment. 'This is nothing against Louie, but Byron really cares about me. He loves you too, Romaine. He saw something special in you, so he understood… Don't look at me like that. And I know what you're tempted to ask.'

'You don't.'

'No, it had never happened before. I don't consider myself to be gay. Byron and I aren't swingers. But that's not the point.'

'Okay,' Romaine smiled. 'So, you do know what I wanted to ask!'

'I've thought about it a lot.'

'And?'

'And it won't happen again.'

'I knew that all along. Somehow, it was too perfect. It was enough.'

Alison reached over and stroked her cheek.

'I'm glad you said that. It was *so* special to me. Something pure and distilled. I hoped that you felt the same way. And then when he called, I thought something had been destroyed between us.'

'Why?'

'Because Louie was shouting at me about abuse of power, taking advantage of you, sexual harassment. I wondered if it was him I was hearing or you.'

'Alison!'

'I know. But you left. When I woke up, you were gone. I didn't know what to believe.'

'I needed to get home. You were already at home.'

'You needed Louie. You can tell me that, Romaine. That wasn't what hurt.'

'No, I needed to be at home.'

'So where to we go from here?'

'I hope we can go forward, Alison. You know you're very special to me. You were what I needed then. I still need you. I'll always treasure that night.'

'Good. That's what I hoped to hear.'

In spite of the confidence with which she seemed to have approached the conversation, Alison was relieved to have got it over. She had instinctively felt that the friendship with Romaine was repairable, but the few doubts she'd had were stoked by the recollection of Louie's venomous anger. A tight little ball of rage, insecurity and regret had formed from the moment of that telephone call and it had grown relentlessly over the weeks and months forming itself into an almost Indiana-Jones-type insurmountable rock of resentment.

She was disappointed in herself too. How many times had she told herself not to mix her business and social life? And when she did make the one mistake, boy did she make it in a big way! Although, was it really a mistake? She'd had discovered something profound within herself and she couldn't bring herself to regret that.

Alison headed for the taxi rank, head bent against the wind, striding purposefully along, oblivious of the strangers who jostled past, heading in the opposite direction.

It had been natural that they should form an alliance. Though Alison would never have shown it, she was weary of being the only black person in that office. Sure, everyone was deferential, friendly even, willing her to pretend to be white and, at first, she'd been prepared to, once a week, join them in the local pub. They'd talk about work, having little else in common, but she got the feeling that they were all waiting for her to leave, that they'd be more at ease once she'd gone. She knew she was taking a risk when she insisted that Romaine be appointed to the position, even though she was the best-qualified candidate. She could imagine the conversations that would take place in Human Resources if it turned out that she'd made the wrong choice. But she doubted that would happen. There was something about the way Romaine held herself, the determined set to her jaw when challenged, the interested tilt of her head when she listened; here was a kindred soul, someone who would persevere until the job was done.

Alison tightened her scarf around her neck and stamped her feet. It was getting colder and there were no reassuringly bright yellow 'For hire' signs heading in her direction. She didn't know how long she had been waiting, but the ice was creeping into her bones. She sighed and reluctantly headed for the tube. Mercifully, she stepped into a compartment that was almost empty.

Daily, as they worked closer together, Alison would mentally pat herself on the back. She was a good judge of character and had made an excellent appointment when she chose Romaine. And, oh, the relief of having someone else there who understood. It wasn't something they discussed or ever needed to say. Someone in the office would make an offhand comment and Alison would see her own expression reflected on her assistant's face. Or a client would ask an imbecilic question like, 'So where do you come from?' And Romaine's immediate, firm but polite put-down would forestall her own. And when they were far away from the office, geographically and psychologically, they would laugh together about all of this.

It wasn't even that she'd allowed herself to drift into a close friendship. She had actively pursued it, drawn by the lure of something shadowy that her soul was seeking. She didn't have the words to articulate what it was. She had tried to explain it to Byron, but couldn't. And he hadn't insisted. Her darling bear of a man loved and trusted her enough not to demand any more than that she still loved and wanted him. Alison hugged herself. She appreciated how lucky she was. Look at what had happened to Romaine. Louie had left her. She wondered about the two of them. She had always thought that they seemed like the ideal, textbook couple, relaxed, confident and loving with each other. And now, what?

The carriage was getting more crowded with each stop and Alison began to feel claustrophobic. The tinny sound of her neighbour's personal stereo began to seep its way into her brain, the high-pitched tinkling irritating the hell out of her. There wasn't even enough room for her to move without making it obvious. At this time of night, it was probably best to be diplomatic. So she tried to close her ears, to blot out the noise with her thoughts.

Even though she knew it would be fruitless, she couldn't stop herself asking the same question, over and over: how?

How had they got to the position where that night was possible? Had there been any signs that she should have recognised? Had she given out signals without knowing it? But then, she wasn't sure who it was that had initiated the first touch, the first kiss. Of course, Louie had wanted to blame her. And she supposed that the fact that he'd walked out on Romaine meant that he had found a way to blame them both, not himself of course.

The train reached her stop and she squeezed her way through the tightly-woven commuter bodies. Unthinkingly, she sighed. It was always a relief to get to the end of a London journey safely. She had just about enough energy to walk up the escalator but emerged into the dark night feeling as if a huge weight had been lifted from her shoulders. She asked herself again, how? How was it that each time she thought of that evening with Romaine, she couldn't help the smile that curved her lips.

The house was dark and she felt a slight hint of disappointment. She'd hoped to see her husband, to tell him all about her meeting with Romaine. She wanted to make him understand. He hadn't said that he would be home late, but Alison was sure that he'd be back very soon.

❧

Romaine had preferred to walk for a while in an attempt to clear her head. When necessary, she could hop on a bus, but for the moment, she'd had enough of crowds, being hemmed in by people. She craved the kind of open space impossible to find in the capital city, but her feet instinctively took her towards street lights, glowing shop windows and the safety of the herd.

It was good to have cleared the air with Alison but, she admitted to herself, during the whole conversation, there had been an undercurrent of Louie. Thoughts that didn't quite reach the surface, but echoed back and forth: where could he be? Was he okay? Surely he could just call to let her know! He must know that she would be worried.

By the time Romaine arrived in front of the darkened house, she had worked herself into a state of anxiety, seeing shadows everywhere she turned, hearing footsteps behind her, watching a car drive off from outside her front gate, feeling a presence watching her every move. She felt her walk becoming less and less natural, more edgy, stilted.

She hurried to lock the door behind her, to attach the security chain. If Louie decided to bring his sorry ass back home, he could damn well ring the bell and wait until she was ready to let him in. Not even knowing why, she peeked round the wooden shutters as she closed them. There was someone standing across the road, staring straight at the house, or so she thought. It was difficult to tell in the gloom. Romaine half closed her eyes, trying to peer further into the darkness. No, there was nobody there now. It must be the effect of being alone in this big house. She was beginning to imagine things.

Romaine turned on the bright overhead light in the sitting room, the hall lights, upstairs and down as well as the security light outside the door. From outside, it must look like Christmas. As she walked towards the study, she sensed that something was different, but she couldn't work out what it was. The soft whirr from the computer sounded somehow louder, dominating the silence of the house. Romaine pressed the light switch and looked around. The desk was unnaturally tidy, cleared of the mounds of paperwork. The shelves, too, were almost empty, the outline of dust testifying to the disappearance of several files. So, there she had been worrying about him, but he'd been fine all the time. So concerned about work that he'd been efficient enough to collect whatever he needed. And he'd made sure that he did it while she was out. She should have guessed that he wouldn't let anything get in the way of his work. Well, she damned well wasn't going to worry about him any longer.

Romaine sat at the desk, switched on the computer and worked her way towards the site. She clicked through to the screen that awaited her details. Her fingers flew across the keys.

Medium height, firm, full breasts with sensitive nipples, shapely legs, rounded buttocks made to be caressed, skin the colour of Virginia tobacco, tasting of molasses. Long, dark, waist-length hair, elegant, ver-

satile fingers. Eyes almost black, shaped like a panther's, thick, curved brows, nose a little too broad, lips a little too full, made to be kissed. Searching for a lover, friend and soulmate to dance to the rhythm of my heart, to make my body tingle and my soul soar.

She closed the program and stomped into the kitchen, still seething with anger, slamming cupboard doors, striding round the room, eventually releasing the nervous tension.

She pulled chicken out of the fridge, found garlic, ginger, and escallions. She stood on tiptoe to look for what seemed like appropriate herbs and spices. Curry powder, allspice and pimento. She spent a few moments examining the ingredients. She knew they all made some kind of sense, but what to do and in what order seemed to be beyond her. The theory was all in place, but the practice was sorely lacking. She put the ingredients back, picked up the phone and dialled for a takeaway.

She climbed the stairs and checked each room, wanting to know how meticulous Louie had been. There were few signs of his absence except for a couple of missing suits, a pile of shirts from his side of the wardrobe and a few ties that he'd obviously pulled out at random. Probably in a hurry, wanting to avoid her at all costs. She deliberately moved her clothes to cover the gaps. Never did have enough room in that damned wardrobe, she muttered to herself. She was hot and sweaty by the time she had finished, more from annoyance than physical exertion. She was just about to step into the shower when the doorbell rang. Must be the takeaway—she had completely forgotten about it.

She grabbed her robe, pulling it on as she dashed down the stairs. She rummaged for her purse in her handbag and was tying her belt as she opened the door. There, in front of her was a figure in black holding the familiar plastic bag decorated with the logo of the local Chinese above his face. He lowered it slowly, laughing as he did so. It was Colin and she was standing there in a flimsy dressing gown, clutching her purse.

'I don't charge extra for delivery.'

'I don't understand. What…'

'Arrived just at the same moment as the delivery guy. He was happy to let me do his job. You goin' let me come in before your food gets cold?'

So what could she do? Why did Colin have this uncanny knack of arriving at the most inconvenient of times? Now she'd have to invite him in and share her meal with him. Whatever she did, though, she would have to make sure that she did it fully clothed.

'Sorry. Come in Colin. Have you eaten?'

'Yes, but I'm still hungry.'

She ignored the look in his eye. 'I'm sure there will be enough for two.'

His look travelled the length of her body. Romaine held the collar tight around her neck.

'I'm sure there is.'

'Colin, if you don't mind, I was just about to hop in the shower. Go through to the kitchen and I'll be down in a couple of minutes. Fix yourself a drink.'

She dashed up the stairs before he could make any further comment and hurried into the bathroom, locking the door behind her. She showered as fast as she could, dried herself and eased the door open before slipping into her bedroom and pulling out the baggiest combination of clothes that she could find. Somehow, she wanted to create an impenetrable barrier between Colin's probing eyes and her bare flesh.

She could hear him moving about downstairs and noted how her husband's noises, usually so reassuring, sounded compared to that of someone who was not Louie. Colin was in their sitting room now. Romaine heard Luther Vandross' bass voice floating up the stairs as he turned on the stereo. She felt irrationally irritated. She and Louie had always encouraged their friends to treat their home as if it was their own. So she couldn't really blame Colin. But Louie was no longer there and Colin's every action seemed… well, presumptuous, like he was attempting to take her husband's place.

Romaine took the stairs slowly, making each step as deliberate as possible. She ignored Colin in the sitting room and headed for the kitchen. She reached up to the cupboard to get plates and felt Colin's arm around her waist. She turned towards him, a reproof on her lips and he moved her to one side, as if his only intention was to get to the plates before her. There was nothing she could say but 'Thanks'. Still, there was something a little nerve-wracking about the way he crept up so silently.

As she shared out the food, Colin found glasses and poured her a drink: vodka and tonic. He found a lime in the fridge, cut it in half, and squeezed a few drops into the glass, adding a couple of cubes of ice. Romaine wondered how he knew how she liked her drink, but realised he must have watched often enough as Louie prepared it for her.

'Thanks, Colin.' She was tempted to take a long gulp, but the way Colin looked at her reminded her that she needed to keep her wits about her.

'So, what are you doing round this way?' It was blunt, but the only way she could think of approaching the subject.

He looked momentarily embarrassed. But not for long. 'I been hearing rumours and just wanted to check them out.'

'What kind of rumours?

'Folks been saying that they ain't heard from Louie in a few days. I've been calling. Left a few messages on the answering machine today.' Damn! She hadn't checked.

Romaine put the plates on the table and rummaged in the drawer for knives and forks.

'So you thought you'd find out for yourself?' She sat at the table and gestured for Colin to join her.

'I wanted to make sure that you're okay, Romaine.'

'I'm fine.'

His fork hooked a few tendrils of noodles and swirled them around. 'In this big, old house on your own?'

'Who said I'm on my own?'

'I can tell that Louie's not around. Ain't that so?'

Romaine put down her fork and stared at Colin.

'He might just be working late for all you know.'

'He might. But he's not, is he?' His fork dropped to the plate. Romaine noticed that he hadn't taken a single mouthful. She lowered her eyes and concentrated on her own plate, acutely aware of the moment when his hand rested on her thigh, just above her knee. She moved her leg, away from him but he held fast and that only brought his hand in contact with her other thigh. She opened her legs fast and looked up to catch his satisfied grin. It lasted for only a split second, to be replaced by a concerned expression. But she had seen it.

'Rome, we've been friends for so long. I know when there's something wrong between you and Louie. I've known for a while. I told you so. I came here because I want to help.'

'You can help by being a good friend, Colin. That's what I need now.'

'Is it because of us? Did you tell him?'

This time, Romaine's head snapped up and she looked straight into his eyes, trying to judge what, precisely, she was seeing there.

'What do you mean?'

'Come on, Romaine. You know that there's been something between us for as long as... well... forever. You tried to suppress it. I tried, but I always knew that it would erupt like a volcano. You thought the feelings we had for each other were dormant. That's why you married him, isn't it? You know, it's not just synchronicity that brings me here whenever you need me. I feel so deeply for you that I'm bound to know when you're in trouble. Believe me, sweetheart, I'm meant to be here.'

It was eerie. There was something fundamentally true in what he was saying. Yes, Colin did appear at key moments in her life. He was like some supernatural spirit. But she still wondered whether he was on the side of good or evil. She was in the house alone with him, no Louie-type cowboys likely to ride over the horizon. She chose her words as carefully as she could.

'Louie is away, Colin. But it's nothing too serious. We decided to have a little time apart. That's all.'

He looked sceptical. His hand was moving up her thigh. She placed her hand on his, stilling the movement, not wanting to precipitate any eruption. Colin was making her feel more than nervous. It was as if he felt that he'd metamorphosed into a husband. His hand on her thigh was proprietorial, his physical bulk dominating the room, as if to displace her absent man. But she was still nervous, rather than frightened. She could deal with Colin. Just didn't want to have to.

She stood up, scraping the dregs from her almost-full plate into the bin, standing, pushing the hair back from her face, still turned away as she ran water into the sink. And then she moved suddenly, not wanting to allow him the opportunity to creep up on her. But when she finally turned and looked at him, he hadn't moved. He was pushing a Chinese mushroom around the plate, concentrating on it as if his life depended on it.

And then Romaine's defences were shot to hell. She looked at the bowed head, the rounded shoulders, the dejected curve of his back and wondered if, incredibly, Colin's bluster held some kind of real emotion. She walked towards him, reached out and traced a finger along the back of his neck, slowly registering each vertebra. He looked up at her then, something vulnerable and infinitely moving for a split moment before he opened his mouth.

'You know you can't resist me, Rome.'

It was blunt, crass. Romaine wondered it this was his way of making her back off from what might have been a significant moment. He was abdicating responsibility. Romaine laughed. It felt genuine.

'It's late, Colin. I need to sleep.'

He stood and leaned towards her as if to kiss her, but instead, he ran a finger along her cheek and took her hand, pressing it for a moment.

'I'll be here whenever you need me.'

She simply nodded.

He left while Romaine finished the remains of her glass.

And then she was suddenly furtive, calculating as she left the lights on downstairs and crept up the carpeted flight. She chose the windows of the spare bedroom and looked out. Yes, the car was still there. Colin. Sitting out there. Watching. Waiting.

It was twenty-seven minutes before he left and Romaine counted out each one of them, not knowing what to do.

She went to bed and, for a couple of hours dreamed of being surrounded by men. All of them faceless. Impossible to know whether they were looking away from her or towards her. And there was the background sound of drums, but not tom-toms, more synthesised, impossible reverberations, irregular rhythms, impossible to predict, though she tried. Though they all tried. And whichever way she turned, they were moving closer, as if they held hands and they glided forward, intending to crush her. Within minutes, dream seconds, they were close, their bodies touching hers, crowding her, and their clothes melted away, hers too and she could smell their sweat, their fear as they turned their backs to her, still pressing against her. The silent command told her that she had to grope her way to each of their cocks. It was imperative to keep them hard, otherwise she would pay the price. They formed an ever-tighter circle, forcing the breath from her and her hands were everywhere, wherever she might elicit a moan of passion. The silent voice shouted that she was failing and she broke through the circle, dancing around them as the circle tightened. She stroked, fondled, not stopping to enjoy the feeling of power, not aroused by the size of them, caressing, placing a kiss here, the tip of a tongue there, licking, squeezing, understanding the swelling of flesh, feeling her own reciprocal flowering of passion until she danced around the circle and looked down at the one instance of flaccid, shrivelled flesh. She touched. Held him in her palm, rounded her fingers, caressing with her thumbs, creating a tender pouch. And still he held himself aloof. The voice was screaming. She needed to survive. Had to make him hard.

Romaine knelt and, reluctantly, placed her lips against him, hoping to hear a moan or, at least, a sigh. His limp penis curved against his thigh. She nestled her lips around him, exhaling a warm breath, feeling a hint of movement. She opened up and took him further in, laving the head of his cock with her tongue. No response. She sucked gently, then harder, not knowing what more to do. She looked up, letting him fall from her lips in the moment of surprise. She pulled away and looked into his eyes, the features coming slowly into focus: Louie.

She awoke with a start, heart beating fast. Wondering if she had heard a sound. In an instant all the stories her mother had told her about duppies and ghouls came to life in the darkness. She recalled those nights in front of the coal fire, listening to the tales. She could hear the sinister keening, the low moans. She pulled the duvet over her head, hoping, even as an adult, that the fear would go away.

❦

Louie looked around the dingy hotel room. He hadn't wanted to go to any of his usual haunts. Didn't want anyone to find him. Couldn't explain to Sheldon, or Matthew, or Colin, or, God forbid, his mother. How could he tell them about Romaine and Alison? For so long now, it had been Louie and Romaine. Before her there had been Louie and 'some new piece of ass'. Gina had come close to being 'Louie and Gina' but she had been eclipsed by LouieandRomaine.

So, let's look at this rationally: how the fuck was he going to explain that his wife, the one he'd taken so long to choose, to be certain of, to place all his trust in, had chosen a woman instead of him. No point her telling him that it was nothing to do with making a *choice*, that she still loved him more than anyone, that it wasn't to do with *him*. All right, so other people might never find out. He might not have to tell them. But still, however hard he tried to avoid thinking about it, he would *know*. He had been softening towards her, allowing himself to fall back into the old, familiar passion. And then he'd had to hear that voice on the phone. Could he never be rid of her? As long as Romaine worked at that place, there would be a constant reminder. And she showed no sign of wanting to resign. Could he force her? How?

There were times when he wished she had never told him. Shit, the woman was so sure of him that she felt she could tell him about that *nastiness* and he was supposed to just accept it?

'I adore you', she'd said.

'And that's supposed to make me feel better. I guess you're going to tell me that you weren't even thinking about me. Well, gee, thanks for that Romaine. How do you expect me to take that? You tell me that you rejected me and made love to that fucking—'

'I wasn't rejecting you, Louie. But while we're at it, what about you? It's not as if you're a saint yourself. Am I suppose to have forgotten about that little "ting" you had with Gina, even after we were together?'

'I might have known you'd bring that up again. You goin' always throw that in my face?'

'I'm just trying to make you understand that it doesn't matter, Lou—'

'That was different.'

'Why?'

'I have to spell it out to you?'

'Yes. Why don't you just do that?'

And yet, he couldn't. He couldn't because each time he tried to summon up the words, what came to mind, reluctantly or willingly, he didn't know, was the image of Romaine, naked, clasped in the arms of Alison. Alison who he'd never before seen as a sexual, desirable being. And yet now, she was never far from his mind. Especially when he tried to make love to his wife…

Louie got up from the bed. The mattress was so cheap that his imprint remained and it would probably take the next guest a few days to usurp his outline. He'd been lying there, motionless, for the best part of the night, alternately thinking and trying not to think. It was morning now, though difficult to tell even with the curtains open, just as he'd left them. He looked through the window, not close enough to the front to see the sea, though if he raised the window and craned his neck around the corner, it might just be possible. Instead, he stepped back and looked around. A small tray with the regulation stainless steel teapot, electric kettle, powdered milk and brown and white sugar lumps. Brocade-covered armchair with an antimacassar and cigarette burns in the seat. Dark mahogany single wardrobe that held his sparse clothes and two spare blankets. 60-watt light bulb under a shade that hung by a single thread. 14-in television screwed to a bracket, reception weak enough to show only two stations.

What the hell was he doing here, after all? Louie Webster who had boasted of staying in some of Europe's finest hotels. Europe's? Hell, the world's finest. And here he was in one of England's most anonymous bed-and-breakfasts. Just so that she wouldn't have the first idea of where to start looking for him. Thank God for modern technology and the laptop. He'd probably move around the country, staying just ahead of whoever might be trying to find him. If anyone. He smiled to himself, not really amused by anything at all. At least he was in the right profession to disappear for as long as he chose. He plugged the modem cable into the phone line. He needed to make contact with Sheldon. He had to hang on to his business at least, while everything else seemed to be falling around him. He guessed he'd have to call his mother too, though God alone knew what he would say to her. He wouldn't put it past her to get the police out looking for him. It might be best to ring at a time when he knew she'd be out, simply leaving a message on the answering machine. And Romaine? Well, what was there to say to her?

He'd managed to convince himself that he had been unfair on her, punishing her too harshly for one incident, one lapse that she promised would never be repeated. And he believed her. It was not in Romaine's nature to lie to him—if only it were, then all this might have been avoided.

There were times, many of them, when Louie asked himself whether he truly believed it would have been better for Romaine not to tell him. And there was the Catch Twenty-Two: yes, he wanted not to know, but he also didn't want a wife who could not tell him, a wife who could lie by omission.

Louie sat on the edge of the bed and balanced the laptop on the small bedside cupboard. He dialled in to the office computer and left a message for Sheldon. It was much too early to call, but he wanted Sheldon to know on his arrival in the office. He would talk to him later, but he would need time to formulate what he would say.

So what was stopping him telling Sheldon everything? They'd know each other almost forever but try as he might, Louie couldn't say those simple words: *Romaine's been with someone else*. To his brother, yes, but Sheldon was another matter. And Sheldon's inevitable question would be: who? Louie stood and looked at himself in the narrow mirror set in one panel of the wardrobe. There wasn't room to move back far enough to see the whole of his frame, but all he wanted to look at was his own face. To convince himself that it was really him, that he knew who he was, that he hadn't dreamed himself into the life of someone else.

He was looking at the face that he'd seen each time he brushed his teeth for the last twenty years. The same face he saw every time he looked at Matthew, but older, clean-shaven. Something had changed: he'd always before been able to smile, to look into those eyes and remember something that had happened to make him laugh. Now, he stretched the muscles at the side of his lips, but only managed to produce something that resembled the rictus of death. He gave up trying and simply said the words aloud: *Romaine's been with someone else*. The answer to the next question just wouldn't come. He imag-

ined himself saying other names: Jimmy, Stanley, Anthony, Oliver…
All perfectly possible. Each one almost flowed from his lips. But…
Alison? No.

And yet, he needed to vomit up the name, to rid himself of the bile.
Otherwise, there would never be a cure and he could find himself irrevocably sick at heart. Louie grabbed his mobile, hesitated for just a
moment and then dialled a number he hadn't meant to: Grace.

❧

Romaine was sleepy and unbelievably nervous as she waited for the
page to load. Just suppose no one had responded to her. Imagine the
shame of being rejected by millions of men she didn't even know. Probably not as bad as having your husband walk out on you, she told
herself, not sure if she really believed that. At least there was a reason
why Louie had gone that was to do with something that she had *done*,
an act that she could have resisted. To have these strangers ignore her,
meant that there was something about her, or about the individual she
was projecting, that repelled them.

It was with a childlike sense of relief that Romaine looked at the list
of messages. She almost hugged herself when she saw that there were
eleven e-mails. So four of them were from HandyMan—did the guy
spend his whole time in front of his computer?—but that still left seven.
And another three were from companies trying to sell her sex toys; she
supposed they were right to presume that she might need one. But that
still left five men who wanted to get to know her better.

The first was from Rampant:

Hey, sweet thing. Take a look at what I got for you.

He had included a photograph that left absolutely nothing to the
imagination. Romaine was grateful, but stunned at his courage. She
knew that looks weren't everything, but she was amazed that he thought
any woman would be turned on by him. And she got the feeling that
this wasn't a personalised message, but one he sent to every woman (and
possibly every man) on the site. Romaine felt sorry for him, but not
sorry enough to reply to his message. She deleted it immediately, just in
case she might get desperate.

The next one she commended for his honesty:

Hey Scarlet, you sound just what we've been looking for. We got married a month ago. We're childhood sweethearts and we've been screwing for years. Thought it was supposed to get better after the wedding. Realise we're just bored with each other. We both love the sound of you. Would you care to join us? We'll both make your body tingle. Fleur wants you to eat her pussy while I fuck you from behind— Into the recycle bin.

So just two to go. Romaine wasn't holding out a lot of hope.

Scarlet. I hope you're nature suits your name. I imagine you as wanton, ripe for the taking. Were you the same Scarlet who allowed a stranger to touch you in a train while your husband watched? I love to watch. Didn't the stranger turn you on, just because he was anonymous and allowed you to do whatever you want with no sense of guilt? Well, imagine me as that stranger. You'll never see my face, but every time you touch yourself, every time you choose to make love, I'll be there, watching you. Does the thought excite you?

It did.

Then let's talk. Dark Knight.

He gave details and she knew what to do. Yes, she would talk to Dark Knight sometime, but there was just one more message to check. Romaine clicked on it.

I can tell you've maybe come to this site looking for Prince Charming to ride up on his white horse, but I've read your profile and all you say is that you want a lover, one who can make your body tingle. If you've been looking without success, perhaps you might think more laterally. I've found my Sleeping Beauty. I didn't go looking for her, but she found me and every day, my heart sings. Maybe I can introduce you if you're open-minded enough. Charlene.

Wow! Well, that certainly gave her something to think about. But with both messages, there were complications that Romaine didn't want to analyse right now. She turned off the machine and sat for a while listening to the acute silence. She realised for the first time that this house hadn't been truly quiet in years. It lived against the background of a computer continually whirring. Louie never turned it off, just like he never closed the shutters. Well, it looked as if things were going to change.

For no apparent reason, Romaine felt empowered. Seeing no more fleeting shadows, she switched off every light and, in the darkness of her bedroom, crept into the bed and slipped into sleep.

CHAPTER 8

This was going to be harder than he thought. It was always obvious that battle lines would be drawn, but not this soon. So Sheldon had been his friend first and his first contact with Grace had been as a business colleague. In spite of that, they'd always worked well as a group of friends and he'd never before detected any hostility. Looking at her now, he recalled his almost-forgotten nickname: praying mantis, or was it *preying* mantis? There was something truly scary about Grace that he hadn't experienced to the full before, but the way she looked at him now, eyes half closed, made him want to run for cover. She obviously had no intention of making this easy for him.

'I was surprised to get your call, Louie. Are you sure it's me you should be talking to? Maybe a psychiatrist? I think you need to have your head examined, the way you been treating your wife lately.'

She was making it clear whose side she was on.

'Grace, I don't think you know what's been going on between me and Romaine.'

'I think I do.'

'You only know what she's told you.'

'Louie, believe me, I know a lot more than Romaine's told me.'

'What do you mean by that?'

She had agreed to meet him in the Euphorium bakery and coffee shop not too far from the station. He suspected that it had been chosen because she knew he'd feel out of place. The space seemed to be designed for mothers-who-coffee after dropping off children at one of the local schools. He had seen her sitting at a small table at the back and had fought his way around pushchairs and snot-nosed toddlers to reach her. None of which, he was sure, was accidental. He was definitely on female territory and felt large, awkward and thoroughly male—in short, at a total disadvantage.

Grace looked at him not as if she was planning to devour him, but more like she'd already decided that his bones weren't worth picking. She'd be known as 'the vulture' in future.

'Before I met Sheldon,' she began, seeming to change the subject, 'I met so many guys who were just like you, Lou. Good-looking, charming, smooth… full of themselves. It's like you think that the only reason the world was created was to revolve around you. I fell for Sheldon because he's the opposite of you: no bullshit. Sheldon knows just what he wants and how to go about getting it. I guess most people would look at you and Sheldon together and think that *you* had all the advantages in life—but only until they get to know you both.'

'I never realised you felt this way about me, Grace. What have I ever done to deserve this?'

'Don't get me wrong, Louie. It's not that I feel any way about you at all. I'm not really concerned with *you*. It's Romaine I'm worried about.' Her anger sizzled.

Louie was silent for a while as Grace stirred her coffee.

'Why did you call me, Louie?'

'I'm beginning to wonder.' He laughed, but she didn't.

'I know exactly why. You were too proud to talk to Sheldon or any of the guys. Didn't want to admit that you might not be man enough for your wife. And then you thought to yourself, "I know. It would be so much easier to talk to a woman. They've been genetically modified to put up with the bullshit. So, I can't talk to my wife, who's the next best thing?" Am I right?'

'It wasn't exactly like that, Grace.'

'But pretty much, huh?' They stared at each other for a moment and then, surprising themselves, they both laughed. Laughed until the tears rolled down their faces and other customers began to stare.

'I was right to call you, Grace. You might be just what I need.'

'If you leave behind the bullshit. So, what do you want, Louie? Talk.' And he did.

❦

The call came before Romaine had started the morning coffee and her brain was still slightly fuzzy. Grace was struggling against the roar of traffic in the background, so she was brief.

'Girl, get yourself to The Sanctuary. We've got plenty to talk about. See you there in about forty minutes. My treat.'

The line went dead and Romaine held the phone, staring at the receiver as if the message hadn't yet got through to her brain. When she finally came to her senses, she realised that she would have to hurry. She replaced the tin of coffee in the fridge and ran up the stairs for a hurried shower, then slipped a swimming costume and a pair of flip-flops into her bag. She knew the routine well. Before her Louie-imposed exile, she had spent many a Saturday morning at the women's health spa and then the rest of the afternoon shopping in Covent Garden with either Alison or Grace or both.

When Romaine arrived, Grace was already there, impatient, a look of suppressed excitement on her face.

'Hurry up, girl. I got plenty things to tell you.'

'What's happened?'

'Let's get changed and go for a drink. I'll tell you everything then.'

They made their way up the narrow stairs to the reception area and signed in, Grace handing over her platinum credit card. It was impossible to speak about anything significant in the crowded changing room, so Romaine waited until they were both wrapped in their towelling white robes and were making their way to the Koi Carp Lounge. Even though groups of women chattered away, the atmosphere was calm, quite unsuited to the buzz of excitement that Romaine felt emanating from her friend. Her curiosity was roused.

Grace got coffees for them both—none of that healthy herbal shit, she protested—and they settled themselves into the cushioned chaises beside the pool where they could watch the hypnotic motion of the carp.

'So, don't keep me in suspense, Grace. What's happened.'

'You're not going to believe it. I got a call this morning.'

'Who from?'

'Louie.'

Romaine was momentarily speechless. From the look on Grace's face, it was obvious that Louie hadn't called looking for Sheldon. It had to be something more than that.

'Why was he calling *you*?' Romaine wondered why she felt a little hurt. Why was he phoning Grace and not her?

'He wanted to meet.'

'And?'

'And so I agreed to meet him. In Euphorium.'

'When?'

'This morning.'

Now, Romaine began to understand Grace's suppressed excitement. Louie must have said something that Grace felt she needed to know. There was a little flutter in her solar plexus.

'So, what happened?' She tried to maintain a calm exterior.

'Well, the first thing—'

Grace's words were halted by the figure approaching. Tall, shapely, blonde with her hair tied into a straggly bun, cup of steaming herbal tea in her hand. Elaine.

'Hi, you guys!'

'Hi, Elaine.' It was hard for Romaine to hide her disappointment at this woman, who she didn't particularly like, interrupting their conversation at this precise moment. 'I didn't expect to see you here.'

'Oh, I'm often here in the mornings during the week. Just to relax before work in the evenings. Can I join you?'

Romaine and Grace looked at each other. What else could they do?

'Of course,' they chorused, smiles glued to their faces.

They had little in common with Elaine that there were a few moments of awkward silence and Romaine wondered why she had chosen to join them. It wasn't like Elaine to make any gesture of friendship towards either of the two women, her attention normally focussed on Matthew and his every move. Elaine was usually so aloof with them both. Romaine wondered if just the fact of being smothered in the white robes, faces bare of any makeup, brought down to the same level as everyone else made her less confident, a little more vulnerable, a little more likeable.

It was Grace who started the polite conversation about work that broke the silence and as the other woman responded, Romaine had the opportunity to look at her more closely than she had before. She noticed the blue rings under Elaine's eyes and wondered if the late-night job really suited her. As she talked, Romaine saw that she picked at the cuticle of one finger, leaving it raw and bleeding and she brought it to her lips as if to bite the nail before silently reproving herself and allowing her hand to fall into her lap. There was a tight undercurrent to her voice that Romaine had never noticed before. God, this woman was wound so tight that she might snap. And Romaine thought that *she* had problems!

Romaine waited until there was a gap in the desultory conversation before suggesting a visit to the hot spa pool, almost hoping that Elaine would prefer to stay and finish her drink but, surprisingly, she rose to follow them. Just what they needed: Elaine following them around all morning like a lost lamb. Grace and Romaine glanced at each other, a look of mild exasperation passing between them. Grace shrugged her shoulders as she led the way down the stairs into the sultry humidity. There were only three other women in the pool, so they hung up their robes and descended into the shock of the sudden heat from the bubbling water, but not before Romaine had time to notice that, whereas she and Grace were in simple black costumes, Elaine wore the skimpiest turquoise bikini—and looked fabulous in it. Another black mark against her.

The three of them leaned back and closed their eyes, pummelled by the water and inevitably feeling their muscles relax. Romaine only opened her eyes when she felt someone trying to get past. She moved round to allow her room and only then noticed what looked like tears on Elaine's face. At first, she wondered whether it was just sweat—Elaine just wasn't the kind of woman who would cry, was she? She was uncertain until she heard the soft sniff and watched as the other woman raised a hand to wipe away the now-steady flow of tears. Romaine nudged Grace and nodded in Elaine's direction. Grace immediately took Elaine's hand and led her out of the pool. Romaine followed and draped the towelling robe around her shoulders. She noticed the other women in the spa looking at them curiously as they led Elaine up the stairs, round past the carp and up the stairs to the Meditation Suite. As usual, it was empty. Ideal.

Grace sat holding Elaine gently, stroking her hair until there were no more tears to come.

'I'm sorry,' she sniffed. 'This is so embarrassing. I don't... know... why...' she hiccuped.

'Shh!' Grace continued, soothing her. 'Don't talk. Not until you're ready.'

As she looked up, Romaine noticed that Elaine's skin was blotched and her eyes rimmed with red. She looked so vulnerable that she wondered how she could ever have considered her daunting. She was actually quite young. Romaine had never noticed that before. Her heart went out to the girl and she took her hand, noticing the bitten skin once again.

'It's over with Matthew.'

Romaine was surprised. Although she and Louie had often joked that Elaine had got her claws firmly into Matthew and though their relationship had been stormy at times, they'd been together for so long now, that Elaine was almost a fixture in their lives. At least, she'd lasted a lot longer than any of Matthew's other women.

'What happened?'

'I'm not sure. It's all just... well...' she sniffed, wiping her nose with the tissue that Grace handed her. She took a deep breath. 'It's all so weird. Everything was fine with us until, well, until the night he spent at your house, Romaine.'

'He seemed perfectly okay then. He called you, didn't he? I didn't have any idea that there was anything—'

'That's what I mean. There *wasn't* anything wrong. As far as I knew, anyway. That's why I was glad to see you here today. I wanted to ask you if you know what...'

'Matthew didn't say anything to me, if that's what you mean.'

'I just hoped... I'm just trying to figure it all out.' For a moment, she regained a little of her old, belligerent self. 'Whatever you guys thought, Matthew and I worked well together. Okay, so we had the odd row every now and again. Doesn't everyone?' She looked from Grace to Romaine who both nodded obediently. 'I thought we loved each other. I've never been with anyone for as long as with Matthew.' The tears flowed again and she stopped talking.

Neither Grace nor Romaine said a word. It felt a little like voyeurism to be witness to her grief. The tears still rolled down her cheeks as she spoke again.

'Sex was great.' She didn't blush. It was a straightforward, matter-of-fact statement but both Romaine and Grace felt a flush of embarrassment and the irrational need to laugh. They didn't look at each other. Matthew was family; they didn't really want to know about his activities in the bedroom.

'Then he got weird.' She was silent until Grace felt it was her cue to ask.

'In what way?'

'As I said, it was just after he got back from staying over at your house.'

Romaine felt two pairs of eyes on her as if she'd been accused of some horrible crime.

'He came round the next night, just as normal. We had a relaxed evening together, a few glasses of wine and a couple of joints...'

Well, well. How little you knew of people. She just didn't seem the type.

'...And then, when we get into the bedroom... Normally, he can't keep his hands off me... And now... all he wants me to do is to touch myself... so that he can watch.' She lowered her eyes. Luckily. She missed the blush that rose to Romaine's cheeks.

'So what's so freaky about that?' Grace asked, innocently. 'As Romaine and I can tell you, there's much weirder shit goes on.'

'What do you mean?' Elaine's eyes brightened for an instance as she was distracted from her troubles. Romaine wondered where Grace was headed, but she guessed that distraction was the general idea.

Grace lowered her voice. 'Believe me girl, if you look at some of these internet sites that Romaine and I been checking out, you'd soon find a bit more adventure. What's the name of that one you just found, Rome?'

Romaine blushed and muttered the name, wishing that Grace had kept her out of this one.

'You don't understand, Grace. It's not that I was shocked or being prudish. Believe me, I was more than happy to do it for him.' There was a definite sparkle returned to her eyes just for one instant. 'But it was the same thing the next night, and the next... and he didn't want to touch me. Wouldn't come anywhere near me. Just wanted to watch me as he jerked himself off. I begged him, but he wouldn't make love to me any more.'

Grace nodded slowly and put her arm around Elaine's shoulder again. 'Did you talk to him about it?'

Elaine nodded, her eyes distant as if she was replaying the scene in her head.

'I got the crap about how it wasn't anything to do with me, it was all his fault, the relationship just wasn't going anywhere. I couldn't believe it. I wondered if there was someone else. I thought back to when things changed. You know, Romaine, I made myself believe that he was lying about that night at your house. I thought he'd probably been with someone else. That's really why I asked you. I half expected you to not know what I was talking about.'

Romaine shook her head. 'No, Elaine. He was telling the truth. He did stay at our house that night.'

'You're not just saying that?'

'No.'

'I know you're not lying. I guess I just hoped to find some answer, something that would explain...'

She wiped her eyes with the sleeve of her robe and stood.

'I'm sorry.'

'Don't be. Where are you going?'

'I have to go.'

'But you don't have to get to work yet. Why don't you stay and have lunch with us?'

'No. Thank you, but I need some air. Goodbye.'

They let her go. As soon as they watched her walk down the stairs and across the walkway, Grace pulled Romaine back into the darkened room.

'So, Romaine, spill.'

'What?'

'You know exactly what I mean. What did you do to Matthew? What happened that night at your place?'

'Why do you think it's got anything to do with me?'

'I saw the look on your face when she told you what Matthew wanted her to do. What went on?'

'Oh Lord, Grace. It's all my fault. Or rather, your fault.'

'Where do *I* come into this?'

'You were the one who bought me the vibrator and told me to enjoy it next time I was on the net.'

'And you took my advice. So?'

'I wasn't sure until now, but I felt as if someone was watching.'

The two women stared at each other, horror dawning on their faces until they both saw humour in the situation, collapsing in laughter until tears flowed down both their cheeks.

❦

They'd booked lunch in the dining room and checked that Elaine had, in fact, disappeared before they allowed themselves to be shown to their table. Romaine knew that she wouldn't be able to look at Elaine again without feeling terribly guilty. She didn't know how the certainty that Matthew had watched her in the study made her feel about him. She certainly didn't think that she would ever again be able to just call him for a casual drink. The thought made her feel a little nostalgic already. But even so, Matthew wasn't the most urgent matter on her mind.

They ordered blackened cod with lentils and the obligatory salad.

'So, Grace, what did he have to say?'

'Girl, it was like pulling teeth at first, but once he got started, there seemed to be no stopping him. Like the dam burst and he couldn't control the flow.'

'Come on, Grace, get to the meat. What did he have to say about us, about me, about Alison.'

'Okay, let's start with the easiest one first: Alison. What he feels about her seems to be fairly clear cut. He's mad as hell with her. Sees her as some kind of predator who's been grooming you for the kill.'

'That's absolutely ridiculous.'

'I know. And I think he knows it really, but it's like that's the only way he can deal with the second part of your question: how he feels about you.'

Romaine sighed, mentally preparing herself for the worst.

'I think he's hurt, Romaine.'

'Doesn't take a genius to work that out.'

'Remember about not shooting the messenger? You might think it's obvious, but it seems to me that you forget that. You focus on the fact that he's angry, not how much he's hurting.'

'I don't think that's true, Grace. I've spent a lot of time in the last couple of months feeling guilty about how much I've hurt him. It's just that his behaviour has taken me past that. He's made me hurt too.'

'I know. I'm not taking his side, Romaine. Just telling you like I see it. He feels as if you've betrayed him—'

'Just like he did with Gina.'

'Yes, but ancient history. And it's not just that. Funnily enough, I think—and Louie knows—that it would have been easier for him if you'd been with another man, a group of men or even a herd of wilde-beeste! His masculine pride is hurting.'

'I don't get it. What difference does it make?'

'Just think about it rationally, Rome. If it was another guy, he could do his rutting deer bit. You can just imagine the two of them circling each other, antlers to the fore, ready to fight each other to the death. Can you see that happening with Alison?'

Grace smiled and Romaine had to laugh at the image that arose in her mind.

'I guess not.'

'Underneath it all, he still loves you. And I guess you love him.'

'I'm not sure any more.'

'Romaine, don't try to kid a kidder. And besides…'

'What?'

'Well, in spite of all I said about Louie, I think I can see a bit of what you see in him.'

'You're joking! After all this time?'

'He's kinda cute when he's desperate.'

'That's not funny, Grace.'

'No, but it's true.'

'Okay, so where does that leave the question of "us"?'

'Well, that's the tricky part.'

𑁍

'So where does that leave you and Romaine?' Grace had asked, wondering whether she, herself, could glimpse the answer to that. All her instincts told her that she should be advising her friend to walk away from this man who had been mentally abusing her—that's the way Grace saw it—for weeks now. And in a curious way, she had enjoyed the way in which Romaine seemed to be gaining her independence. Give her a few more weeks of this, and she'd be ready to leave Louie and go out into the big, wide world on her own. That's the key, Grace thought to herself: when you're in the dominant position, you need instincts that are finely tuned, instincts that tell you how far you can go with any kind of punishment without pushing the other over the edge.

Looking at Louie's bowed head, Grace thought back to the night before with Sheldon. Every time she reviewed one of their sessions, she wondered at how close she came to crossing that knife-edge boundary.

Last night, he'd come home very definitely not in the mood. From the few words that he offered over supper, she guessed that he was worried about Louie. But so typical of him not to say. She had let him eat silently, watching him processing and then filing his thoughts. They'd relaxed to music on the stereo; Miles Davis' *Tutu* always managed to calm him; you couldn't help concentrating on the rhythms and inflections. So they were both feeling mellow by the time they got to their bedroom.

He relaxed on the bed, still chatting idly while Grace changed. She still liked to wear the high-heeled leather boots, the tight, constricting cat-suit and, when she was in an especially adventurous mood, the mask. They'd gone past the point where Sheldon needed any kind of restraint. They'd dispensed with the whips, handcuffs and other props. Instead, They played the games that Grace had rehearsed with Keith, and the others, refining them along the way.

'You know, Grace, in the office today—'

She wheeled on him and stopped his words mid sentence.

'How dare you address me like that. Since when am I "Grace" to you?' The look on her face was severe, unrelenting. She stood glaring at him, legs apart, arms akimbo, as tall as she could make herself.

'Get up off that bed, you runt.'

Sheldon was instantly obedient, hurrying to stand up, but not before his wife noticed the stirring in his trousers. She smiled inwardly, but nothing of it showed on the surface. She stepped closer to him until he could feel the warmth of her skin radiating against him. Grace said nothing more and yet she could see the beads of sweat forming on his upper lip. At her full height in the high-heeled boots, she was at least two inches taller than Sheldon and she used those extra inches to the full. Looking down her nose at him, she ran her fingers along the line of his jaw.

'You know I like your skin baby smooth, don't you?'

'Yes, Miss.' She could see his eyes flickering from side to side, wondering whether she was going to use any equipment tonight.

'Get into the bathroom. Now!'

Sheldon scurried away and she followed close upon his heels.

'Sit!' She pointed to the chair placed in front of the mirror. On the shelf above the basin, neatly arranged was a brush and a pot of shaving soap. Sheldon watched as Grace lathered the brush and held it for a moment, examining the layer of foam. She brought the brush to his cheek and lathered carefully, stroking his skin like she was creating an oil painting. He was beginning to almost enjoy the sensation of the cool, smooth circles, relaxing under her tender ministrations. And then she stopped and, instantly, his body became rigid as he watched her raise the old-fashioned shaving blade and twisted it in her hand, watching the bluish glint of the tempered, sharpened metal. She brought it close, closer to his cheek and it seemed they both held their breaths as the sharp edge angled against his skin. He could feel the cool heat of panic as she pressed the knife gently against him and with a rapid glance, swept away the foam and the shallow layer of five o' clock shadow. Sheldon felt the breath exhale from his body in a whoosh and, at the same precise moment, he sensed the rush of heat to his groin. The fear had excited him and he felt his penis swell further as he watched the blade approaching again.

One more stroke of the knife and Grace stepped back, blade still in her hand, regarding him like a painter admiring her handiwork. His eyes were transfixed to her strong fingers clutching the blade. And then his gaze was distracted to her other hand as she slowly, excruciatingly painfully unzipped the rubber suit that she was wearing, exposing her full breasts that looked too large for her slender frame.

She straddled the chair, still holding the sharp blade upright. She leaned forward, allowing her breasts to come to rest at Sheldon's eye level. A line of sweat was forming along his brow and beginning to trickle down towards his left eye. She reached for a tissue to gently wipe it away. And then, while his eyes were fixed on her nipples, she touched the blade to his skin again and gently, infinitely carefully continued to shave him, knowing that the sight and scent of her naked flesh so close to his eyes, his nostrils, his lips excited him. She knew too, that he didn't dare to squirm. Not while the cold metal touched his flesh.

Grace could feel the tension drain away as she reached for a warm, damp towel to wipe the traces of foam from his skin. She let herself sink to his lap, her crotch resting against his prominent erection as she leaned against him and allowed him to kiss her lips, press his tongue against hers. But only for a moment. As soon as she felt him relaxing against her, she stood again.

'Get up.'

His eyes widened, but he knew better than to ask any questions.

'Strip naked.'

Her eyes didn't leave him as he hastened to extricate himself from the layers of clothing. When he stood before her, exposed, defenceless, she ran her fingers along the muscles of his arms, like a livestock buyer examining a potential purchase. She nodded as if satisfied and reached for the shaving brush again.

'Sit.' She ordered.

This time, there was a definite hint of apprehension in Sheldon's eyes. It was obvious that he both feared and longed for whatever was about to come.

Grace kept him on tenterhooks, twirling the brush between the fingers of one hand, brandishing the razor with the other.

She took a pace forward and stood between his legs, spreading them with her own knees. She looked down to his groin where his penis seemed to shrink with fear. She watched as it came to rest against his thigh and then looked into Sheldon's eyes. Whatever he saw in her face obviously didn't reassure him, since he shifted nervously, drawing away as his knee brushed against her leg again.

'Tut, tut! You really need to learn to control yourself, Sheldon.'

Grace turned away and replaced the brush and the razor on the shelf, watching him in the mirror as his tongue slowly emerged to lick his dry lips. She turned back to him and as soon as he raised his eyes to her body, she tugged the zip lower, peeling it away from her shoulders, her arms, her wrist. Smoothing it down over hips until the thin strip of pubic hair was revealed. She felt a gush of moisture as she acknowledged that her husband couldn't take his eyes away from her body and that the sudden stirring of his desire was making itself evident.

'Naughty, naughty, Sheldon. What's 24 times 638?'

She saw a moment of deliberation in his eyes and then he frowned in concentration.

'Fifteen thousand…'

She used two fingers to hold her pussy lips apart.

'…three hundred and…'

The index finger of her other hand hovered above her exposed clitoris as his eyes widened and his breathing became more and more shallow. Grace watched as a flush of red rose to his chest.

'…twelve.'

'Well done, Sheldon. Keep it up!' She laughed aloud at her own humour. Sheldon didn't seem amused as she began to caress herself, letting her finger descend further, down, under, until it eased into her vagina. She watched as his cock twitched in a desperate attempt to rise.

'Sheldon! 762 times 147.' She was throwing out numbers at random, not knowing or caring what the answer might be. Grace continued to play with herself, all the time watching the cogs turning in his brain.

'One hundred and twelve…'

She picked up the brush again and walked towards him, holding it like a sword. As he struggled with the words, '…thousand and…' she pushed his thighs wider and brought the brush down against his flesh, beginning to later his balls, the triangle of fuzzy hair above his cock. His eyes widened with shock and he began to shake his head as she reached for the sharpened razor.

She held it high, just at his eye level as she asked, 'Twelve thousand and...?'

His eyes didn't move from the blade as she lowered it towards his cock. 'Twelve thousand and... um... er...'

She touched it against his skin, the blade leaning away from his cock as she held it steady for a moment before sweeping upwards, away from his wilting manhood. Grace felt the relief herself, but renewed the suspense as she brought it down again to hover a millimetre from the fullness of his testicles.

'And...?'

Grace watched the tight furrow between his brows. He was concentrating hard, searching for the answer, on not allowing the fear to overcome him.

'Fourteen,' he finally breathed as he felt the sharp breath of the razor across his sensitive flesh. He nervously wiped the sweat from his brow as he felt the intense pleasure of relief sweep through him. The rush of adrenaline hardened him again and he gasped as he felt his cock twitch against the hard metal.

'Whew! That was close,' Grace breathed and he could see the cool smile on her lips. For a moment he felt a mixture of terror, hatred and the most intense desire. He wanted to fuck her, drill his cock into her until she knew what this fear felt like, until she begged him to stop, until she told him that he was too much of a man for her. But, for now, he didn't dare move. And then she was at it again, that freaky shit, holding the blade so close to his skin while she frigged herself, her nipples getting so tight, her pussy getting so juicy that he couldn't stop the tightening in his balls, couldn't stop his prick hardening, rising so close to... Oh Lord!

At the last moment, Grace swept the blade across him. For as long as she could take it, she kept Sheldon in a state of blissful terror, arousing herself until she knew that *she* couldn't bear it any longer. And then she raised herself up, straddled his waist and, without warning, plunged down on his cock that was now hard and free to respond as she writhed and twisted around him. It was always like this when she'd held him back for so long; he was ferocious, vengeful and she delighted in the size and strength of him as he drilled into her and held her hips, raising her as if she were light as a feather and he was all powerful. Over and over, raising her up, pulling her down, tilting his hips to plunge ever deeper into her. And she watched the jut of his jaw as he clenched his teeth and thrust as hard as he could, forcing the scream of delight from her, making her come in long, sweeping waves until she rested against his chest. And as soon as she was done, he picked her up, lowered her to the floor and entered her again from behind, squeezing his hand beneath her and fingering her clitoris, grinding hard into her until she came again and his body became rigid in a final thrust as he bit into her shoulder.

❦

So she hadn't been concentrating too hard on what Louie was saying and only caught the end of his sentence.

'…think I still love her, but don't know if I can forgive.'

She felt exasperated. 'Well, Louie, you haven't been listening. I don't think it's a question of forgiveness. What on earth did she do that was so awful? But if you don't think you can forgive her, then you might as well just walk away and let her have her freedom. That way, you can both get on with your lives.'

It was as if he hadn't expected the severity from her. His head jerked up and he looked at her as if she'd said that her name was Charles Babbage and she'd just invented the computer.

'You think she'd want to go back to Alison?'

Grace was willing to slit his throat and possibly her own wrists.

'No, of course, I don't. If that's what she wanted, she would have left long ago. I think she loves you, but what's the point if you're not prepared to move on from this situation, if you're just going to keep dissecting it over and over?'

He was silent for a long while and Grace wondered if he'd gone into a coma. She put her hand on his arm.

Louie looked up at her and she recoiled at the glimpse of deep, deep pain. 'You really think she still loves me? After what I've made her go through? I don't know why I've been treating her like that. I just wanted to lash out.'

'Of course she loves you.'

'Then, I guess, I have to give it a try.'

❦

'He doesn't need to do me any fucking favours.'

Grace was stunned at her friend's reaction. 'Romaine! I thought that's what you'd want to hear. He's prepared to give it another go.'

'You know, Grace, you sound as if you're on his side now. Did you fall for him, or something?'

Grace almost blushed. No, she couldn't fall for someone like Louie, but as she'd watched his pain, he'd aroused something soft and warm and liquid inside. Something that she had almost allowed herself to feel for Sheldon's son. Something that she'd always suppressed before. Something unformed that might make her want to collapse to the ground in a puddle of sentimental mush.

'I'm not taking sides—'

'Exactly. That's what you say now. I always thought you were on *my* side. Well, if you're going to be a messenger, you can tell Louie that he's too late. You made me realise that I've taken too much shit from him these last few months. I've seen a side of Louie that I don't think I like very much. I think I stayed with him because I was scared of being without him. But you know what, Grace? I'm not frightened any more. This particular worm is not only turning, it's going to rise up and bite his bum!' Her face was serious, but the analogy was so ridiculous that they both laughed until Grace gave her a huge hug and they waved to the waitress and ordered chocolate tart with mascarpone cream.

'He's going to be calling me, Romaine. What do you want me to say to him?'

Romaine thought for a moment.

'Tell him that I need some space.'

❦

Well, well, well! One half of Grace felt like skipping with delight. At last, Romaine was finding some backbone where her husband was concerned. Romaine, who would take no crap from anyone else and yet she'd go all wide-eyed and misty whenever Louie was around. Grace had always felt that there was something a little unhealthy about her devotion. Sure, he was good-looking, intelligent, funny and, by Romaine's account, sensitive and caring too but, in Grace's view, a woman should always hold a little something back. Otherwise, what would she have to offer to the next one who might come along if it all went wrong?

Now that she had talked with Louie, though, understood a little of what made him tick, she no longer wanted to take sides, but if her sympathies were going to sway in any direction, it would be towards Romaine. Although the sight of Louie, dejected, hopeless, fragile had touched something within her, she suspected that it was a part of a woman that only a child should touch, not a grown man. Maybe something instinctive had warned Louie of that and so he'd come to her, rather than his wife. If Romaine had seen him like that, she might be wondering who, exactly, was the worm and she might feel a little like squishing him.

❦

Louie, on the other hand, returned to the dingy hotel room feeling as if a few ounces of the weight had been lifted from his shoulders. If anyone knew what Romaine was thinking, it would probably be Grace. Unless... unless it was Alison, but he didn't want to go there. Both Romaine and now Grace had assured him that he had nothing to fear where Alison was concerned. How had Grace put it? 'Something she needed to do, but she'd done it now. Over.'

But how could it really be over? Ever since Romaine had told him about that evening, he had been unable to get the image of Alison out of his head. More often than not, Romaine and Alison together. He would first of all recollect the gentle intimacy that he'd witnessed between them first at that summer barbecue and then on numerous occasions since. He examined each frame in his memory to see if there were signs that he'd missed. Surely if they'd had... feelings towards each other, he would have been able to tell. Try as he might, he could find no coded signals, no significant words. And then, almost inevitably, he'd try to imagine the two of them together... making love. However hard he tried, the picture didn't quite fit. Romaine was *his* woman, belonged in *his* arms, was designed to fit *his* body. But—and he only admitted it to himself now—each time, he also felt a prickling of sensation that he tried to deny and suppress. Alison and Romaine. Making love together. He shook his head to rid himself of the pictures that rose before him.

He sat on the bed looking at the laptop. He should, he knew, contact Sheldon and get down to some work. Instead, he sat, as still as a block of ice. He was trying to recall every word that Grace had spoken.

❦

Romaine was walking on air. She could pretend that it was just the effect of spending a day at the spa, but she knew it was a lot more than that. She felt liberated. First, she'd admitted to herself that she felt a little jealous that her husband should choose to discuss their relationship with Grace, her best friend. Then she'd felt a column of ice rising along her spine as Grace described what Louie felt his problem to be. Finally, she'd felt a sense of almost physical lightness as her anger at his willingness to *forgive* her dissipated any lingering guilt that she had felt. Hell, she'd served her sentence, made penance and paid her debts. If Louie still cared about her and wanted their relationship back on track, then he was going the wrong way about it. She hadn't, after all, murdered anyone, hadn't walked out on him, hadn't rejected him. She didn't actually need him as much as he thought. She knew that she had alternatives and if he wanted her back, then he could damn well prove that he deserved her.

Romaine was so engrossed in her thoughts that it took a little while to sense the presence of a car that seemed to be cruising alongside. As she turned her head, it sped up and turned left into a side street. She might just have imagined that the car had been following her, but there was still a prickling of unease at the back of her mind. Louie? But why would he be following her when he knew where to find her at virtually any time of the day or night? Romaine quickened her steps; she was only yards from her gate, so there was no sense in worrying. But, up ahead, wasn't that the same car coming towards her? She stopped suddenly and then, hearing steps behind her, ran to her door. In the dark entrance, she fumbled for the lock, berating herself for not leaving the security light on. It was so dark that she could hardly see what she was doing and her hands were trembling as she breathed hard. Finally, she let herself in and braced herself against the door, bent almost double trying to catch her breath. She crept silently into the dark sitting room and looked out of the window. Nobody there. No cars. No shadows. In fact, the whole street looked warmly lit and welcoming. Romaine smiled as she switched on the lights. What on earth was happening to her? Just a few days of being alone in the house and she was becoming a gibbering wreck. What kind of danger could there be? She'd walked these streets thousands of times without any mishap. And who would want to do her any harm, anyway? She straightened her shoulders and walked towards the darkened kitchen telling herself that unless she began to think a little more rationally, she was in danger of becoming paranoid.

Romaine looked towards the study and, immediately, her mood lifted. Once before the screen, she lost no time in logging in to check for messages. HandyMan again, getting desperate. More spam. And one new correspondent.

It's night. A warm night. Moonlight. A few stars. We're in my car, parked by the shore. We can hear the rush of the waves. Prince is on the car stereo. 'Scandalous'. Have you ever heard a sexier song? 'Tonight I'm gonna be your fantasy…' Oooooh. 'Anything's acceptable…' he croons, and how could he be wrong—he's the prince, after all. Where do you want me to take you?

Computer Expert. Nothing more about himself, just his instant messenger details. Romaine read the message once again. Phew! Only a few words and he'd got her hot and bothered already. God, if only he knew what that song always did to her. In any chart of erotic music, it would have to be her number one. Just the opening bars could set her in the mood for loving. In the days when she and Louie first got together, if they were in a club and he wanted to leave, he would request that track. In their bedroom, it would always be close to the stereo. Now, she wasn't sure that she would know where to find it.

She walked into the sitting room and searched in the racks of CDs and, after several minutes, found it, blew off the dust and return to insert the shiny disc into the computer.

The song didn't fail her this time either. Immediately, she felt a tightening in her stomach and her nipples began to pucker. It had been so long since… since she'd listened to this track. This must be an omen, she told herself and she sat down, ready, eager to talk to Computer Expert, whoever he might be.

As she leaned towards the keyboard, there was a rattling at the front door. More pizza delivery menus, Romaine told herself. But as her fingers hovered over the keyboard, she recalled the shadowy sense of someone following her home. She got up and walked to the front door. Nothing on the mat. In the sitting room, she looked through the windows. Was that someone walking away, or the shadow of the rowan tree swaying in the wind? In any case, how could she, like Louie, have left the shutters open all this time. She hurried to close them, forcing the bolts into place.

Once again, she climbed the stairs, ever so slightly cautiously, check- ing every room, turning on every light. Please don't let it be that, without Louie, she was becoming a scared, pathetic female. She refused to let herself be cowed simply by the lack of a male presence.

She poured herself a brandy and, as if it were a job that needed doing, Romaine returned to the study and started the Instant Messenger program. She entered Computer Expert's details and sat back to wait. She noticed that HandyMan was online and knew that it would only be a matter of time before he noticed her presence. There was nothing she could do but ignore him; he was becoming more than a little persistent, but still a minor annoyance. For the moment, she would push him to the furthest reaches of her mind. She re-started the Prince track and began to type, letting the words take her wherever they might.

♥

<Computer Expert, I appreciate your choice of music. I agree: maybe the sexiest track ever. Where do you want to take me in your car?>

<I hardly know you. Tell me something about yourself.>

<What do you want to know?>

<First chocolate you'd pick from the top layer.>

Romaine was surprised. She would have expected something more overtly sexual given her previous chats with HandyMan, JellyRoll and FrenchKiss. She thought for a while, wondering if there was some underlying reason for the question.

<It's not a trick question...> he typed, as if he could read her mind.
<Rum truffle.>

<Hmm! Soft centre. Favourite drink?>

<Vodka.?>

<Don't tell me: with tonic and a twist of lime?>

<How did you guess?>

<You seem calm and cool. Where are you sitting now?>

<In the study.>

<What's it like?>

<Why do you want to know?>

<I want to picture you.>

Romaine looked around at the room that now seemed slightly dilapidated without Louie's clutter on the shelves, the absent files leaving dark patches. She felt sure that it wouldn't do a thing for him to picture her as she was.

<The walls are deep blue, lined with bookshelves from floor to ceiling. Thick cream carpet. I'm sitting in an old, oak swivel chair upholstered in pale leather at an oak desk. There's one lamp on, casting a warm glow. I'm listening to music.>

<Prince?>

<Yes.>

<What were you doing before you got my message?>

<I'd just got home. Poured myself a drink.>

<Stressful day?>

<Yes and no.> Romaine wondered why he cared.

<Want to tell me about it?> What was this? Some kind of counselling service? Well, actually, no she didn't want to talk about it with a complete stranger. But still, she appreciated the fact that he'd offered.

<I'm okay, but thank you.>

<Comfortable room, low lights, some alcohol. I hope you're feeling more relaxed.>

<A little.>

<What are you wearing?>

<A gold satin robe.> No need for him to know about the jeans and baggy sweatshirt.>

<If I was with you, I'd massage your back. Would you like that?>

<Yes!>

<Kick off your shoes. Lean back in your chair. Feel my warm, sandalwood-oiled, hands on your shoulders. My thumbs kneading the muscles along your spine, down inside your shirt. Your head falls forward and the deep pressure makes you moan with half pain, half pleasure. I'd ease the tension from the muscles under your shoulder blades, then back down the line of your spine, working on each vertebra in turn. My palms roam across the slick skin of your back, up, down, increasing the pressure. Your sigh of delight fills my ears as I feel you relax under my touch.>

<Don't stop.>

<Are you alone?>

<Yes.>

<I kiss your neck, just beneath your right ear. It's time for me to go.>

<Why?>

<Are you married?> What a very strange question. Romaine imagined that was just the kind of question that was forbidden according to the etiquette of these sites. What difference would it make to him anyway? Her fingers hovered over the N and the O of the keyboard, but she found herself typing...

<Yes.>

<Then you'll understand.>

And he was gone. Just like that. How very peculiar! How very frustrating!

Romaine stood up, stretching, hands rubbing her neck and she stopped, almost guiltily, remembering the virtual massage and how he had made her feel. Warm. Languorous. Perfectly relaxed and comfortable with him, whereas all the others had made her slightly uneasy, even if they'd provided the release she sought. And this guy hadn't even come on to her, let alone anything approaching sexual activity. How very peculiar. But kinda nice in a strange sort of way.

She looked at who else was online. HandyMan, of course and now FrenchKiss was back. Romaine clicked on his icon. His response was immediate, as if he'd been waiting for her.

<It's been a while, Scarlet. Good to see you again. How have you been, my mistress?>

<Busy, FrenchKiss.>

<I've missed you, Scarlet. Didn't know what to do without your instructions. I kneel at your feet, head bowed. Just the sight of your body has aroused me. I dare not look. I know that you don't care for me. I am only one of many who learn from you. That's why you've ignored me for so long. I have imagined you with the others, teaching them the art of love. I know you are in much demand and I have felt no resentment. My heart is just filled with joy that you have enough kindness to think of me again. What must I do. Be strict with me.>

Strict? Romaine could guess what he was hinting at, but she wouldn't know where to start. She wasn't normally into these kinds of games, but hell, this was all so surreal anyway, it wasn't as if there would really be any suffering or humiliation or pain involved. They were separated by miles, both geographical and psychological. It might be fun to play the game. There was nothing better to do and if it made him happy…

<Your homework's late. Have you completed it?> Romaine could almost feel the satisfied smile at the other end of the connection.

<Yes, Miss. Here it is.>

<You're not serious, boy…> Romaine snorted with laughter. After all, she could just see him: probably late fifties, pink mottled flesh, greasy grey combed-over hair, banker by day and wanker by night. She could be completely wrong, but it amused her to think of him that way. She took a sip of her drink; she would need a little Dutch courage to continue in this vein. <What do you call this? Speak up, boy! You know what has to happen, don't you?>

<Yes, Miss.>

<What?>

<You'll have to punish me, Miss.>

<And how do you imagine I might do that?> Playing for time and hoping for a few hints here.

<Please, no Miss, not the metal ruler!> Lucky that she'd asked. Left to her own devices, Romaine would have gone for a hundred lines of 'I must do my homework on time'. She obviously needed practice.

<Drop your trousers, lad...> 'Lad'? Were we talking public school now? Romaine wondered what books she'd read in her childhood to bring this kind of language to mind. And then the picture of Miss Ivanova, her year seven teacher, came to mind. The one who had thought she would get nowhere in life if she didn't know how to decline a verb.

<Don't think you can get away with the dictionary-down-the-pants trick. Over the table, boy. Now!>

<With terrified obedience, I let my trousers fall, revealing slightly grey underpants. I obey your command and lean across the school desk. As you march towards me, I hear the terrifying click of your stiletto heels across the wooden floor...> Romaine understood that from this point, she could lean back and relax. She had presented the appropriate cues and the necessary buttons had been pressed. Now, she was part of the audience that FrenchKiss needed. She would need to provide a prompt now and then, just to let him know that she was watching, but, apart from that, her job was done. She watched as the staccato letters appeared on the screen, but her mind was elsewhere... trying not to analyse how and why Computer Expert had touched her.

<Your gentle fingers stroke the tender skin of my buttocks, lingering a little longer than really necessary.>

<Don't you dare think that I'm enjoying any of this. This is purely for your benefit.>

<No, no, of course not. You push my pants down, the fabric scraping my skin. You step closer to the desk and I can feel the trickle of sweat rising to my forehead as a tremor of fear invades the base of my spine.>

<Why are you frightened?>

<Your nails are long and sharp and scarlet as they scrape across my skin, raising welts. There is no pain, just a tickling sensation that is even worse than pain. Your touch is too light, making me wriggle. 'Keep still!' you order, but that's impossible as the ants scamper down my spine, around my balls and up the length of my penis.>

<How dare you! I will not permit signs of insubordination in my students. I have not given you permission.>

<Of course. I apologise, Miss. I cover my shame, force my body to

acknowledge your superior power, to shrink into itself and yet, as I bow my head, the sight of those knife-edged, tapering heels, the tight, formal skirt, the severe cut of your jacket... I can't control the desire raging at the back of my mind.>

<You will control yourself.>

<I know. And you retreat to your desk, stand behind it for a moment, a finger stroking your chin, wondering, staring at my meek body as I wait, patiently for your decision. You rummage in the drawer of your desk and your hand emerges, holding the metal, the gunmetal grey glinting in the pale light. I count your steps as they approach. Seven, eight, nine... ten, and you stop by my side. I feel the heat from your body. I turn my head for just a moment and watch as you raise your muscular arm. I turn away, apprehensive, no, scared, as my breath retreats. I feel the trail of fear slithering from the base of my spine up, up to grip my throat. I can hardly breathe. I'm excited too. But you're right, I must control myself. I wait in expectancy, my breath rasping, harsh.>

<I keep you waiting.>

<I can't bear this. I can feel the stickiness of my skin, damp against the smooth polish of the wooden desk, freckled with years of carved graffiti, the varnish peeling, the grooves indenting my flesh. I scent the aroma of fear mixed with the fine mist of chalk dust. The silence is terrifying. I hold my breath and say my seven times table to still my feverish brain. It's as I get to nine times nine that I hear first the whoosh of air and then feel the sting as the metal connects with flesh, followed by the burning heat of fire. I gasp.>

<Silence!>

<I bite my lip, desperate to stifle any sound as I sense, rather than see, your arm raised again, the cruel, unfeeling line of your lips, the satisfied glint in your eye as, once again, your arm, hand, the ruler descend, this time much faster, much harsher. My teeth are forced into my lips and I taste the salty tang of blood. Heat rushes to my head and I'm dizzy. Blood flows to my groin and my cock is instantly hard. You can't help noticing and the sight of it only spurs you on. Again and again the lashes fall on my reddening buttocks that are now aflame. And

with every touch of the hot metal, my cock is getting harder, fuller, straining towards you, crying out for attention.

The sight of the pleasure I'm feeling only enrages you further and the blows rain down on my flesh, raising welts. You stop for a moment to examine your handiwork and you stand back. I look up, not knowing what is happening and you touch my cheek, gently, with your soft hand, and then the gentle touch caresses my burning flesh, cool, like soothing, flowing water. Instantly, my prick twitches, and a drop of cum emerges. You're furious and—>

For no good reason, Romaine thought of Louie, her confident, yet sensitive, caring, loving husband and she wanted to weep. And then her thoughts turned to Computer Expert and, suddenly, she didn't want to play this game any more.

<And I say goodnight, turn, and leave the room.>

Before FrenchKiss could respond, Romaine quit the program. Tonight, she just wasn't in the mood for him. For a few moments she felt a little guilty about leading him on, but was sure that he'd find satisfaction somewhere else. She sat for a while trying to figure out why, tonight, she hadn't been able to go along with his fantasies and found no logical answer. Maybe because the thought of Computer Expert made her smile. She had to assume that he was married; that was presumably what the 'then you'll understand' meant. But why did he feel the need to tell her? And why had he asked the question? There were no immediate answers, but the likelihood was that she would find out, or at least try.

Romaine checked the shutters, window locks and security chains before heading off to bed.

❧

It was 6:30, at least an hour before Dolores would call, when Romaine's eyes opened to what sounded like mice invading her bedroom. She immediately sat up, wide awake and motionless, listening for the sound again. There was only the noise of a car starting up and then disappearing down the street. She waited for a few minutes to make sure and concluded that it must have been the remnants of a dream or the result of her very vivid but troubled imagination.

Dolores. Sunday lunch with Dolores. There was no way in the world that she could go. She could always ring and say that she wasn't well. She had taken time off work, after all, so it wouldn't exactly be a lie. Well, not strictly speaking. The only problem was that an excuse of that kind would risk Dolores and the others turning up at her door, food in hand, to check on her wellbeing. Romaine hauled her tired body out of the warm bed and dragged herself to the bathroom. She looked at herself in the mirror and the sight of the dark shadows under her eyes only made her feel a thousand times worse. What on earth was the matter with her? Don't say that Louie being away for a few days had led to this? Well, you better get used to it, girl, because it looks like that's the way things are going to be in the future. She looked at his toothbrush in the holder and realised that, apart from the increasingly rare business trip and the more frequent late nights in the office, she and Louie had not spent too many nights apart in the last couple of years. No wonder she was finding it difficult to acclimatise. That's all it would take: a little time.

She debated calling Grace. Not to find out anything about Louie, of course, just to chat and see how she was doing. After all, they hadn't talked about *her* in recent times, being far too wrapped up in Romaine's sorry problems. She looked at her watch. Only 6:45. Who was she kidding. It would be miracle if Grace was awake at this time on a Sunday morning. Instead, Romaine got into the shower and turned the temperature to cold. She needed to shock her system into wakefulness and to stop dwelling on thoughts of how alone she felt in this rattling old house. The cold water was a mistake, because it brought to mind freezing winter mornings and cuddling up to the warmth of Louie's skin and the way he would, instinctively, wrap his arms around her, still asleep, but pulling her close to his heart.

Romaine quickly finished, stepped out of the shower and dressed, pulling her hair away from her face and pinning it up on top of her head. It was deliberate. Louie preferred her hair down, flowing around her ears. He loved to play with if, brushing it away from her eyes with gentle fingers.

But the last thing Romaine was going to do this morning was to think about Louie. If he had chosen to leave her, without really trying to work things out, then so be it. She didn't intend to waste her time going over what might have been. So, he'd told Grace that he was willing to try again. That might have been a possible starting place, but to say that he would try to 'forgive' her! Who the hell did he think he was? Grace was right: he'd set himself up as judge and jury and Romaine wasn't prepared to accept the verdict. She would show him that she could cope on her own.

She looked at the clock and counted the minutes until Dolores' call would come. Why was there a fluttering of butterflies in the pit of her stomach? The possibility that Louie might be there, summoned by Dolores? No, if she admitted the truth to herself, the problem today wasn't just Louie, it was also the thought of having to sit through a polite meal with Matthew, knowing what she knew now.

Romaine left the house before the call could come, hardly taking in the scattering of pebbles across the path. There was no way that she would go to lunch and she wouldn't submit to the tyranny of having to accept a lift from Matthew and then sit through the journey alone in a car with him. To do that would take a bit more front than she possessed at this precise moment. Leaving so early meant that she would have to drive around for a long time, making a huge detour around north London. But that was a small price to pay. Romaine enjoyed driving, particularly when the roads were relatively clear and she knew this part of town well enough to almost go to automatic pilot. She turned the radio on, increasing the volume as she sang along to familiar R 'n' B tunes. It wasn't until she sped away from the lights at Finchley Road that she realised that each time she had looked in the mirror for the last half hour at least, the same dark car seemed to have been behind her. Not directly behind, but two or three cars back. Or was she being paranoid again? God, paranoid or not, she was nervous. And then came the realisation that if she didn't attend Sunday lunch, Dolores would eventually turn up on her doorstep anyway. There was no way of avoiding her. Romaine slammed her fist onto the steering wheel and took the next left turn.

The route to Dolores' flat from there was fairly tortuous, Romaine having worked out her own idiosyncratic route that avoided any possible hold-ups. And for several twists and turns, there it was, some distance behind, but still there, the dark car. She found herself checking with one hand that her mobile phone was in her bag, wondering whether or not to switch it on. And then, as she looked up, she saw that the road was clear behind her. No cars at all. Had she been worrying unnecessarily? Probably some innocent driver making his or her way home. Romaine shook her head slowly as she pulled up in front of Dolores' flat. No dark cars any-where around. She would have to watch herself in case she turned into some kind of screaming, gibbering lunatic.

As luck would have it, Matthew pulled up to the kerb just as she was getting out of her car. There was no way that she could pretend not to have seen him, so Romaine waited by the front steps.

'Hi, Romaine,' he took her hand and kissed her cheek briefly, the same slight, smile on his face as usual, but the obvious difference made Romaine do a double-take. He'd shaved off the goatee. Even up close, he was the spitting image of her husband. She couldn't help staring. And then, remembering the conversation with Elaine, Romaine found herself blushing, mentally berating herself for being so uncool.

'No Louie, again? How you doing?'

'Fine, Matthew.' He looked at her with doubt in his eyes. 'Honestly, I'm fine. No Elaine?'

He simply shook is head and, taking her elbow, ushered her up the steps and rang the doorbell.

Dolores opened the door with her customary hug for Romaine and then did a theatrical look over Romaine's shoulder. 'I thought it was Louie you had with you. You'd think after all these years I would know my children apart. At last, Matt, you shave off that piece of raggedy fluff from you chin. Come in out of the cold, nuh. Girl, for a moment I thought the two of you sorted out your problem and got back together.'

Romaine could almost feel Matthew stiffen behind her.

'What's this about you and Louie?'

Romaine was silent, not wanting to discuss the situation now. As they walked into the dining room, Dolores blithely continued, pointing at Mr James, ensconced at the head of the table.

'Don't worry about him, Romaine. Him not paying us no mind. And today we is family together.' She looked pointedly at Matthew. 'So what happen to that girl you always bringing with you?' Dolores liked to pretend that she couldn't remember Elaine's name.

'Just didn't work out, Mum. Nothing to discuss.'

'Another one bite the dust, eh?' She shook her head at them both. 'You children with you complicated lives!'

'Just like that J2O,' chimed in Mr James.

'J-Lo,' chorused Romaine and Matthew.

'Married she childhood sweetheart in Gretna Green.'

'Britney. In Vegas.'

'And divorce what's him name, Ben Laden. And I can't work out how the Americans them can't track him down. If even Britney can find him…'

Matthew and Romaine looked at each other, rolled their eyes and gave up.

Ignoring Mr James, Dolores picked up her theme again as she ladled piles of food on their waiting plates.

'Why you can't just find the right one and settle down, Mattie? You looking for something you ain't never goin' find? This last one did seem like a nice enough girl…' Romaine nearly choked on her food thinking of the way Dolores had always treated the poor girl.

'…Why you couldn't make do with she?'

Matthew didn't look up from his plate. 'I guess because I don't want to "make do",' he muttered.

Dolores sighed heavily. 'And what that other son of mine up to now? I thought I told him that he should be here this Sunday. And all I does get is a message on the answering machine, not even leaving a number for me to call him back. Must be too frightened to speak to me. Guilty conscience, no?'

Romaine sensed the motion as Matthew looked up at her. She could feel his eyes on her.

'Dolores, you have to stop blaming Louie. I promise you: he hasn't done anything.'

'Don't tell me that. You think I ain't got eyes. I can see the way you troubled, Romaine. You don't have to protect me, you know. I lived my life in this world of suffering and despair. And I does know the way men is…' She eyed her son pointedly. 'I know you probably don't even want to think about it, Romaine, and I can understand why—'

'Dolores!'

'—But he's probably with some trollop right this minute. If I know him, that's why he don't show up—'

'Dolores, for God's sake! Louie hasn't had an affair. It was me.'

Dolores dropped her knife and fork with a clang that resounded in the sudden silence. Even the background drone of Mr James' muttering ceased. All eyes were on Romaine and she couldn't look at any of them.

'What you saying, girl?'

Romaine didn't respond.

'So all this time, you been letting me think that my son…'

'I didn't let you think anything, Dolores. For reasons of your own, you jumped to your conclusion. I tried to tell you.'

'You couldn't have tried too hard, Romaine. You been playing the innocent all this time when you broken my child's heart. You know where he is?'

'No.'

'So you don't know what kind of state him in? How you could let him leave like that?'

'Dolores, I tried to stop—'

'Seems like you been doing a lot of trying and not much succeeding.' There was a grim, unforgiving set to Dolores' lips as she glared at her daughter-in-law. 'So who was it? Someone you working with, or someone you pick up somewhere?' Her disgust was almost tangible and roused Romaine from the torpor that she was sinking into under the force of Dolores' attack.'

'Dolores, you don't understand anything about what goes on between me and Louie. You don't know why—'

'So why you don't tell me why, Romaine? Yes, why you don't explain how you could cheat on my poor son.'

Romaine looked into the other woman's face and knew that there would be no point. Matthew was staring at her with intense curiosity, as if he was waiting for her to say something. Mr James' eyes were clouded and he stared into the middle distance, a look close to panic in his expression. The raised voices obviously confused him. Romaine folded her napkin and rose from the table.

'I think I'd better go.'

Dolores didn't try to stop her, didn't even look up at her. Romaine walked to the hall, put on her coat and left, closing the door quietly behind her. She stood for a second realising that was the first time she'd ever heard the sound of silence in Dolores' home. She laughed bitterly.

By the time she got into the car, she was shaking, unable to fit the key into the ignition. Before she knew it, her door was being opened and Matthew was taking the key from her hand, gesturing that she should move over. He settled into the driver's seat and started the engine. Romaine looked up to see Dolores staring at them from the dining room window. Matthew glanced at her and pulled away from the kerb without speaking.

He drove in silence, glancing at her now and then. Romaine stared straight ahead, knowing that he was looking at her, but not wanting to meet his gaze. She couldn't trust what her eyes might say to him.

Matthew parked in front of the house, got out of the car and opened the passenger door. Romaine walked to the front door, knowing that Matthew was trailing behind her. She fumbled in her handbag for her keys and managed to open the door. She turned to Matthew, not wanting to allow him over the threshold. She held out her hand for the car keys. Curiously, Romaine was glad of the fact that Matthew was six inches shorter than her husband. At least she wouldn't have to look up at him. This way, she could still be in control.

Matthew dangled the keys above her palm for a moment.

'You going to be okay, Romaine?'

'Absolutely fine, Matthew.'

'So Louie went?'

'Uh-huh.'

'You must hurting.'

'Like Elaine.' It was a cheap shot, but she wasn't in any mood to spare his feelings. Right this moment, she'd had enough of the whole of the Webster clan. She could see the hurt in his eyes. 'I'm sorry, Matt. I didn't mean that, but honestly…' She took the keys and gently touched his shoulder. 'I'll be fine. Don't worry about me. I really just need to be on my own for a little while. I appreciate your concern, but…' But she wasn't going to make any lame excuses; she just wanted him to leave. She could see the momentary hesitation, but in the end, he probably knew that it would do him no good at all to insist.

'Elaine called. We talked. You know, everything's cool with her. We'll be friends.' He paused for a moment as if what he was about to say had great significance. 'She told me that she met you and Grace and that you talked.' Was that meant to be significant? Was she supposed to understand something?

'Why did you shave off the beard?' In a way it was a non-sequitor, but at the same time, it wasn't.

Matthew looked at her silently and then a slow, very slow grin spread across his handsome features. 'Oh, something happened to make me feel like a new man. I didn't feel like hiding any more.'

He leaned forward and kissed her cheek, lingering a split second too long. Romaine pulled away and closed the door.

She ran up the stairs and watched from the bedroom window as he trudged away. She knew that he would face a long journey back to Dolores' flat and then he'd have to face her wrath at what she would see as his betraying the family by going after her. Romaine sighed deeply and kicked off her shoes. She felt guilty, but knew that there was no way that she could let Matthew into the house, not when he was being so mysterious and she was feeling vulnerable. Vulnerable and angry too. How two-faced of Dolores to react in that way. When she thought it was Louie who was playing away, she was willing enough to lend a sympathetic ear, probably thinking that she could sweet-talk her into forgiving her husband. But when she learned the truth, then there was no question of compromise; no, she was all out protecting her precious son. Romaine almost laughed at the thought of Dolores' reaction if she'd known about Alison.

Romaine lay back on the bed, her arms cupped behind her neck, breathing slowly, trying to relax her muscles. God, what a day. She reluctantly wondered what Louie was doing. Probably not a care in the world now that she had, effectively, given him his freedom. Dolores might even be right: he could have found someone else, could be shacked up with another woman even now, maybe even got back together with Gina. Romaine found herself overcome with a deep sadness at the thought, surprising herself. She pulled the duvet up to her neck and curled into a foetal ball. She was hungry and sad and adrift. She didn't want to think about all that had happened in this short day. Romaine closed her eyes and within minutes was fast asleep.

CHAPTER 9

Romaine was startled awake by the screech of the telephone. She reached for it half asleep. As soon as she picked up the receiver, the line went dead. She felt an immediate surge of rage at Louie. Why the hell was he doing this to her now? It wasn't as if he cared what she was doing. If he did care, then why had he walked out?

Still holding the receiver, she looked around the room unsure of where she was and what day or time it was. She squinted at the clock: 3:30. Morning or afternoon? And then it all flooded back: the lunch, Dolores' expression as she pronounced her guilty on all counts. She dropped the receiver back in the cradle and pulled the duvet over her head. She tried her hardest for several minutes to return to sleep, with no success. Instead, she lay awake listening to the well-known creaks and groans of the house, background noise that now seemed so unfamiliar.

Suddenly she jumped at the unexpected shrill peal of the doorbell. Romaine closed her ears, hoping to shut out the noise. Whoever it was, she just hoped that they would go away. She tried to ignore the sound for as long as possible and then threw the duvet aside and hurried down the stairs. She opened the door and there was no one there. She took a step outside and looked along the street in both directions. Nobody. Probably children playing a silly game. But all the same, she needed to remember to use the security chain in future. The skies were beginning to darken, threatening rain or perhaps even snow. Romaine quickly closed the door and leaned for a moment against the radiator, trying to warm her body from the outside in when she knew that the cold was profoundly internal.

She needed to talk to someone. Under normal circumstances, she would talk to Louie. There had been many occasions when they'd returned from lunch with Dolores and then spent most of the rest of the afternoon laughing at Dolores' idiosyncrasies or mulling over some minor irritation or even trying to solve the mystery of Mr James.

'Careful what you say, Lou. He might turn out to be your new stepfather.'

'Well, I could do a lot worse. I'd learn a lot I didn't already know from Mr James.'

For a fleeting moment, Romaine smiled to herself at the recollection. And then she remembered that she wouldn't be able to talk to Louie about this particular family lunch. She walked to the extension in the kitchen, picked it up and dialled Grace's number. The answering machine responded and there was no suitable message that Romaine could leave. This wasn't a message-leaving situation, it was a need-to-talk-right-now kind of occasion. Colin? Not in a million years. Alison? She'd promised Louie that she wouldn't. No extra-curricular contact. That was the deal.

Romaine opened the fridge and retrieved a bottle of white wine. She uncorked it and poured herself a generous glassful. She jumped at a crackling sound outside the window and laughed at herself when she realised that the wind had risen and all she'd heard was a twig hitting against the window pane. She looked out into the gloom. Soon she'd be thinking that those shadows under the trees were lurking figures out to get her! She walked out of the kitchen, leaving the lights on and as she walked past the study, realised how the room that, earlier, she had thought looked dingy and dilapidated, now seemed warm and cosy and welcoming, like a cocoon.

Almost without thinking, Romaine found herself seated in the chair, her hand eagerly grasping the mouse. She now regretted all the years she'd spent laughing at the computer geeks she imagined ensconced in their adolescent rooms, addicted to the machinery. Now, she was turning to her e-mail program as if it were an old, understanding, non-judgemental friend.

And her confidence in the machine was rewarded when she found not one, but three e-mails from Computer Expert. The first, she noticed, was early this morning, long before she'd even struggled awake.

<I imagined you listening to the Prince album and wanted to feel closer to you. I went to HMV and bought it. It's been a long time since I've heard it. Each time in the future, I'll think of you.>

And then:

<I apologise for leaving so abruptly. I missed you.>

And finally:

<I'm here if you want to talk.>

Oh boy, did she want to talk. He must be some kind of mind reader. Romaine immediately launched Instant Messenger. Computer Expert was true to his word: online.

<Hi.> It was all she could think to say.

<I've been waiting, Scarlet. How are you? Hard day?> He must be psychic. For a moment, Romaine wondered if Computer Expert was really a man. And the whole point of the net was that you could be whoever you wanted to be. Surely very few men could be that intuitive. But immediately, Romaine berated herself for the gross generalisation. After all, that's how things used to be with Louie; that's why she'd fallen in love, rather than just lust, with him.

<You could say so.>

<Want to talk about it?>

<Prefer to talk about almost anything else.>

<That bad?>

<That bad!>

<Are you in your blue room?>

Blue room? Oh shit, she'd almost forgotten how she'd described the study to him. She would need to keep her wits about her.

<Yes.>

<Tell me what you really look like.>

<I already described myself.>

<Now tell me the truth.> How did he know she had lied?

<Why do you want to know the truth?>

<Because I feel there could be something between us. Don't you feel it?>

<No.>

<No there couldn't be anything between us or no you don't feel it?>

<Why did you ask me if I was married?>

<Because I wanted to know if you would tell the truth.>

<And how would you know if I was lying.>

<I'd know.>

And Romaine believed him. She found the thought somehow comforting, if a little scary at the same time. Computer Expert, from the beginning had been different from HandyMan, FrenchKiss and the others. From the moment she'd first encountered him, each time she turned to the computer she had been hoping to hear from him. What was it that made him so different? Was it really as simply as a coincidental musical empathy? That had been the catalyst, but Romaine sensed that there was something more that brought her back to these intimate chats, wanting more.

<Scarlet?>

<Yes?>

<Tell me about yourself. What do you most enjoy doing?>

<Being alone.>

<You're an only child.>

<How do you know?>

<Lucky guess. What do you do when you're alone?>

<Listen to music, mostly.>

<When I was in the record store, I got carried away. Bought some sounds that I haven't heard in a while. One song, in particular made me think of you.>

<What's that?>

<A track from Hot Chocolate called 'Are You Getting Enough Happiness?'>

<Why would that make you think of me?>

<What's your answer?>

<You know the Destiny's Child song that says 'I'm a survivor'?>

<Yes, and I also love Millie Jackson's 'Making the Best of a Bad Situation'.>

Romaine knew the track well. It was on a CD that she'd played over and over when she'd first moved into the house with Louie and the other guys. They'd begged her to stop, asking if she was trying to convey some kind of message about the state of the house. It was weird that he'd mentioned that particular song, but she certainly couldn't fault his taste in music so far.

<Tell me about yourself, Computer Expert.>

<What do you want to know?>

<You're married?>

<Why do you ask?>

<Because you asked.>

<Fair enough. Yes.>

<Happily?>

<At the moment, no. But isn't that what they all say?>

<Why? What's gone wrong?>

<How about Frankie Beverley and Maze with 'Too Many Games'?>

<Or maybe 'Joy and Pain'?>

<Marvin singing ' When Did You Stop Loving Me, When Did I Stop Loving You'.>

<I have to go.>

<Why?>

<I have to go.>

Romaine closed the program, struggling for breath. It was like he'd delivered a physical punch in the solar plexus. She'd been enjoying the game, batting a knowledge of music back and forth and then he'd mentioned that track by Marvin Gaye. She'd watched the letters appearing one by one, knowing exactly what he would type. How many times had she and Louie lain in bed on a lazy Sunday morning listening to that particular album, humming along to those lyrics, secretly knowing that they would never apply to themselves? And look at the two of them now: her on a dismal, rainy Sunday afternoon, tempted to share her innermost secrets with a stranger who could be some kind of psycho and Louie who knows where? If she wasn't made of such strong stuff, she could just break down and weep.

Instead, Romaine picked up the phone and dialled Grace's number again. Still the answering machine.

So, she'd promised Louie that she wouldn't call Alison, well, all those vows were invalid now. Louie had walked out on the agreement and she needn't feel constrained by it any longer. Romaine punched out the familiar number that she'd pushed to the back of her mind for so many weeks now.

The phone was answered after several rings by an out-of-breath Byron.

'Byron, it's Romaine.'

'Oh. She's… um… Alison's not here. She… um, she's in the office.' There was no warmth, evidently no wish to prolong the conversation.

'Okay. Thanks Byron. I'll call her—' The line went dead before she could finish the sentence. Romaine's hand flew to her mouth. What they hell had she done, what had they done to this kindly, unassuming treasure of a man? Alison hadn't told her. She'd acted as if Byron understood. And yet he could obviously hardly bear to speak to her. That, more than any promise to Louie, made it impossible for Romaine to dial Alison's office number.

❦

Try as he might, Matthew couldn't get the thought of Romaine out of his head. If he'd needed any confirmation of why it was wrong to be thinking of his sister-in-law that way, then his mother's reaction to her confession provided it. And Dolores had been mad as hell when he returned to pick up his car. She had obviously been waiting by the window since she opened the door and was half way down the steps before he could even unlock the door.

'I hope you does satisfy with yourself, boy. How you could take after she so, when you heard for yourself what she done to your brother?'

'Mum, you don't know what happened between Romaine and Louie. It's not a question of taking sides. You saw how upset she was. I couldn't let her just go like that.'

'Why ever not? You could leave she to go to her fancy man. I sure he would take care of her. Boy, you need to learn where your loyalty lie. You not worried about Louie? You heard from him recently? Goodness knows what happened to him and yet is she you go run after.'

'I wasn't running after her, Mum.' But he knew that he was.

Ever since the night that he'd stayed at their house. Ever since he'd crept quietly down the stairs, stepping to the side, trying to avoid the tell-tale creaks that had signalled Romaine's progress. Well, well, well, he'd thought as he'd eased open the door and looked at the screen, Romaine's a computer geek. Who would have thought. He had been about to turn around and go back to bed when he'd heard the soft exhalation of breath that told him he was about to gain some invaluable insight into what made his sister-in-law tick. He stood to one side, hidden in the dark shadows of the hall and pushed the door further in order to gain full access. It was impossible, from this distance, to read the words on screen.

He'd watched in horrified fascination as her hand reached down to the hem of her thick nightdress and began to lift the fabric, smoothing it upwards, along the curve of her calf, up further above her knees, revealing the tantalising roundness of her thighs. He knew that he should leave, but an invading army could not have forced him to retreat at that point. He held his breath, not daring to make a sound even though he could feel the heat descending to his groin. As if hypnotised, his hand reached down to cup his balls inside his boxers. His overactive brain was telling him that he should go: this was his brother's house, he was watching his brother's wife touching herself. They were alone together in his brother's house, both of them half naked, and the heat was rising so that beads of sweat could be felt on his brow even though he was suddenly freezing cold as he watched her hand reach down to a package by the side of the chair and, oh God no!, she was holding what looked like a rigid phallus and she was about to touch herself with it and his knees were trembling, weak. He'd had to brace himself against the wall as she spread her legs, her head dropping back and he watched the artificial penis mock him as it slid into her moist depths.

🐞

The phone rang again. The third hang-up in an hour and as Romaine hurled abuse at the unhearing receiver, she glanced out of the window and thought she saw a shadowy figure on the other side of the road, mobile held to his ear. She moved closer to the window and she was no longer sure. Besides, what was so unusual about a person in a London street talking on their phone? Romaine mentally berated herself, but as she heard what sounded like a creak in the room above, she instantly picked up the phone again and dialled Grace's number. If you'd like to leave a message… No she wouldn't. She tried the mobile.

Switched off. If she would like to leave a message… As the house creaked again, Romaine dialled the office. Whatever had stopped her before was far from her thoughts now. She was panicky. Outside the window it was pitch black, impossible to make out anything. Romaine reluctantly closed the shutters as she waited; she didn't know whether it was better to block out the darkness or to at least be able to see if anything did emerge from the shadows.

'Brown, Bartlett and Velasco?'

'Alison, it's Romaine.'

'Romaine! What's up? You okay?'

'I'm not sure.'

'What is it?'

'I've had a hell of a day.'

'You don't sound too good.'

'It's just my imagination, I know, but I'm in the house alone and I keep seeing things and hearing noises. It's probably just years of alcohol abuse catching up with me, but…' Romaine made the feeble joke, trying to make light of the situation. Alison, however, didn't laugh.

'I'll be there in thirty minutes, Romaine. Make sure all the doors are locked. I'll call on my mobile when I'm outside the door.'

'You're making me scared now, Alison. I'm sure there's nothing to worry about. I just needed to talk to someone who'd tell me that I'm being childish and imagining things that go bump in the night. You know, like my mum after she'd told me stories about duppies and vampires and evil spirits and then expected me to go to sleep alone in a dark room.'

'You probably are worrying about nothing, but I've almost finished here and I'm not expecting Byron home for a while. Thirty minutes.' She put the phone down and Romaine wondered at the white lie. She knew very well that Byron was at home. Presumably, this was Alison's way of making the trek over to Tottenham seem inconsequential.

Having spoken to Alison, Romaine now felt very silly indeed. Of course there was nothing to worry about. But all the same she checked the locks on the doors and windows before sitting by the phone, waiting for it to ring.

🌢

Alison was as good as her word and twenty-seven minutes later, the phone rang and there she was outside the door clutching a bottle of wine and what looked like a huge bag of groceries.

'I guessed your fridge might be empty,' she said, handing the bag to Romaine.

'You're right, but you didn't need to go to this trouble.'

'Have you eaten all day?'

'No, I had been expecting Dolores' usual Sunday lunch, but I had to leave before we got that far.'

'Louie?'

'No, he wasn't there, but yes, we argued about him.'

'You actually argued with the old battleaxe?'

'You'd have been proud. I stood up for myself. Sort of.'

'And she threw you out?'

'No, I walked out.'

'Go girl!' They high-fived and Romaine surprised herself by breaking into genuine laughter.

By now they were in the kitchen and Alison was rummaging through the cupboards looking for saucepans. 'I'll make a quick omelette. Have you got an omelette pan?' Romaine looked bewildered, so she continued 'Okay, I'll make do with this frying pan. So, tell me all about it.'

Romaine poured glasses of wine and proceeded to relate the day's happenings. By the time she got to the suspicious noises, she was relaxed and played down her fears.

'What about these phone calls?'

'Oh that? It's only Louie, checking up on me.'

'Why would he bother, now that he's left?'

'I guess to show he cares.'

'Seriously though, Romaine, Louie never seemed the type to behave like that.'

'No, you're right. Before all of this, I would never have thought Louie would be so controlling, but you didn't see how hurt he was and how suspicious he became. Besides, I caught him out. He called on my mobile one time and I was just outside the house. He still had the phone in his hand when I walked in.'

'Did you ask him about it?'

'No, he was still pretending to be talking to someone else. It was so childish and I didn't want to get into the pettiness. There were far more important issues to get sorted out.'

'And what about the car you said was following you, and the feeling that someone was watching the house?'

'Just my imagination.'

'Certain?'

'I feel a lot better.'

'I'm glad. You know, all this wouldn't have happened if it wasn't for me.'

'It wasn't you alone, we've talked about this, Alison.'

'And we'll probably have to talk about it many times more before we both understand. I still don't see why you confessed to Louie. You must have known how he'd react. Even I could have seen it.'

'What do you mean? You said yourself that you talked to Byron about it.'

'Yes, but Byron is a different type of man altogether.'

'In what way?'

'This is nothing against Louie. You know I was, and probably still am, very fond of him. It's just that Byron doesn't have any of that macho ego stuff going on. Louie's masculine pride was always going to be hurt.'

'I guess I knew that. But he asked me where I'd been. As simple as that. I've never kept anything from Louie before. He was like my best friend in the whole world, my whole family wrapped into one. It would have burned me up. Keeping it from him would have made what happened between us seem so sordid and I didn't want that.

Alison smiled gently at her. 'You know, Romaine, you might be all of twenty-eight, but you have a whole lot of growing up to do. You knew what the likely outcome of telling Louie would be. And yet you went ahead just because it would make you feel better.'

'I know now. It was selfish. But I can't take it back.'

'So what are you going to do now?'

'I don't know. Louie wanted to give it another try.'

'And?'

'I guess I threw my rattle out of the pram.'

'You said "no"?' Alison's eyes were wide with astonishment.

'Not exactly. I told him that I need space.'

Alison tilted her head to one side, as if analysing Romaine's features. 'You might be right. Maybe you do need the space.' She looked at her watch. 'I'd better get going.' She gathered up her coat and briefcase and Romaine followed her to the door. Alison turned back to her as she was about to close the door.

'You know, it might help if you remember that Louie isn't your only family. You've got Byron and me.' She reached up and tenderly stroked Romaine's cheek. Romaine hugged her warmly.

'Thanks, Alison. I'll remember.'

She closed and bolted the door behind her, making sure that the security chain was in place. And now the house seemed even emptier now that Alison, too, had gone.

❦

She started up the program and within seconds he was there. As if he had been waiting.

<What did I say?>

<Nothing. I just had to go.>

<I understand. You probably needed a little space. Feeling better?>

His choice of words was unfortunate, but he obviously did understand.

<A lot better.>

<You know how I think of you?>

<How?>

<As someone who needs a lot of tenderness, treasuring, warmth, nurturing.>

<Is that what you're offering?>

<I'm not sure that any one person can provide all of that.>

She could see where this was heading and felt a sense of disappointment. Not another one with a partner who wanted to swing! Maybe she'd chosen the wrong site. Perhaps there was some code that she just didn't understand. She could see now why he'd asked if she was married; he was just leading to this moment. She knew, but still had to ask, just to be one-hundred-percent certain.

<So what are you suggesting?>

<That maybe you need a softness, an intimacy, an understanding that I'm not capable of giving.>

<Why not?>

<Because I'm a man.>

Are you really? Romaine wanted to ask. Or is this some kind of mind game. So far, there had been nothing to indicate who Computer Expert might really be. Certainly nothing to suggest a particular gender, until this most recent declaration. What could be believed?

<Why would that stop you being soft and intimate and understanding?>

<Because I'm hard for you now!>

<Is that a joke?>

<No. I'm deadly serious. There's the problem. I can give you what you want, but not what you need.>

<And why do you think you know what I need?>

<Is your husband with you now? Tell me the truth.>

There was a minute's pause. Romaine was no longer sure where this conversation was heading and whether she should be following the path. But what did she have to lose? This was, after all, an anonymous encounter.

<No. But what is it that you think I want?>

<I know that you want to express your innermost desire. It's torturing you. You can't get any rest. I bet that's why your husband isn't with you. You can't tell him, can you?>

<And what do I need?>

<Her?>

<Who?>

<You're not the type to play games. Tell me about her. I'd like to know.>

It was like the flood-gates had been opened. Without knowing why, Romaine trusted Computer Expert. Or perhaps she didn't know if she trusted him, but in the end it didn't matter. What did she have to lose by pouring her heart out to a complete stranger who could never betray her, even if this was just his fantasy? He'd never know the truth.

<She was like my best friend. I felt I could talk to her about anything. She didn't judge. Just accepted the way I was. She's beautiful, too. Soft curves, silky skin, the scent of warm perfume always present.>

<So what happened?>

<We made love. Or rather, we made real, beautiful friendship. That's what it was: deep, meaningful caring for each other.>

<Friends don't usually make love to each other.>

<That's not true. My husband was my friend.>

<Okay. You got me there. But have you made love to other women?>

<No>

<Do you want to?>

<I don't think so.>

<What was special about her?>

<The softness. The gentle curves. The fullness of her lower lip, the silkiness of her hair, the creamy feel of her skin. And yes, the heaviness of her breasts as I touched them, the roundness of her hips, the way her nipples puckered, the generous forest of hair, the hot wetness between her legs, the smooth touch of her inner thigh against my skin. The fact that she was so familiar and so new, too. She knew what I wanted, how I needed to be touched, without words. And more than that, it was the moment. We both recognised the moment.>

She wrote without even pausing to consider, the words flowing out as if they'd been pent up for too long. And it was as she wrote that she understood that, yes, that's why it had happened. They had both understood, without discussion, without games, without awkwardness, that the right moment had arrived. It wasn't a question of making a decision or trying to resist or having to finely judge where the balance of power lay. At that sudden, unexpected, unrepeatable moment, they were equal, equal in their affection, their love and their desire.

<As we held each other, I knew that this was going to be the most important sex of my life. The passion was slow burning, lit the moment I looked at her lips, touched them with mine. It smouldered when her

fingers reached for me and stroked my flesh lightly, adoring, and I recip-
rocated, not able to resist running my hands along the swell of her
breasts, cupping them, wondering at the size, the shape, so different to
mine. And as I watched her nipples pucker, I wondered at the knowledge that it was me causing this arousal in her, that someone other than
my husband, someone whose judgement and taste were exquisite,
wanted me. And making love to her was like nothing I'd ever known
before. Her touch was achingly tender, powerfully gentle and she waited
for my pleasure before taking hers. We both did.>

    <Did she make you come?>

    <Are you getting excited by this?>

    <Would it worry you if I said yes?>

    <Perhaps.>

    <I'd be lying if I said no.>

Romaine was grateful for his honesty, but she was uncertain about
sharing with him something that was, as yet, not fully formed. He was
pushing her in directions that she wasn't sure she wanted to go, making
her find answers to questions that she had hesitated to ask herself. They
were, though, questions that needed to be answered and maybe now was
the best opportunity she would have. She could tentatively explore what
had happened with Alison without having to see concern or anger or
suspicion on Computer Expert's face.

    <Sex has never been a problem with my husband. I need to say
that from the start. I fell in lust with him before I fell in love with him but
the two melded together. I never needed anything else, would never
have gone in search of anyone else.>

    <But you did.>

    <No, I wasn't looking for her. Didn't plan for it to happen. Didn't
want it to happen. There were no thoughts involved. Just feelings.>

    <Was it alcohol?>

Romaine wondered at the question. When she'd confessed all to
Louie, he'd immediately picked up on the couple of glasses they'd
drunk together, the bottle of wine taken into the sitting room, sipped
before the fire. As if alcohol would be the acceptable camouflage that
they could both hide behind. To pretend that the wine had anything

to do with it would have been disloyal to the reality of her feelings for Alison.

<No. I don't know if I can make you understand. I'd had some wine, but when it came to this, I was sober. I knew that at the time. My senses were alive with the sight, the feel, the scent, the thought of her, not a result of the wine. We touched each other, exploring parts that we thought we didn't know but found we knew from time immemorial. We didn't have to move into the right positions, we were already there. We didn't question the caresses that would arouse, we knew them by heart. And when she touched her lips to my clitoris, it was with a certain knowledge, a precision of touch, the gentlest, most fleeting, most profound caress that I could ever imagine. Her tongue explored me in ways that I had only imagined possible. And I knew that, at that moment in time, she was where she wanted to be, not because she would demand or expect anything in return, but just because she wanted to give me the pleasure. I opened myself to her, maybe the first time I've ever, ever done that.>

<Why?>

<Because I'd trust her with my life.>

<And your husband?>

<Well, he left me!>

Romaine had no more words. She didn't want to read any more words. She clicked on the X and walked out of the room, shaken. It was not just the admission to a complete stranger what Alison meant to her, but the sudden realisation too of just how much the fact that Louie had left affected her. Did this really mean that she would never be able to trust him? Even though she was the one who had 'cheated' on him?

❦

At first Romaine thought the fuzziness was to do with the unnatural hour of the morning. She'd reached for the phone, startled from sleep.

'Look out the window.'

'What?' She glanced at the clock. 2:35 am. Must be some crazy lunatic who'd got the wrong number.

'Look out of your bedroom window.'

'Who is this?'

'Just do as I say.'

'Louie? Is it you? Stop playing games.'

She could hear breathing. This had to be a wrong number or some kind of practical joke. Romaine put the phone down and covered her head with the duvet, hoping to get back to wherever she had been in her dreams.

Within seconds, the phone shrilled again.

'Look out the window.'

'For God's sake, who is this.' The voice was making her more than a little nervous now. Romaine got out of bed and tiptoed over to the window. She moved the curtain aside by the merest millimetre. At first, there was nothing to see but the pitch black and then, as her eyes focussed, it seemed that she could make out a shape on the other side of the street. She couldn't be sure that this wasn't her imagination because whoever it was, or might be, was motionless. She let the curtain fall back into place and picked up the receiver again. It was as if he had seen her every movement and was waiting for his cue.

'Did you see me?'

'No.'

'I want you to know I'm here.'

The line went dead and Romaine felt a shiver of fear spiral up her spine. The hairs on her arms were standing on end and she knew that it wasn't just the cold. She made her way back to the window as silently as she could and peeked out again. This time, there were no shadows to lift the inky darkness of the night. Had there really been a person there, or just someone wanting to spook her? And who? Why would anyone want to scare her? Louie might be angry with her, but he wouldn't want to do that to her. And who else was there? Matthew? Not his style. Colin? He might be trying to get her into his bed, but frightening the life out of her was not the most successful seduction technique she could think of. But what if it wasn't a man? The voice had been so muffled that it was impossible to tell. Romaine almost laughed at where her thoughts were heading. Why on earth would a woman want to be out in the early hours of the morning, stalking her? The name immediately rose to the forefront of her brain: Elaine.

Romaine wouldn't put it past her, but there was no reason why Elaine would have anything against her in particular. She thought back to what Matthew had said: they'd talked. About what? Romaine wondered. But now she really was letting her imagination run away with her. It was probably someone who'd just dialled her number at random and was playing a pathetic game.

Romaine climbed back into bed, trying to get warm. She shivered and then wondered whether it might not be sensible to call the police. But what could she say to them? So, she'd had a couple of crank phone calls and she couldn't be certain that there really was anyone watching the house. They'd write her off as paranoid or drunk. And who else could she call at this time of the morning?

Wrapping her robe around her, Romaine crept down the stairs, not turning on any lights. She double-checked that the front door was securely locked and that the security chain was in place. She suddenly recalled the scattering of pebbles and the rattling noise that had woken her the previous morning. Had someone thrown them up at her window? Was that what had awoken her?

She groped her way into the study and turned on the desk lamp. She powered up the computer and clicked on the Instant Messenger program praying that Computer Expert would be online. Somehow, as if he knew her so well, he'd always managed to soothe her taut nerves. She was relying on him to do so again. She was alone and vulnerable. Romaine almost laughed at the thought that her husband had left and she was now reliant on a complete stranger.

The night was so still that she could even hear her teeth chattering. Pulling the robe tighter around her, Romaine waited for the program to open. At last, the familiar window appeared. And sure enough, HandyMan was on line. It was as if he was always waiting for her. Romaine found herself wondering about HandyMan. What had he said to her in those early messages? *You are disobeying me… You are forcing me to cause you pain… Respond or else.* Just seeing his name made her feel uncomfortable but, surely, that was as much harm as HandyMan could cause; he didn't even know her name and she thanked God that she had made sure of that..

Romaine scanned the list once again, fervently praying, hoping to conjure up Computer Expert. Surely he would understand and be there when she needed him? Try as she might, though, he wasn't. She couldn't conjure him up. She would, somehow, have to get through this night alone.

CHAPTER 10

The regular, monotonous hum of the train lulled her body into a state of suspended animation. Romaine felt like a robot and just wished that she could shut down the activity of the computer that was her brain. She would have to get through the day on automatic pilot having spent the rest of the night sitting bolt upright in the gloom of the shuttered sitting room, with only a glass of medicinal brandy as company.

She bought strong coffee from the optimistic seller who had set up a table and chair, complete with striped umbrella on a grey, misty morning. It would be her fourth cup of the morning and she hoped that it would dispel the gloop that was seeping into her head. Now who was being more foolishly optimistic: her or the coffee seller?

Romaine did little more than shuffle papers around her desk waiting for the moment when she could be sure that Grace would be at home, and reasonably sure that she would be alone. Sheldon would certainly have left for the office by now . She found herself biting her nails, something she never did, while she waited for the endless ringing to be interrupted by the sound of Grace's voice. She was about to give up when she heard her friend's breathless tones.

'Hello?'

'Grace, it's me. Romaine.'

'Girl, I was just thinking about you. Haven't talked to you for a while. How you doing?'

'Not good, Grace.'

'What's happened.'

Romaine explained about the telephone call and the subsequent night-time fears. And the fact that things hadn't seemed that much better in the morning.

'Even if it was just a random hoax call, whoever it is has got my number. It could happen again. And maybe there really was someone watching the house.'

'Girl, you don't need to be taking no chances. You get a few things together and you come and stay with me and Sheldon. I'll come over and help you. Can't you get off work now? I'm sure Alison would understand if you explain to her.'

'I'm sure she would, Grace and thank you so much for the offer, but what good would it do in the end? I can't stay away from home for ever. I guess I just needed to talk about it. Now, it doesn't seem so bad. I think it's probably someone playing some kind of joke. You know: they know that once they tell you to look out of your window, then you're bound to imagine something scary out there.'

'And what's in it for him?'

'Or her! Probably the same kind of power that all those computer geeks get dreaming up new viruses.'

'You might be right, Rome, but I don't like the idea of you taking any chances. If you don't want to come here, I'll come to you. Just for a couple of nights—'

'No, I can't let you do that, Grace.'

'No arguments. Just one night if you insist. I need to see for myself. Talk to Alison and call me back when you're ready to leave. I'll be here.'

Romaine looked up as Alison walked into the office. She was surprised at how fresh and relaxed and confident she looked. Not that Alison ever looked much different, but having been through the night that she had, Romaine found it incredible that other people's lives hadn't been disrupted too.

'Hi, Romaine...' Alison's smile froze as she noticed the dark circles under Romaine's eyes and the tense lines at the corners. 'Come into my office.'

Alison waited and closed the door behind them both. She put her arm around Romaine and led her to the chair.

'What's wrong, Rome?' Alison never called her 'Rome' in the office. She must really look bad. Romaine explained all that had happened the previous night.

'And Grace is going to stay with you? Tell you what, I'll stay too. Byron's away for a few days so I'd be on my own at home anyway. And there's safety in numbers. We need to get to the bottom of this. You're probably right that there's nothing to be worried about, but I'd like to make sure.'

'There really is no need,' Romaine tried to laugh, but it came out like a strangled sob.

'Just indulge us. Do you want to go home?'

'No, I'd rather stay busy.'

❦

For the rest of the day, Alison watched Romaine, noting how her hand shook every time she reached for a ringing phone and how her eyes flickered around the room as she spoke. However much she might pretend otherwise, it was obvious that the phone calls and the shadowy figures had spooked her more than she would admit. Alison suspected that this had to have something to do with Louie. Although she, too, would never have suspected this of him, she could imagine that it was his way of getting some kind of petty revenge. In her heart she knew that he would never do anything to physically hurt his wife, but she could also believe that he wouldn't understand how much more damaging this kind of mental torture could be. Romaine might be unwilling to point the finger, but Alison knew where she would place her bet.

It wasn't really clear how staying with Romaine in the house would help the situation at all in the long term, but right now, she might at least be able to sleep knowing that there were others in the house. And it looked like untroubled sleep was what she needed more than anything.

She would have to go home to pick up a few things. She'd call Grace and get her to agree to meet Romaine at the house and stay at least until she could get there. She'd prefer it if Romaine didn't have to travel home alone, but there was no point in frightening her any more by insisting that she wait for a bodyguard. Although there might be no very logical reason, Alison was surprised to find that she was feeling very, very nervous herself so she forced herself to concentrate hard on the current project that she was dealing with.

She left the office earlier than usual and went home to pack an overnight bag. She called Byron's mobile and left a message telling him where she would be. She didn't want him to worry if he called and didn't find her at home. She would have preferred to talk to him, to explain all the details, but if he wasn't able to answer, then a voice message would have to do. She would try him again later. Alison checked all the door and window locks in the house, admitting to herself that Romaine's experiences had made her more safety conscious than usual. She double-locked the front door behind her and threw her bags into her car and drove off not looking behind her, concentrating on where she was heading and why.

As she turned into Romaine's road, she accelerated. She could see even from a distance that there was something wrong. She could see two figures: Grace, her arms around Romaine in front of the gaping front door. She screeched to a halt and dashed out of the car not even stopping to close the door behind her. There was no need to explain. She could see the devastation for herself. Every shrub had been truncated, bulbs ripped from the soil, the hedge surrounding the front of the house savagely chopped, dry brown swathes in the grass, obviously the effect of a strong weed-killer. She looked at Romaine, her face almost white with horror. Alison's eyes met Grace's and she nodded silently. As if receiving a coded command, Grace turned and ushered Romaine inside. Alison retrieved her bags and followed them.

Grace made tea and Romaine sat at the kitchen table. Alison couldn't sit. She paced around the room.

'You should call the police now,' Grace said.

'No.'

'Why not?'

Romaine was silent, just slowly shook her head from side to side.

Alison answered for her. 'She thinks it might be Louie.'

'Louie? No way he would do something like that. He knows how much you love your garden. Louie's not mean-minded like that.'

'I know. That's what we'd all like to think, but who else?'

'Let's think about this sensibly,' Grace insisted as she poured tea. She wouldn't let herself believe that anyone who had been close to Romaine could do this to her. 'Why would Louie want to scare you?'

'Maybe because he wants her back. Wants her to think that she can't survive without him.' It was clear that Alison wouldn't be fighting his corner.

'Yeah, but if he knows Romaine at all, he'll know that this is the worst way to go about trying to win her back.'

'But he probably doesn't think that she'll ever find out.'

'Please stop it, you two. I don't think it's Louie. Grace is right: it's just not the kind of thing he'd do. Whatever has happened between us, I still know him. Louie just wouldn't.'

'So why won't you call the police.'

'It might be someone else I know. Or it might be my fault.'

'What do you mean *your* fault?'

Without a word, Romaine stood up from the table and led the way to the study. She opened the e-mail program and pointed to the list of messages. 'Have a look at these.'

Alison sat at the desk and Grace looked over her shoulder as she clicked through the messages. Romaine leaned against the wall, her arms coiled tightly around her body as if holding herself together.

Finally, Alison turned to her. 'What is all this?'

It was Grace who explained about the site that Romaine had found. Alison looked at Romaine, puzzled.

'I'll admit that some of these messages are a little kinky, but what's that got to do with the phone calls... or the garden? After all, they don't know anything about you.'

'No. And just as important, I don't know anything about them either.'

'So?'

'Don't you see? I've been e-mailing these people, talking to them in chat rooms, all the time assuming that these were all anonymous words floating through the ether. But what if... what if one of them knows more about me than I thought?'

'But how could they? Surely you just picked them out at random.'

'Except for one. Computer Expert. He—or she—contacted me first. Right from the beginning I felt as if I'd found a kindred spirit. He—and I always assumed it was a he—almost seemed to read my mind. So much seemed like coincidence, like we were soulmates. But what if it seemed like that because he really *did* know me.'

'But how would anyone be able to contact you through the site?

They couldn't possibly search through the thousands of sites out there. And how would they even know that you'd signed up?'

'Oh God!' It was Grace's turn to go pale.

'What is it?'

'Don't you remember? We told Elaine.'

'And Matthew was here, watching me when I was online that night.'

'But I still don't understand,' Grace protested. 'I don't see why either of them would do something like this.

'I don't either,' Alison replied, 'but I think we need to find out. Romaine, can you try this Computer Expert again? See if he's online.'

'And then what?'

'Talk to him for a while. Just the same as usual. As if there's nothing wrong. Just see what happens. If it's him doing all this stuff, then he'll expect you to say something. That would only be natural. Maybe you can force him to reveal his hand.'

'So what do I do then?'

'You try to arrange a meeting.'

'What?'

'Don't worry. You wouldn't have to go through with it, but at least we'd be able to find out who it is. We'd be with you.'

'I still think it would be safer to go to the police,' Grace argued.

'You might be right, Grace. But I don't think Romaine will agree to that, do you?'

They both turned towards Romaine. As they watched, her eyes seemed to clear and her shoulders straightened. She pushed herself away from the wall and walked towards the computer. Grace and Romaine made way for her.

She could immediately see that Computer Expert was online. Maybe he'd been waiting. *Play it cool*, Romaine told herself although she could feel the anger rising.

\<Hi, C.E.>

\<Hi, Scarlet. Good to hear from you. How are you doing?>

\<Great.>

\<Really?> Why didn't he believe her? Did he know something?

\<Yes. I'm fine.>

<It's just that the last time we spoke, you left suddenly. You were talking about your husband.>

<Yes.>

<Doesn't sound as if he was understanding about what happened.>

<I don't blame him. I'm not sure I understood myself.>

<I think I understand. You explained and I could feel what you were feeling. Something clicked as you talk. I promise you, I understand.>

Romaine turned and looked up at Grace and Alison.

'Ask him what made him understand.'

<So how comes you think you can understand when he doesn't.>

<Oh, I've learned to listen. Without any outside distraction and without being able to interrupt, I hear what you say. And it makes sense.>

<Wouldn't you be jealous in my husband's place?>

<Not now that I understand. I can see how important friendship and caring and tenderness and sharing and love can be between women. I think I could make room for someone else in your heart.>

<And what about trust?>

<You haven't lied to me. Why shouldn't I trust you?>

<How do you know I haven't lied?>

<I know you, Scarlet.>

The stillness in the room was absolute as each letter appeared on the screen.

'I think that does it, Romaine,' Alison finally said. 'Go for it. Try to set up a meeting.'

'Hold on a second, guys...'

<Are you still there, Scarlet?>

'What is it, Grace?'

'I'm not sure about this amateur detective stuff. It always seems so easy in those thrillers, but this isn't a book. It's real life. This could be dangerous.'

'What on earth can happen to all three of us? I don't think we've got any choice. What do you think, Romaine?'

<You seem like the ideal man! I feel as if I know you too. Would like to get to know you better. Could we meet?>

<Yes.>

'I don't like this. He doesn't even ask where you are. You could be anywhere in the world and yet he says "yes" just like that.'

<When?>

<Tonight. We could meet tonight.>

'Romaine, please say no. Or put him off. We could get the police onto him. Or get Sheldon or Colin to come with us.'

'What use would either of those guys be? If we arrange to meet somewhere that's quite crowded, somewhere where we can see him—'

'Or her.'

'—Or her, before they see us.'

Romaine typed:

<Where and when?>

They arranged to meet at the All Bar One, Cambridge Circus at 9:30, Grace agreeing that it would be relatively busy at that time of night and they'd quickly be able to spot a lone person from the outside.

<How will I recognise you?>

<I'll carry a small bunch of yellow freesias.> And he was gone.

Romaine was shaking and she realised that her palms were sweaty. She turned to the others, her face pale and strained.

'How does he know that they're my favourite flowers?'

Romaine dressed carefully in dark colours, hoping to blend into the night. And then she felt too much like the man in the Milk Tray advertisements. She tied a gold chiffon scarf around her neck, remembering when Louie had brought it home for her, an impromptu gift that he'd spotted in a shop in Marylebone High Street. He'd immediately thought of her and knew that it would please her. For a moment she wished that she could just magic away the last few months and take them back to the way they were. But that just wasn't going to happen. As she put in the discreet diamond studs that they'd bought together in Hatton Gardens, she tried to push thoughts of Louie to the back of her mind. She would have to deal with the state of her marriage at some stage, but right now, there were more urgent concerns. And without Louie in her life, she was going to have to deal with this problem before it could escalate.

As they left the house, Romaine tried not to notice that Grace discreetly stooped down to pick up several large stones, which she secreted in her handbag. She smiled to herself: at least one of them was forward-thinking. They managed to hail a taxi quickly and Romaine thanked God. It would hardly be sensible for a group of women to be loitering around the streets of Tottenham, especially when one of them was carrying a concealed weapon in her handbag.

The journey became quieter and quieter as they each retreated into their own thoughts, all of them unwilling to admit how anxious they were becoming with every kilometre.

They got out in New Oxford Street, not wanting to arrive too early and needing to walk for a while. Glancing nervously at their watches, they stopped to look into every shop window they passed, checking out the musical instruments, shoes, luggage and books without actually seeing any of them. Too soon, it was 9:55 and they were metres away from the bar. Alison squeezed Romaine's hand and Grace took her other arm. They looked at each other.

'Ready?'

'Ready.'

They were now at the smoky plate-glass window, their view partially obscured by a large group of men in dark suits talking loudly, beer bottles in hand, laughing uproariously. Slowly, they inched their way past, peering into the depths, looking for the solo figure. They all spotted him at the same moment.

'What the hell is *he* doing here?'

Romaine turned to her companions, an unreadable smile on her lips.

'It's okay. I'll be all right. I think it's best if I do this on my own, don't you?'

Without faltering, she walked straight towards him. He stood as she approached and moved towards her. Romaine avoided his touch and took a seat opposite him. She looked out of the window and could see Grace and Alison peering in at her. She discreetly signalled to them to leave, smiling to herself as she did so.

Her favourite vodka and tonic waited on the low table, icy condensation beading the glass. She pushed it to one side.

'Dry white wine, please.'

He raised one eyebrow, but made no complaint. He walked to the bar. Romaine watched the easy grace of his movement. Shit, just the sight of him could still raise flutters in her stomach.

She took a slow sip of the wine, relishing the silence between them. She was in no hurry to open this particular conversation.

'So, Scarlet...' he smiled.

'How did you know?' She didn't return his smile though there was an involuntary twitch at the corners of her lips.

'You know I can dial into the home computer. I could see that Instant Messenger had been used. I'd never opened it myself. I looked at the contacts list. You'd left a trail in the history folder of the browser. It wasn't hard to find the site. Remember I *am* a computer expert.'

'But why did you do it?'

'I wanted to talk to you.'

'Louie, you could have talked to me any time.'

'I know, honey, but there were a lot of things getting in the way.'

'Like what? We were in that big house together. A lot of the time it was just the two of us.'

Louie looked uncomfortable, twisting his glass in his hand, making patterns in the condensation. 'Ever since you told me, it was never just the two of us; she was always with us. Sure, sometimes there were the guys—'

'And what a dumbo I was to go along with that shit that you put me through. What was all that about.'

'Rome, you gotta understand… I was hurting… I thought you didn't want me any more. I thought you wanted someone else. The only thing I could think of was to keep you close by all the time.'

'What for? As soon as we were alone together, you just ignored me. How do you think that made me feel.'

'I know. I've had a lot of time sitting in lonely hotel rooms. I realise that I was trying to punish you.'

'For what? For needing something different? Something that you couldn't give me, simply because you're the wrong gender. Something that I wouldn't expect you to provide?'

'I understand that now, Romaine. Scarlet explained it so well.'

This time she did smile at the memory of their online conversations.

'I think I kinda liked Computer Expert.'

Louie returned her smile. 'You know, that's who I am. Really! Don't give me none of them badass black woman looks! Seriously, I haven't changed that much. It was just a temporary malfunction of the circuits.'

'And how do you feel about Alison? I'm still working with her. She's still a good friend. And always will be, Louie. Remember that, at least, she and Grace were around while I've been going through all this crap with you. At least they didn't walk out and leave me on my own.'

Louie had the grace to look shamefaced. Romaine reached across the table and touched his hand, her first gesture of conciliation. He held on to her finger, bringing it to his lips.

'You know, honey, no matter what I did, whatever I said, I never, ever, for one minute stopped loving you. If I'm going to be honest, I still feel… I feel… threatened by her. Don't worry! I know it's *my* problem and I'm going to have to deal with it. I promise you, honey, I will. I just don't want to lose you.'

Romaine felt something soften inside her, something that she had to hold at bay for a while longer. 'Louie, I can understand how you felt and I can deal with that. But what worries me is how you changed. How could you have done all that stuff?'

'What stuff are you talking about in particular?' There was a teasing look in his eyes that disconcerted her for a moment.

'You know what I mean. The phone ringing—in the office, at home, my mobile—and the hang-ups—'

'Honey, I don't know what you're talking about.'

'Come on, Louie. I thought tonight was all about honesty. You know you were checking up on me…' As the words left her mouth, Romaine could see that she was on shaky ground. The look on Louie's face suggested that he really didn't know what she was talking about.

'Louie, I caught you out. Don't you remember? You called me on my mobile just as I was getting home. You hung up and when I came into the house you were still holding on to the receiver, pretending that you were talking to someone… Oh God, it really wasn't you, was it?'

Louie looked totally bemused. Romaine could tell that this wasn't any kind of play-acting. A frown crossed her brow mirroring that on Louie's face. She looked into his eyes and knew, without any doubt at all, that Louie just wasn't capable of what she was accusing him. Another case of things that go bump in the night, she thought. She had let the demons grow so out of proportion that, in the terror of the silent, lonely darkness, she'd allowed her imagination to run riot, totally disregarding the truths that she knew.

'And it wasn't you who made that phone call. It wasn't you who demolished the garden, the pebbles at the window.' Louie was looking totally blank and more than a little worried. Romaine moved closer to him and, surrounded by the lively background chatter that signalled the end of a working day, she explained to her husband all that had been happening.

Anyone looking at them would have thought that they were a couple newly in love. Louie pulled Romaine into his arms, stroking her hair, caressing her neck, letting his fingers roam across her body as if he wanted to confirm possession of all of her. He wanted to hold her, to protect her, to keep her from harm, to make up for all the potential danger that he'd, inadvertently, exposed her to.

'God, Romaine, I'm so sorry. I shouldn't have left. If I hadn't behaved like a spoiled brat, a total jackass, this would never have happened to you.' They were both silent for a moment as he did his best to comfort her, to allay her fears. They almost sank into a state of stupor until they both, simultaneously, had the same thought: if it wasn't Louie, then who the hell was it?

'I can't let you go home alone, Romaine. We don't know who's out there, who this weirdo is. Let me, at least, take you home, make sure you're safe.' He pulled away from her. 'Then I'll get back to the hotel.'

'You don't have to go back tonight. It is your home too, after all.'

'I didn't want to presume. I don't have my things.'

'I'm sure we could find a few things to fit in my husband's wardrobe.'

❦

Although Louie was holding her close, Romaine looked up as she instinctively knew that the taxi was approaching their home. Her first thought as she spotted the house was: I keep wishing that Louie wouldn't leave the shutters open and now I've done the same thing. And then she stiffened. She knew that they had definitely not left the lights blazing. She worked back in her memory: Grace bending to pick up the stones. There was no back lighting. No, the house had been dark as she'd turned to lock the door.

Louie sensed her alarm and they both mentally urged the taxi on. Louie clutched at her hand as they got out. The driver, white, middle-aged, looked as if he would do anything to avoid the trouble that he saw looming and zoomed off before Louie could even get his wallet out.

The front door had obviously been smashed and hung from just one hinge. With the bright illumination in the sitting room, they could see that the furniture had been slashed, stereo and television obviously flung across the room and now in a million shards, pictures torn from the walls, the glass splintered, books gutted and scattered like snow in a blizzard. Louie's hand tightened around Romaine's as they slowly picked their way through the debris into the hallway.

'Stay here,' Louie commanded, but there was no way that Romaine would stay on her own. She followed her husband as he turned towards the door to the sitting room. She felt his sharp intake of breath and peered round his shoulder, looking in the same direction as him. There, huddled in the corner, head bowed, curled into a foetal position, shoulders heaving as his body shuddered was Alison's husband, Byron.

He must have heard their footsteps, but he didn't look up. Louie walked across the room and closed the shutters. Then he returned to the front door and did his best to close it. Romaine was amazed at his calm. She could hardly move from shock. And then Louie did something that she would not have expected in a million years. He walked over to where the older man was, crouched down and put his arms around him, pulling Byron's head into his shoulder, holding him, rocking him the way he might a young child. And she stood and watched as Byron's body heaved with earth-shaking sobs and her husband stroked his head, murmuring 'shh!'.

Romaine's initial anger faded immediately. She walked to the sideboard and poured a glass of brandy. She she handed it to Byron. She sat cross-legged before him as he sipped the liquid, and waited. It was a few minutes before he could speak. He shrugged off Louie's touch, not ungratefully, but almost as if he didn't deserve the attention. He began to speak though he couldn't bring himself to look into Romaine's eyes.

'Why… why are you both being so kind? After what I've done.'

Romaine looked around at the devastation in the room. It could all be put back together or replaced. That didn't immediately seem important. What was, though, was whether there was any way of putting Byron back together. Romaine wanted to ask him why he'd done this, but before she could articulate the question, there came the first stirrings of understanding of quite how hurt and angry Byron must have been.

'Byron, what exactly have you done?'

Louie looked at her as if that was a pretty bizarre question to ask under the circumstances, but Romaine couldn't take her eyes from Byron. He looked as if he was in a fog, desperate to navigate his way out. His jaw was clenched as he raised his head and stared at her, unseeing, the veins in his neck bulging.

'She told me it was over between you two. That it wouldn't happen again. She was so matter of fact. As if she just expected me to understand and to accept what you did. As if that kind of stuff happens every day and even though she described to me how important you are to her, how significant that evening was in her life, how it didn't affect our relationship, how much she still loves me, she expected me to believe her. How could I? If your feelings for each other were so strong, why wouldn't you do it again? Don't make any sense that I can understand.' He paused for a moment and took a long sip of his drink. 'I watched her.'

'You watched me too.'

His eyes seemed to focus for a moment and Romaine caught the embers of his confusion. She shivered and then her eyes misted with tears for the old Byron and for the easy affection they had shared.

'You both betrayed me. I thought you were my friend.'

'The calls? It was you, wasn't it?'

'I wanted to know if you were together. If I lost her, I wanted to know if she was with you. You were together nearly every day in that office. I couldn't see what was going on in there. I was getting more and more angry with her, with you, with all of you.' He stopped and looked at Louie as if expecting some kind of affirmation. Louie nodded his head slowly and patted Byron's shoulder.

Byron looked at his hand as if it was an alien object. He took a deep breath. 'And before… you embraced, right there on the doorstep, flaunting it. And tonight, I saw her come here—'

'Only because I was scared, because of all the hang-ups, the pebbles thrown at the window, the phone call last night, what you did to the garden…'

'But she had her bag with her. I hadn't seen Louie coming and going for days. I knew she was going to leave me. I watched as the three of you women left in that taxi. It was like you were going out celebrating or something. I couldn't control the rage any longer. Just wanted to take it out on you. To make you know how bad the pain I'm feeling is.'

'Byron, believe me, Alison had no intention of leaving you. She was going to stay for a couple of days just because I'd become frightened of being on my own. Because of what you were doing. She wasn't lying to you, Byron. She does love you, just the same way that I love Louie. What happened between us… well, I can't pretend that it wasn't important to me too. But it won't happen again because it doesn't need to. We learned what we needed to learn about each other and it was wonderful and magical, but we know now. And that's enough. I promise you.' She reached out and took his hand in hers. It was cold and she instinctively rubbed it with her other hand. 'Louie's back and I hope he'll be staying. Alison's at home, waiting for you and probably worrying.'

Louie stood up. 'I'll drive you back, Byron.' He reached out a hand to help him up and waited until Byron took it. Louie smiled down at Romaine and tousled her hair. 'Shut the door behind me any way you can, honey, and put the chain on. I'll be as quick as I can.' He ushered his charge out of the door and into the night.

For a second, Romaine debated calling Alison to warn her of what had happened, but she decided it would be best to stay out of this one, to give them room, not to add any further complications. Gingerly, Romaine picked her way across the broken glass and walked into the hall. As she turned to the door, she was momentarily shocked to see a figure there, his hand raised to the bell. This time, she was relieved to see Colin and realised that she shouldn't be surprised. Once again, he'd appeared at a moment of crisis. It was destined to be this way. Romaine sighed, knowing that she was going to work hard to transform their relationship into what could be a very special friendship, once he understood once and for all that, sexually, she was out of bounds.

'Rome, what's happened here?' His voice was full of genuine concern.

'Don't worry, Colin. It's okay. I'll explain as you help me clear up. Louie will be back soon.' She thought she might as well get that in and start the way she intended to continue.

Colin grinned at her.

'Fine. Just show me to the nearest screwdriver.'

It was the early hours of the morning. Colin and Louie had worked quickly and efficiently together to make the house safe. Now Romaine and Louie were exhausted, sitting up in bed together, his arms tight around her, his fingers stroking her hair.

'Alison was there, you know. She was frantic with worry. She'd been trying his phone all day and getting no answer. I left them together.'

'If anyone can make him understand, I'm sure Alison will, once she sees that there's a problem.'

'I'm amazed that you didn't want to hit him after all he'd done.'

'It didn't click at first. I just saw him and the sitting room and I wasn't thinking about all the other stuff.'

'You were still pretty sympathetic when you realised.'

'I guess I wasn't as surprised as I might have been. I always wondered how he could have taken it as calmly as Alison suggested. Byron never struck me as being that worldly, but—and this is really ironic now—I envied her for having such an understanding husband.'

'When yours was just a stubborn, pig-headed fool.'

'You took the words out of my mouth.'

'Hey!' Louie took the opportunity to tickle Romaine until she begged him for mercy.

'Seriously, though, Louie, all I could think of when he was talking was how hurt you had been and if I couldn't forgive Byron, then I'd never be able to forgive you either.'

'And have you forgiven me?'

'I'm on the way there. What about you? Have you forgiven me?'

'Rome, I really have learned that there is nothing to forgive.'

'You've certainly learned the script. We will get through this, won't we, Lou?'

'I know we can.'

'There's only one problem.'

'What's that?'

'Explaining all this to your mother. She's pretty mad at me.'

'Really?'

'Really.'

Louie leaned down and gently nuzzled her neck. Romaine immediately felt a spark of electricity slither down her spine. She turned her head to him and sought his lips. They were gentle as they brushed against her. 'Mmmm,' she moaned.

'I'm not scared of my mother, you know.' His tongue whispered against her lower lip and she eased her breasts closer to him, her nipples demanding the caress of his skin.

'Uh-huh?' Even with his mouth muffling her voice she sounded sceptical.

'No,' he rolled across her so that he was lying on top of her. 'I'm a big boy now.'

'So I can feel.'

'I'll show you.' Louie's tongue probed her mouth, slightly reticent, awaiting her response. And Romaine felt, suddenly, strangely, shy, as if this were the first time and, in a sense, it was. This was a new Louie, but a Louie who could still prompt the same arousal in her. Her fingers stroked the nape of his neck, pulling him closer as his hand sought her breast. She gasped as he found her nipple and held it tenderly between thumb and forefinger. He pulled away and she immediately felt bereft, wanting him as close as possible to her, to protect her, to drive away the last residue of fear.

Slowly, carefully, Louie undid the buttons of her blouse, parting the fabric to reveal her lacy bra. He gently caressed the swell of her breast placing a reverential kiss at each spot that his fingers touched. Romaine watched as his soft lips touched her flesh and she felt a surge of love and tenderness and overwhelming desire for her husband. She pushed the straps of the bra off her shoulders and he reached behind her to undo the fastening, allowing it to fall and reveal the golden sheen across the satiny skin, the tiny black buds of her hard nipples. He took each in turn, sucking gently allowing his wet tongue to swirl around them. Romaine was breathing hard now, her body trembling with pleasure. Louie pushed himself up on one elbow and watched her, the sight of her arousal making him, in turn, harder. He couldn't keep away from her and his fingers as if of their own accord returned to her breasts, experimental, tracing decreasing circles towards the nipples, watching in amazement as they shrank and puckered further.

Romaine reached for him and, as her fingers brushed against the skin around his waist, she pushed his T-shirt up, stroking his skin, pulling the garment over his head. He waited, wanting her to lead the way. She continued touching his skin, the tips of her fingers barely dancing across his flesh, the electric charge as fiery as if she'd drawn blood. And when her lips touched his nipple, it was a touch of fire and yet as light as a breath and he groaned deep in his throat as her tongue played round it. She laughed and pushed him back against the bed, straddling him, her knees tight around his waist. She leaned forward, and he reached up to push the hair away from her face, to savour this woman he'd longed for the minute he'd walked out of the door. Romaine returned his gaze, amazed that he was here, that she still couldn't resist the sight of his gorgeous, tempting body. She recalled the first sight of that mysterious internet nude, smiling inwardly as she acknowledged how much better the real thing was. His hands trailed the length of her body, caressing the swell of her hips as she rocked back and forth against him. Inevitably, the movement was too much for him and, with a moan, he pushed her to one side and got up from the bed. An 'Oh' of surprise silently formed on Romaine's lips.

'Don't worry, honey. Give me one minute and I'll be back.'

She watched in astonishment as he ran across the room and she heard the rapid beat of his steps down the stairs. There was the sound of rummaging in the sitting room, items being thrown around, Louie's muttered curses and then his footsteps padding to the study. Moments later he was back, a CD case triumphantly brandished in his hand. 'It must be fate. Byron didn't get hold of this one.'

Before he could insert the disc into the player, a smile tugged at the corners of her lips. Even as the bells sounded, she was reaching for him and Prince didn't even have to whisper 'Come... closer... feel what you've been dying for' before she was... ready... to... explode.

And almost not soon enough, Louie was by her side, nibbling at her ear, whispering 'tonight I'm gonna be your fantasy...'

Romaine reached for her man, found the buckle of his belt and unfastened it, lowering his zip, smoothing the fabric of his trousers down over his hips until he helped her by kicking them away, along with his boxers. She ran her hands down the length of his chest and looked down at his penis, so familiar and yet so new. And still she turned away again. She looked up tentatively into his eyes, knowing what she wanted to see there, and fearing what she might. Sure, his erection told her that Louie wanted her, but she had to see something more. And there was the heat of desire in his eyes as his pupils dilated, but he didn't reach for her and Romaine recognised in an instant what she had sought in another person's gaze: patience, self-sacrifice, the desire to learn, to know and, in addition, the confirmation of her ability to arouse, to satisfy. She'd seen all that in Alison's eyes.

Louie moved to take her in his arms and Romaine relaxed into him, determined to hold nothing back, this time. She was secure, there was no need for any self-defence mechanisms. As he fumbled for the zip of her skirt, Romaine pushed his hands away and stood. She lifted her skirt and rolled down her stockings, as slowly as she possibly could, tantalising him, knowing that each moment would be a test of his endurance. She reached up under her skirt and eased her knickers down until she could step out of them. She made no motion towards him, just stood and waited.

Where the shadows didn't caress her, the light sparked golden highlights on her hair and skin, moulding the contours of her breasts. Arms akimbo, legs apart, she looked more powerful than Louie had ever seen before. She didn't need to speak or gesture, he understood the command in her stance.

Louie stood and walked towards his wife a look of almost reverence in his eyes. He stood before her, close, nose to nose, breasts to chest, legs almost touching. Briefly, he brushed his lips against hers. Romaine made no response and he touched her shoulders, sliding his hands down to her fingertips, to her hips, holding here there for a while longer, appreciating the powerful directness of what her eyes were saying to him. He knelt before her, letting his hands travel the length of her thighs, over the coarse fabric of her skirt until they found the warmth of her skin. With the barest glance of his fingertips, he moulded circles into the backs of her knees, whispering a touch upwards along the curve of her inner thighs, allowing his lips to follow as he pushed the skirt up, further up until the first tendrils peeked out and he stopped for a moment, holding himself back, just thanking the gods that he was with her again, so close that he could feel the heat radiating from her, smell the tangy, salty, musky aroma of her sex.

Romaine had wordlessly told him what she wanted and now, he was so close. Submissive, at her feet. She could just tilt her hips slightly forward and he would be touching her, but something held her back. A memory that remained a little too near to the surface. Louie arousing her to the point of release and then leaving her flat and frustrated. This time would be different, she knew, but there still lingered a scintilla of doubt. This was his test. With Alison, and the recollection would never fade, there had been no need for instruction, for guidance. There had been only the unselfish, desire to give each other pleasure and maybe that was at the core of what they had taken from each other. So Romaine forced herself to remain still, even though her nerve endings were screaming to move towards his soft, warm lips.

Louie tilted his face and looked at Romaine's face, the pout of her lips slightly apart, her eyes half-closed, drowsy. He edged closer and watched the tiny involuntary shivers that rippled through her frame. He increased the pressure of his fingers, clasping her thigh, allowing his thumbs to inch nearer to her pussy lips, closer, closer until he touched the soft folds, holding them apart. He heard the gentle gasp from Romaine and felt his balls tighten, his cock twitch upwards towards his belly.

She didn't know that the sharp gasp had come from her own lips; she could only concentrate on the touch of his rough thumbs on her flesh sending a jolt of hot, molten sweetness up through her belly, flooding her breasts, making her nipples tingle. Romaine looked down at her husband's bowed head, wanting to caress the vulnerable nape of his neck, force him closer to her hardened clitoris, but she made her hands remain in place, silently screaming at him: Now Louie, oh God Almighty, Now! Her knees began to tremble, her thigh muscles contracted as she saw the tip of his tongue emerging from between his lips, zeroing in on her vagina, she felt the heat building, concentrating, but didn't know if was coming from her or from him. And then, oh, oh, oh, his tongue was tracing the contours of her pussy lips as he held them gently apart, readying her to his lips and, Lord, moving downwards, circling her opening and up again, slithering towards her desperate clitoris. Romaine's knees buckled and she screamed, 'Oh Louie!' as his pillow-soft lips closed around the tiny hard bead and he played his tongue round and round making the muscles in her vagina tense with pleasure. And he released her for just an instant and he was back, down between her thighs, lapping at the wetness that flowed, burying his nose into the black triangle of hair. His broad tongue licked upwards, over and over sending shudders of unadulterated ecstasy through her. He suddenly stopped and pulled away. Romaine moaned, but held her breath. He'd taken her to this point before. Please, please don't let him be so cruel again!

But Louie stood up and Romaine wanted to claw at him, to hurt him. Her eyes tightened as he reached behind to unzip her skirt. He watched as it fell to the ground and she could see the movement of the bulge in his trousers. She smiled inside, allowing nothing to show on her face, challenging him to do the right thing. And then he was lifting her, swooping her up in one fluid motion, laying her on the bed, her legs dangling over the edge and before any more thoughts of disappointment or frustration could surface, he was kneeling, pushing her legs up, forcing her thighs open, exposing her. And now his tongue was back again, just where she wanted, but his touch was harder, faster as he shook his head from side to side, his tongue pointed like a weapon, bruising the sensitive flesh, concentrating sensation until Romaine felt the prickly heat rise to her breasts and her own fingers pinched and squeezed her nipples. She felt his tongue slip inside her, probing, in and out, more and more insistent until she felt herself relax completely and give herself to him as his finger took the place of his tongue, then two fingers, forcing their way in, almost brutal against the softness of his tongue back again on her clitoris, this time moving painfully slowly, excruciatingly gently and she knew that, this time, now, there was no stopping. Every muscle in her body clenched and every nerve ending screamed and the world went red and then silver and then gold as she came in ripples, rolling waves that built and built until they burst against the dam and she felt something give inside her, something that brought and unexpected explosion of freedom and peace. She opened her eyes and Louie was holding her safely in his arms, protecting her, cherishing her.

It seemed to take forever for the waves to subside and Romaine realised that Louie was staring at her, a question in his eyes that she didn't want him to ask even though she knew it would lurk at the back of his mind until she could find a way to reassure him. God, for a strong man, his ego was so fragile. The thought was objective, without blame, an acknowledgement of the depth of his vulnerability where she was concerned and, therefore, her own power over him, which she didn't intend to abuse. She felt a rush of undiluted tenderness for this man she'd loved for so long. She reached up and trailed a finger along the curve of his jaw-line. 'That was so, soooo good. Thank you.' She let her nail scrape gently down the line of his neck, and she placed a brief kiss behind his ear letting her lips barely caress his skin as she headed down his chest towards his nipples. She rubbed them, squeezing them gently between her fingers, rolling them until the points hardened. At the same time, she fumbled with the buckle of his belt, needing to fell the effect she was having on him. Louie pushed her hand aside and did it himself, unzipping his trousers and awkwardly extricating his feet from his socks. Romaine laughed at his desperate urgency.

'What is it?'

'It just struck me as funny, that's all. We've got plenty of time. No need to rush.'

Louie laughed too and then they held each other for a while, loving the feeling of bare flesh against bare flesh. Their hands roamed lightly over each other's bodies, relishing the relaxed intimacy hiding the tension for the moment, knowing that each was aware of the other's continued arousal.

Romaine felt Louie's cock stir against her inner thigh and the corresponding fluttering in her stomach. She tilted her hips towards him, holding his buttocks, pressing hard against him. She slipped her knee between his thighs, allowing the slick wetness at the head of his penis to trail across her stomach. She reached down to take him in her hand and circled his wide girth, allowing her thumb to smooth up the ridge of protruding vein and over the softness at the tip, then round and round. Louie groaned, a low, throaty sound that reverberated against her chest. Over and over, she teased him, loving the feel of his reaction, the flow of blood into his penis, the tightening of his balls. She cupped them in her palms, enfolding them in her warmth, caressing with her thumbs.

'God, I can't take any more, Romaine. Be careful.'

'I want you inside me, Lou.'

'Now?'

'Now.'

Louie sat up, his back braced against the headboard, his knees wide apart. His erect, reddened cock proudly beckoned to her and Romaine was willing to follow wherever it led. She crawled towards him on all fours until she was close enough for Louie to reach for her. He lifted her buttocks and raised her up until her knees straddled his waist. He held her there, hovering above his prick as he leaned forward to lick the underside of her breast. Romaine arched her back as her breasts seemed to reach for his touch. There was a melting inside as his tongue set her nipples on fire and he lowered her until the head of his cock merely breathed against her vagina. She leaned forward, trying to force the pace, longing to feel his hardness filling her, but he held her away, rotating his pelvis so that his cock traced slippery circles as she tried to tighten her pussy muscles, to suck him in.

'Louie. I can't take any more. Please.'

'Please what?' He smiled, but there was something forceful in his look that sent a shiver of nerves down her spine.

'Please fuck me, Lou. Now.'

'How do you want it, Rome? Gentle like this?' He lifted her slightly and she clutched at his hips fearing his withdrawal, but he just held her there, so that she could hardly feel his touch against her gaping lips, almost as if she was imagining it. This was torture. She knew what he wanted to hear. She clenched her teeth, her sharp nails digging into his flesh and making him wince.

'Soft and gentle, Romaine? Or hard, like this?' He pulled her down, thrusting hard into her, forcing the breath from her body. He held her tight, stopping her movement as he strained against her, impaling her, possessing her.

She flopped against him then and he released her hips and she began to move, raising up slowly, her head still buried in his shoulder, then descending equally slowly as his fingers reached for her breasts, grasping the undersides, pushing them upwards, squeezing, bruising the nipples, squeezing hard in time with each thrust of his cock.

As he quickened the pace, Romaine's need became more frenzied and her thighs tightened around his as she rode his manhood, swallowing it deep inside, taking everything he offered and demanding more. Faster, deeper, give it to me, more, more, more, she screamed as she bounced up and down.'

'Harder?'

'Yes!'

Louie pulled out of her and pushed her back onto the bed. He pushed her knees upwards and she allowed them to fall open, making herself vulnerable now. He knelt in front of her, his reddened erection brandished in one hand as he stroked himself almost lovingly. Romaine's breathing became more and more shallow as he neared, looking as if he was about to stab her with a sword and that's how it felt as a pit-a-pat of apprehension made her stomach muscles tense. And then he was above her, poised, ready, a question in his eyes as he sought certainty. She reached for him and before she could touch him, with one strong movement, he'd thrust violently, his skin slapping against hers as he used every inch of his strength to claim her. Back and forth, round and round until her head thrashed from side to side in the violence of her passion.

'This what you want?'

There was only one possible answer. 'Yes, yes, yeeeees, oh yes!'

He bent over and took her nipple between his teeth, biting hard as his fingers sought her clitoris, rubbing, teasing arousing until her own movements became more and more rapid and her body tensed, rising up against him as she felt the hot rush of wetness around his cock and she arched her back, forcing him as far as he could go and her legs clasped around him as she came in a shuddering climax.

Louie was still moving against her, concentrating now on his own pleasure, his chest hard against hers, his lips close to her ears. His whisper was so low she almost missed it as she reached for his balls, wanting to give him the pleasure she had just felt.

'She couldn't give you that, could she?'

'No, Louie.'

'But you know what, Romaine?'

'What?'

He raised up and looked into her eyes, continuing to thrust hard, the sinews in his neck strained. His voice emerged, almost strangled, through clenched teeth.

'It makes my cock hard has hell to think of you and Alison

together. Makes me so horny, so fucking hot... aaah! God, I'm coming... coming babe.'

As he subsided against her, Romaine turned to him and kissed his cheek gently. She held him against her breast as he drifted into sleep. In the black stillness of the room her fingers crept stealthily down and nestled between her thighs. Romaine thought again of that one perfect night. She smiled very slowly.

About the Author

CRYSTAL HUMPHRIES is thirty years old. She works as a free-lance computer programmer. In her minimal spare time, she also volunteers at a local cat sanctuary. She is married with two children and lives in Enfield, North London. *Online Wildfire* is her first novel.

Also from Brown Skin Books

Josephine Baker became a sensation with her nude dancing in Paris in the 1920s and 30s. Her fantastic life history forms the basis for *Scandalous*. She had prodigious talent and a sexual appetite to match, but in this fictional tale, she meets her match in Drummer Thompson. He's a handsome rogue of a Canadian journalist who knows how to touch her in all the right places and fill the sensual and emotional needs she never even knew she had.

The backdrop to this erotic thriller is a city of seedy cafés and fashionable nightclubs that hides sexual secrets. And it's not long before Josephine discovers that Drummer is not all that he seems. He raises suspicion by delving into her past and attempting to dredge up a lust-filled episode that Josephine would rather keep buried—one that is somehow connected to a Nazi plot to take over France itself. Josephine must join forces with Drummer and foil an assassination attempt that could trigger disaster.

Inspired by Josephine's life and her adventures in the French Resistance, *Scandalous* is a story of one woman's search for ultimate sexual fulfillment—and her own political conscience.

❦

Angela Campion was born and raised in London. She read History at university and later took her Master's Degree at Oxford, in the process becoming an expert on black musicians, writers and artists who lived in Paris between the wars. She now lives in Surrey with her husband and daughter.

A young journalism professor, Faith Graham, finds herself the target of a carefully-planned seduction–not by a man, not by a woman, but by a couple. On one side is Tim, a handsome, ambitious and charismatic magazine publisher who knows how to satisfy raw need. On the other is Sally, an intriguing white American actress who opens Faith's eyes to a new world of sensuality and tenderness. Erotic games evolve into an ongoing relationship–the French phrase is *ménage à trois*–that spells the best sex of Faith's life, whether with one, the other or both!

In this sensual context, Faith attempts to solve the unexplained murder of a young black girl in an inner-city park. She explores a London ready to boil over from racial and political tensions. Her determination to uncover the truth leads to shifting alliances, divided loyalties and the discovery of guilty secrets. There are tests of character waiting for all three as Faith finally discovers who she really is and how she wants to love…

ψ

Playthings is based on a real episode in the life of the author transformed by Faith Graham's inventive imagination.

Brown Skin Books' first anthology of meltingly hot, satisfyingly sweet short stories. Slip into the voluptuous but illicit desire of 'Hourglass' and the furtive, frantic passion of 'Snatched'. Then stoke your passion higher with the guilty arousal of 'Brown Skin' and the tantalising teasing of 'Address Book'. Smoulder through the dark sensuality of 'New Year' and the playful eroticism of 'The Learning Game', winner of Brown Skin Books' first annual short story competition. You'll scale the heights of sultry sensuality with these stories.

Written by black women writers from Northern England to North America, Southern England to South Africa, *Hot Chocolate* is a collection of exceptionally raunchy, intimate and funny tales about what it is to be black, female—and positively, confidently, gloriously sexual—in the twenty-first century.

🍷

Search no further for sizzling, sexy fantasies—take our creamy, steamy *Hot Chocolate* to bed with you and savour its tempting delights!

Brown Skin Books titles are available from bookshops
or to order direct, contact **info@brownskinbooks.co.uk**
or visit our website **www.brownskinbooks.co.uk**.

BROWN SKIN
B O O K S

Warning: never, *ever*, mix business with pleasure. Especially if your whole future is at stake. But don't blame Jewel Chambers if she can't resist what Ben Petersen has to offer. After all, he's tall, slim, gorgeous, clever, funny, he makes her elbows tingle–and her knickers wet. But he's also dangerous, unreadable and volatile. Jewel has her own particular charms–she invades his thoughts, haunting him, enflaming his senses. Can either of them resist the magnetic, compelling lure of overwhelming desire?

As Jewel fights to keep hold of her business, she's drawn into the spell that Ben weaves, not knowing whether he'll be her saviour or her destroyer. She's powerless to turn away, needing him financially as well as physically. Jewel's allies include her friends Stuart, Tasha and Ruby, who all bring their own sexual dilemmas to bear on their reactions to Ben.

Ultimately, it's up to Jewel. She makes her choice. And that's when the secrets hidden for a generation, the simmering passions, the powerful consequences of searing, steamy lust erupt in an unpredicted, shattering climax.

Isabel Baptiste runs her own fashion design company and travels extensively in the United States and Europe. Born in Jamaica, she has lived in England since she was two. Now thirty-three, she lives in the South of England with her partner and two children. *Personal Business* is her first novel.

Brown Skin Books titles are available from bookshops
or to order direct, contact **info@brownskinbooks.co.uk**
or visit our website **www.brownskinbooks.co.uk**.

BROWN SKIN
B O O K S

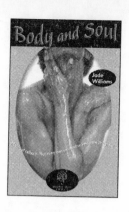

You're a judge on the latest reality TV show and your co-judge is one of the sexiest men on two legs. He also happens to be your former lover. One of the contestants makes you hot and horny, and he knows it. A few short weeks ago you were trekking through a barren sexual desert, now every hot-blooded male in sight is clamouring at your door and then, if that weren't enough, you're suddenly at the centre of a national, tabloid scandal.

Put yourself in the position of Carol Shaw, carefree, sassy, frustrated, music journalist who, experiencing more than just a bad hair day, well, *sexual gratification interruptus* to put it bluntly, gives in to a moment of irresistible passion, unaware of where it will lead. Then, thanks to a drunken, opinionated outburst, she's plucked from contented, if dull, obscurity and thrust into the glare of a nationwide television audience. As luck would have it, that's when a past indiscretion catches up with her–inevitably in the form of a man. And someone wants to make sure everybody knows about it. And that 'everybody' is several million viewers.

You survive all that and then you're faced with a choice of: young, horny and on the rise; been-there-done-that, but sexy as hell; funny, loving, warm but down-and-dirty. Who would you choose? Yeah? Then maybe you *are* Carol Shaw.

❦

Born in England, of Barbadian descent, **Jade Williams** is in her late 20s, single 'but continues to visit the gym with optimism'. A freelance journalist, she has worked in television and radio and has contributed numerous articles to newspapers and magazines. *Body and Soul* is her first novel writing under this name. She currently lives in Sydenham, south London.

BROWN SKIN
BOOKS